Whiskey and Soda

Other novels

in Nina Wright's Whiskey Mattimoe and Homefree series can be found at Amazon, Barnes and Noble, and Kobo bookstores world-wide:

Whiskey on the Rocks
Whiskey Straight Up
Whiskey and Tonic
Whiskey and Water
Whiskey with a Twist

Homefree
Sensitive

Praise for the Whiskey Mattimoe Series

It's rare to find a good mystery that also makes you laugh out loud. This series does that for me every time!--- Gwynn Russell (Lancaster, PA)

Whiskey Mattimoe could be me. It seems as though whatever she does, no matter how good the intention, something goes wrong.
----Bonnie J. Brandburg "Bonnie Joan"

With each new mystery in this series, I become a bigger fan of Nina Wright. Anyone who has ever laughed at (or groaned about) the behavior of an actual dog will love the canine and human characters in the Whiskey Mattimoe mysteries.--- Molly McHugh Baylord (Scottsdale, AZ)

I have read all of the Whiskey books and can hardly wait for the next one. They are great reads. I love the afghan hound Abra she is such a diva and is so funny. Nina Wright really captures the spirit of the hound. All of her books are great reads. They are great page turners and the story lines are terrific. Once you read one of these books you will want to read all of them.--- Nancy L. Smith "Puppyseed" (Las Vegas, Nevada)

Whiskey and Abra are back for another funny mystery. Once again, the antics of Abra and her canine associates steal the book.
--- C. Breedlove (Deep South)

Whiskey and Soda© 2012 Nina Wright

All rights reserved. Except for brief passages quoted in newspapers, magazines, radio and television reviews, no part of this book in any form by any means, mechanical or electronic, including photocopy and recording or information retrieval system, may be copied without written permission from the publisher.

This novel is entirely a work of fiction. Though it may contain references to products, places or people, living or dead, these references are merely to add realism to the product of the author's imagination. Any reference within this work to people living or dead is purely coincidental.

Published by Martin Brown Publishers, LLC
1138 South Webster Street
Kokomo, Indiana 46902
www.mbpubs.com

ISBN: 978-1-937070-19-9

For Holly Weaver Gardner, the true heart of Texas

Acknowledgments

I thank the following individuals for their unique and vital assistance during the creation of this novel: Richard Pahl, alpha reader and writers' advocate; Nancy J. Potter, real estate guru and savvy early reader; and Charles O. Yoakum, wise advisor in many matters.

Also, I curtsy to my personal role model, Rose Hemstreet—born and bred in New Orleans—a witty and gracious southern lady.

I send hugs to Linda Jo Bugbee and her beloved Afghan hounds, and sweet memories of Bailey the toy poodle to his human, my pal Bernie Paul.

Finally, here's to every reader who asked for more Whiskey: Cheers!

Whiskey and Soda
by
Nina Wright

Author's Note:

My own experience in private schools has been with teachers, staff and parents who consistently put children's needs firsts.

1

"Whiskey, repeat after me. 'I am a nurturing person.'"

"But I'm not. Really. I'm no good at it, and I don't like doing it."

Noonan Starr narrowed her eyes in a way that suggested she was losing patience with me. That's saying a lot because Noonan was probably the most patient person on the planet.

Today I was paying her to be patient. In desperation, I had hired Noonan as my personal counselor. She wasn't licensed, except in massage therapy, but lots of people paid her to help them sort out their lives.

"Contemplate this, Whiskey. You've provided care for Avery's twins, and you still take care of Chester."

"I don't think I should take credit for Chester. He crawls in through my kitchen window when he gets locked out of The Castle. And he earns his keep by being Abra's keeper."

"Okay," Noonan said slowly. "But you've nurtured Avery's twins."

"They're Leo's grandchildren which makes them my step-grandchildren. Leo would have done the same if I'd died and my lazy, estranged daughter showed up nine months pregnant. Anyway, the nanny did the nurturing; I just signed the checks."

Noonan ran a hand through her spiky white-blonde hair. I understood her frustration. We'd been at this for over an hour and any real therapist would have stopped after fifty minutes.

"You have maternal instincts," she insisted. "Why else would you attract children and dogs?"

"Bad karma?" I suggested.

Noonan glowered at me. "Attracting life forms is good karma."

"But I've never wanted children. Or dogs. And yet they keep showing up."

"The Universe knows what you need."

"How about what I want? Does the Universe know what I want?"

"The Universe is about growth and opportunity."

"Opportunity to get what I want?"

"Opportunity to grow. Opportunity to develop the talents and insights that will define you."

"I'm thirty-four. I'm defined already. Realtor, divorcee, widow, though not necessarily in that order—"

Noonan's complexion was taking on the color of annoyance.

"Whiskey, those words define the external you. Not the real you. The Universe is in the process of revealing the real you to you. Let's work with that. Repeat after me, 'I love children. I am a nurturer.'"

"But—"

"Repeat after me."

That was the closest I'd ever heard Noonan come to yelling. It reduced me to whispering.

"But I'm not. I never have been. Sorry. I'm no good at this."

"Of course you're good at this. This is your life."

"But—"

"Look at the facts, Whiskey. Chester loves you. The twins love you. And, whether you admit it today or not, you love them."

That much was probably true although, as Noonan well knew, I wasn't inclined to use the "L" word. So help me, I wasn't raised that way. In my family, we tried to do the right thing, mainly, but we never discussed deep feelings.

Noonan dabbed at her brow with a towel usually reserved for her massage clients.

"Your capacity for denial is profound, Whiskey. Everyone in Magnet Springs knows that. Even so, taking care of those you love is as natural to you as breathing."

"Taking care of others is something I mostly forget to do. Sipping wine with Odette after work is as natural to me as breathing."

Noonan gasped. "Don't tell me you drink alcohol in your condition."

"Of course not. I only drink soda now. I have no booze, no caffeine, not much salt, very little sugar, and virtually no fun at all."

"Wonderful." Noonan beamed at me. "The Universe rewards us for our choices."

"Really?" I patted my obviously rounded belly.

"Oh yes," Noonan said. "There is no darkness in the Universe except that which we create for ourselves. Life is light, Whiskey. Go forward and illuminate the world."

"I thought that's what streetlamps were for."

With a graceful flourish, Noonan indicated the rear exit. "I have a massage client in the lobby and I don't want her to pick up your negativity."

On that note I rose less than gracefully from the sagging vinyl couch. Though not a member of our local animal rights advocacy, Noonan was too invested in the Universe to use leather. As usual, I tried in vain to pay her for our session.

"My payment is good karma," she protested.

That was one way to put it. If Noonan didn't take cash from me now, she would take it later, in the form of a rent kickback, as I was landlord for both her massage studio and her small house on the north side of town.

The studio's rear exit was technically the delivery door, although I couldn't imagine what Noonan would ever need delivered. Her business was almost entirely intangible except for towels, which I was pretty sure she laundered at home. As I closed the metal door, a stiff wind almost knocked me sideways. I glanced up at scuttling clouds in a gunmetal-gray sky framed by tall leafless trees, typical of December in west Michigan. The issue was the temperature, which was bizarrely mild. Downright balmy. Ten days before Christmas and it was nearly 60 degrees. It had been every day for a week.

Whiskey and Soda

Ordinarily, I didn't complain about the weather, whatever it was. A proud Magnet Springs native, I took our bitter winters, wet springs, humid summers and crisp autumns in stride. As a Realtor, I did more than that. I sold each season for its specific scenic and sports-related benefits. By December, I should have been selling Winter Wonderland, as in knee-deep snow and the pleasures that accompany it—sledding, skiing, skating and snowmobiling. Plus shopping for fleecy clothes in our quaint shops and drinking too much hot buttered rum in our pubs. Who wouldn't want to rent a cozy cabin here? Or, better yet, buy one?

And it wasn't merely wintertime, it was Christmastime. Nobody, but nobody, does seasonal spirit better than Magnet Springs. Pine boughs, red velvet bows and clusters of mistletoe adorned every shop window. Signs and lamp posts held discreetly placed loudspeakers filling our downtown streets with classic carols. Our mostly empty downtown streets. I had to admit, didn't feel like December without the threat of frostbite. Nothing in nature glittered and nobody even needed a sweater.

Except me. I needed a big sweater. At six months pregnant, I couldn't find anything else in my closets that fit. Never a slave to fashion, I was now a certifiable slob. I couldn't zip up my slacks or skirts and I couldn't button my blouses. I depended instead on stretched-out pullovers to cover everything. As was my habit, I still wore beige. But now it was old, lame, baggy beige. I knew I looked bad not because anybody had said so exactly, but because Odette Mutombo, my best sales agent, wouldn't let me see clients or prospects anymore. To be accurate, she wouldn't let clients or prospects see me. My role was now limited to phone contact.

Technically, since I owned Mattimoe Realty and was the broker, Odette wasn't my boss. Realistically, since Odette made most of our sales and brought in most of our revenue, she might as well have been. I listened to her. I respected her. I deeply feared losing her to a competing agency.

I had just yanked open the driver's side door of my SUV when my cell phone rang. Since the howling wind made identifying the tune difficult, I clambered into my seat, closed the door and listened. My blood ran cold. I would have to take this call as it was almost Christmas.

"Hello, Mom," I said.

"Hello, Whitney. How are you, dear?"

I winced, as I always did, at the sound of my legal name. As far back as middle school, I'd hated the name I was born with—Whitney Houston. I wasn't black or beautiful and I sure as hell couldn't sing. Whitney Houston wasn't yet a celebrity when I was born. My mother read about a heroine named Whitney in a romance novel, and my fate was sealed.

Leave it to Jeb Halloran to give me my nickname. He told our sixth-grade classmates that I sounded like someone who smoked and drank every day. Coming from a family who liked their liquor, Jeb knew a whiskey voice when he heard one.

"I'm okay, Mom. How are you?"

"I'm fine, dear. How's Jeb?"

"How would I know? I haven't seen him."

"Oh, Whitney," my mother moaned. "Why must you be so stubborn?"

Jeb—my first boyfriend, my first husband, my ex-husband, and then after my second husband Leo Mattimoe died, my boyfriend again. Now Jeb was my estranged boyfriend or maybe my ex-boyfriend. In any case, he was the father of my unborn child. But I wasn't sure I should commit to him. Jeb loved me, but he loved all women at least a little.

"I'm not stubborn," I said.

"Are you pregnant?" Mom said.

"You know I am."

"Does Jeb want to marry you?"

"You know he does."

"Then why must you be so stubborn? You're going to have a baby. Jeb is the father, he wants to be your husband, you've always loved him—

"Not always, Mom. We got divorced, remember?"

"And then you hooked up again. Isn't that what they call it? You need to get married, Whitney."

"I don't want to get divorced."

"So don't get divorced. But do get married. It's not complicated."

"It's very complicated."

"No, it's not. You just want to make it complicated. In my day, when a girl got knocked up, and the boy was willing to marry her, they got married. It's still that simple. You're just stubborn."

Other people had been known to make the same observation. Could my mother actually be right? Nooooo. That couldn't happen. Could it?

My mother's ringtone was "Born Free." While I was growing up, she used to croon that overdramatic movie theme song from her youth. The thing about my mother and her favorite songs is she never gets the lyrics right, but that doesn't stop her from singing. Loudly. In this case, she endlessly warbled "Born free" followed by a few rhyming lines that made no sense. She said the song inspired her. It inspired me. Every time I heard my mother belt out "Born free," I couldn't wait to test my freedom. I ran off with Jeb the day after I graduated from high school. Cancer had killed my father a few months earlier. I might have acted out a little.

"Well, I'm not going to argue with you on the phone," Mom said.

Relieved, I was about to ask if she'd like a new bathrobe for Christmas when she added, "I'm driving up from Fort Myers right now."

"You can't do that," I said.

"Of course I can," my mother replied. "I'm more than halfway there already. Last week I leased a new Chevy Volt and I want to see how she runs. Besides, you need a good talking-to."

There was no point arguing. Mom was born free.

"I need a vacation from Florida, anyhow," she said. "There are too many old people and one of them wants to marry me."

This was huge news. In the sixteen years since my dad had died, I couldn't recall Irene Houston ever mentioning another man.

"You—you have a boyfriend?"

Now there was a question I'd never planned to ask my mother, especially after she'd qualified for Medicare. As soon as I said it out loud, I knew it was ridiculous. I may have even giggled.

"Not a boyfriend, dear. A fiancé."

"What?"

"Howard and I are engaged, but we haven't set a date. We've been living together since March, when the college kids came down for Spring Break. Watching all those young lovers got us going."

"Mom, I don't need the details."

"I wasn't going to give you any. Howard's a sweet man, Whitney, but I do miss my privacy." She sighed. "It's complicated."

"I just said that," I reminded her. "Marriage is very complicated."

"Not in your case, dear. You got a bun in the oven. You need a hubby."

Mom said she expected to be in Magnet Springs by this time tomorrow. I was afraid to ask where she planned to stay. Following my advice, Mom had leased out her house last year when she moved to the Sunshine State.

"Peg Goh is renting me a room in her house," Mom informed me.

"Peg Goh is going to charge you rent?"

I was stunned. We were talking about our mayor, one of the nicest folks I knew and also my mother's closest friend.

"That was my idea. In fact, I insisted on it," Mom said. "I'm going to stay awhile and Peg needs the money. Business is terrible in Magnet Springs. You of all people should have noticed."

"Our weather's bad, too," I told her. "It's almost like Florida, minus the sunshine. Winter tourism is way down."

"I'll do my part to help," Mom vowed. "And so will Howard."

"Howard? I thought you were taking a break from him."

"I am. But he'll follow me north, you'll see. Howard needs me."

"Do you need him?" I was genuinely curious.

"It doesn't matter, Whitney. When two people fall in love, they take turns needing each other. Right now you need Jeb. But you haven't figured that out yet."

"Because I'm stubborn?" I hoped Mom could hear my cynicism.

"Because you're in denial," she said. "Everybody knows that."

2

I had nothing more to say to my mother, especially since I was going to see her within twenty-four hours. Who knew how soon Howard, my potential stepfather, might turn up?

Adjusting the driver's seat to accommodate my expanding belly, I marveled—and not for the first time—at how fast life could change. I had lost Leo in the blink of an eye. Actually, I hadn't even blinked. I was asleep in the passenger seat when his aorta burst and we sailed into a ditch. I woke up to find him dead beside me, Abra howling in my ear.

That was almost two years ago. For months afterwards, I was numb with grief. Then I was lonely. And horny. About that time, Jeb returned to Magnet Springs. For better or worse, he remembered how to touch me in all the places that drove me wild. Such fun, such comfort. Suddenly life seemed nearly perfect again, even though Leo was gone.

Then I got pregnant. How the hell did that happen? I mean, I knew how it happened. I just didn't know how I'd let it happen. Or why. Noonan believed the Universe was trying to show me the real me. I was inclined to believe I'd just got lazy.

The "why" didn't much matter at this point. It was the "what happens next" that scared me silly. So far, all the increased estrogen in my system hadn't added up to a single surge in maternal instincts. No matter how many visualization exercises I did with Noonan, I still couldn't picture myself raising a child. Hell, I couldn't even admit I had a dog. I certainly couldn't keep track of her.

That morning was a case in point. Activating my overhead garage door while simultaneously shutting the door to my breezeway, I had balanced a mug of coffee, my laptop and my briefcase. I could have made it all work, even with the sun in my eyes. Except that Abra managed to bolt from the kitchen just in time to squeeze past the closing breezeway door, her sight hound mind fixed on the prize, a day of blissful play chasing shiny objects along the coast.

Before I could scream "No!" or—more appropriately—"Stop, bitch!" she had knocked me sideways, spraying my coffee like an arc of hot lava and scattering my bags. The sleek blonde beauty vanished into the dewy morning, ready to wreak havoc with tourists, if there were any. Abra lived to steal purses and jewelry. She was also inclined to seduce every male dog she met. My only solace was knowing that Fenton Flagg, Noonan's estranged husband, was back in Texas, where Abra couldn't corrupt his medical companion dog, Norman the Golden. Though well trained and devoted to Fenton, Norman had no will to resist Abra. My dog was one bad seed.

Full confession: I lived with and consistently failed to control a felonious canine. I frequently forgot to feed or groom her, much less track which side of the door I'd last seen her on. What the devil would I do with a baby?

These thoughts tumbled around my brain as I drove Broken Arrow Highway toward home. Leo and I had named our rural estate Vestige because it was built on land that once belonged to a large farm overlooking Lake Michigan. We'd saved the original tumble-down barn but built everything else from scratch—our house and out-buildings, our decks and dock. After Leo died, it had almost killed me to come home alone, but my young neighbor, Chester, made sure I didn't do it often. Ignored by his musical superstar mom, he was only too happy to hang out at Vestige and attempt to reform Abra. Before Chester could reform her, or I could remember to spay her, she had provided a puppy for Chester.

I rounded a bend and hit the brake. Ahead of me, on the gravel berm, were Chester and that very puppy. The dog—whose papa was Norman the Golden—had recently celebrated his first birthday; Chester was eight but looked six and often acted forty. To my amazement, Prince Harry the Pee Master and Chester were running, and no one was chasing them.

I honked and pulled over about fifty feet ahead of them. I rolled down my window and waited for them to catch up.

Whiskey and Soda

Chester waved and Prince Harry leaped straight into the air, acknowledging his share of Afghan hound blood.

"Hey," I said, when the panting boy and dog arrived at my vehicle. "What are you guys doing?"

"This is what jogging looks like, Whiskey," Chester said. "Didn't you used to do it?"

"Before I wised up and got a bike. Why are you all the way out here? We must be a mile from The Castle."

Chester consulted some kind of shiny techno-gizmo attached to one skinny ankle.

"Point-eight-nine miles, to be precise."

Prince Harry proceeded to lick the gizmo as if it tasted like cheese.

"To dogs, this pedometer tastes like cheese." Chester explained. "I bought it online, at Dogs-train-you-dot-com. It's guaranteed to keep your dog running by your side, and to keep you running because the dog's tongue tickles."

Chester emitted a high-pitched giggle. Suddenly, I noticed something about my diminutive multi-millionaire neighbor that I'd never seen before.

"Chester, you broke a sweat. Why on earth—?"

"It's an order, Whiskey. Direct from my headmaster."

"Headmaster?"

For a nanosecond I wondered if he was referring to a new hire at The Castle. Until recently Cassina—Chester's harpist/pop singer mom—and her paramour Rupert, who was Chester's sperm donor, had employed a handsome though mysterious Scotsman to drive them around and fix their mistakes. MacArthur called himself a "cleaner." On the side, he sometimes sold real estate, part-time, for me. Chester adored him, and I must admit, I lusted after him until the cleaner made his own mistake, which was a whopper. MacArthur somehow fell under the spell of my shrill ex-stepdaughter, Avery. He even had her sour face tattooed on his sinewy arm. One minute they were living together, with her twins, in a wing of The Castle, and the next minute MacArthur was gone. As far as I knew, he never even left a text message.

I continued cautiously, "Did Cassina hire a replacement for MacArthur?"

Prince Harry whimpered softly, as if the name stirred a fond memory. Chester blinked at me from behind his round wire-framed glasses.

"I'm talking about the headmaster at my school."

"Oh. Your headmaster gives orders?"

"He calls it homework. But Mr. Vreelander makes it sound like an order. He used to be career Army."

"I thought teachers gave homework," I ventured.

"Not at my school. And that's the problem, according to Mr. Vreelander. He says we've gotten soft at The Bentwood School. This is Mr. Vreelander's first year as headmaster, and he's cracking the whip."

Chester mimed doing exactly that. In response Prince Harry performed a perfect back flip.

"Things are changing big-time," Chester said. "Now we have to learn stuff."

"But you've always learned stuff. You're the smartest third grader I know."

"Thanks to my personal assistants."

"Assistants?" I asked, stressing the plural. "How many do you have?"

He held up three fingers.

"One to tutor me in math and science, and the other to tutor me in literature and fine arts."

"That's two assistants," I pointed out.

"My third assistant keeps my calendar and feeds me. She's a Cordon Bleu chef. Everything I know about cooking, I've learned from her."

While I couldn't personally vouch for the first two assistants, I owed a great deal to the third. Using the meager contents of my consistently under-stocked kitchen, Chester often created elaborate meals.

"You're saying the only way you've learned anything at The Bentwood School is by hiring personal tutors?"

"'Til now. But the headmaster is shaking things up. That's why Prince Harry and I are out running. Every student in the Lower School is required to jog two miles a day. Mr. Vreelander says our whole student body is out of shape."

"Is Mr. Vreelander's body in shape?" I inquired.

"Judge for yourself."

Whiskey and Soda

My gaze followed Chester's index finger to focus on a broad-shouldered Spandex-clad cyclist heading straight for us. Other than a helmet, he wore no more clothing than would be required for a summer afternoon workout. I appreciated every bulging muscle.

"That's your headmaster?"

I stepped down from my vehicle for a better view.

"Buff, isn't he?" Chester said.

"That's one word for him."

Other words included "taut" and "hot." But I didn't go there. Instead I observed aloud that the headmaster may have been buff, but he wasn't following his own order to run.

"That's because a landmine in Afghanistan blew out his knees," Chester explained. "He's got titanium knees now, but he can't run. So he bicycles twenty miles a day no matter what the weather."

I couldn't imagine anyone bicycling twenty miles along the coast of Lake Michigan in winter weather. In real winter weather, that is, not the fake Florida stuff we had right now.

"Keep running, son," the headmaster said, briskly saluting Chester as he sailed past, a yellow and white Spandex blur.

"Yessir!" shouted Chester, returning the salute. "Whiskey, I gotta go. Next week is the President's Fitness Challenge, and I need to improve my time."

Prince Harry yipped his encouragement.

"You're sure you don't want a ride to The Castle?" I said. "I'm going your way."

Chester studied my stomach, which wasn't rude since my stomach was eye level.

"You might want to work out with us," Chester suggested.

"I'm pregnant, not flabby," I reminded him. "That belly contains a baby."

"A baby who will be healthier if you exercise every day."

"Which personal assistant taught you that?"

"I saw it on the Oprah Winfrey Network." He sighed heavily. "Starting next week, the headmaster's restricting how much TV we can watch."

"Wait a darn minute," I said. "Schools can't control what

you do in your own home."

"Sure they can. It's called homework. Teachers at The Bentwood School never gave any, but Mr. Vreelander is giving it now. He's changing everything. We've got new rules, new policies, a new curriculum and new textbooks. We may even have to wear uniforms."

"You already wear a school blazer."

"I'm the only one who does." Chester shrugged. "I bought mine online because I liked the brass buttons. Almost nothing is required at my school. Except tuition, which is steep."

"How steep?"

I had always wanted to know what it cost to attend The Bentwood School, an elite academy for the super-rich dating back as far as my grandparents' day.

Chester motioned for me to bend down, which wasn't as easy as it used to be before the bundle in the middle. He whispered a five-figure number in my ear.

I whistled.

"The Bentwood School is just a day school, right? No boarders?"

Chester nodded.

"And it's K through 8?"

"Preschool through 8," Chester corrected me. "Preschool parents get a twenty-percent price break. But they have additional fees for paper products. Those kids tend to be wet."

He had barely finished before an oncoming cherry-red Mercedes convertible, top down, issued a sustained honk and swerved toward the berm where we stood. Instinctively, I threw myself in front of Chester and Prince Harry. I was protecting Chester on purpose; the dog just happened to be there.

A petite blonde bombshell with shoulder-length poker-straight hair and enormous breasts exited the Mercedes. She tottered toward us on five-inch heels, texting on her smartphone. I could only hope she hadn't been doing that when her car stopped six feet away.

"Chester!" she shouted without glancing up from her phone. "Don't you dare try to protect him. Which way did he go?"

3

Chester gulped. "Uh—hello, Ms. Kellum-Ramirez. How are you on this fine day?"

The woman, who was not yet thirty, tore her eyes from her smartphone. Her white-blonde bangs were so straight and long that they collided with her thick, surely fake, black lashes.

"Don't talk to me like that," she snapped. "Call me Kimmi, like a normal kid. I don't know where you get that formal crap."

"From my very first personal assistant—my nanny."

"Whatever," Kimmi said. "Which way did the headmaster go? And don't pretend you haven't seen him. The PTO is tracking him."

"Why?" Chester asked.

"Why what?" Kimmi said.

Distracted, she was texting again. That gave me time to consider her dress, which matched her vehicle: expensive, red, sexy and small. Very small. The bodice dipped low enough to expose two perfectly orb-shaped breasts, the kind God never gave women. The hemline was a foot above her knees. Kimmi Kellum-Ramirez also wore lots of shiny gold and diamond jewelry, including rings, dangly earrings, tinkling bracelets and gobs of necklaces. If my errant Afghan hound were nearby, Kimmi would be Abra-bait.

"Why are you looking for Mr. Vreelander?" Chester said.

"We need to talk to him. To set him straight."

After Kimmi pushed the send-button, she noticed me.

"Who's that?" she asked Chester.

"That's Whiskey."

"You have a personal assistant who gets you booze?"

"I'm Whiskey Mattimoe. I'm a Realtor."

"Chester has his own Realtor? Great. That will be Vreelander's next requirement."

She resumed texting.

"That's not how it works, Ms. Kel—, I mean, Kimmi," Chester said. "Mr. Vreelander isn't raising requirements because of anything I do."

"Ha! You learn things. Now he expects every kid to do that."

"He just wants the school to be stronger," Chester said.

"And as a result, our children are abandoning their PlayStations and Xboxes. Vreelander's got them outdoors, running around like they're—they're—."

"Regular kids?" I offered.

"Poor kids," she revised. "Underprivileged. Forced to use their bodies and their minds. It makes me sick."

Just then, another vehicle—this one a sky-blue Mercedes SUV—arrived from the same direction Kimmi had, and screeched into place alongside her. The driver didn't seem to care that she was blocking one half of Broken Arrow Highway.

"Where is he?" she shouted through her open window.

"Chester won't tell," Kimmi replied, crossing her arms over her chest and glowering at my small neighbor.

"Leave Chester out of it," I interjected.

"Which of his personal assistants is that?" The second driver leaned out her window to frown at me. Unlike Kimmi, this one wasn't sexy. Or even young. I'd call her plain and over forty. Without a trace of make-up, she sported shaggy dark hair and a scowl.

"That's his Realtor," Kimmi said.

"We have to get our kids Realtors now?" the second driver asked.

"She's not my Realtor. She's my neighbor, who happens to

Whiskey and Soda

be a Realtor," Chester explained, hopping anxiously from foot to foot.

The women weren't listening; they were comparing geographic coordinates on their smartphones. A third vehicle, this one a silver PT Cruiser pointed in the direction I had been driving, pulled up alongside the second vehicle. Broken Arrow Highway was now completely blocked.

Kimmi minced over to the new arrival and animatedly explained directions through the passenger side window. A discussion ensued, with Kimmi relaying information between the two drivers. As she did so, several vehicles whose drivers just wanted to get somewhere converged on us from both directions. The original drivers ignored them until horns bleated and the second driver leaned out her window and screamed an obscenity.

I covered Chester's ears with both hands. When she graced us all with her middle finger, I shifted my palms to cover Chester's eyes.

"You need more than two hands," he said. "Don't worry. I already know this stuff."

At that point, the driver of the PT Cruiser—whose face I couldn't see—said, "We're on it." and peeled away. The second driver wheeled her SUV around to follow.

Kimmi told Chester, "Vreelander can't hide for long."

"He's not hiding," Chester said. "He's getting a workout on his bike."

"He's going to listen to us. There's no way that asshole is cutting the Christmas play."

"You do a Christmas play at a secular school?" I asked Chester.

"We do *A Christmas Carol*. I play Tiny Tim every year, but Mr. Vreelander wants to cancel the production because the other kids aren't even trying to learn their lines."

"Who cares about the stupid words?" Kimmi fumed. "It's about how good the kids look. I spent three hundred bucks on my daughter's costume. She's gonna be the Ghost of Christmas Past, whether Vreelander likes it or not."

With that, Kimmi wobbled away on her absurdly high heels. They may have functioned effectively as FM shoes, but they offered poor traction on gravel. She gunned her Mercedes and roared past us, spraying small stones.

I used one hand to shield Chester's face, the other to protect my belly.

"What a witch. I can't believe she's a mother."

"They all are—Ms. Kellum-Ramirez, Mrs. Wardrip, and Mrs. Lowe. The kids call them Kimmi, Robin and Loralee. They run the PTO, but they really run Bentwood."

"They run the school?"

"They run Mr. Bentwood, School President. He's the grandson of the founder. Mr. Bentwood wouldn't give the previous headmasters much power, but he let the mothers do what they wanted. Until the board hired Mr. Vreelander."

"Why the change?"

"Recent graduates of The Bentwood School aren't doing well, Whiskey. Most can't pass admission tests for private high schools."

"You mean—?"

Chester nodded gravely. "Our alumni are ending up in public school."

4

"Alumni of The Bentwood School . . . in public school?" I couldn't believe it.

Chester nodded grimly. "Some don't even get into college."

"No way. Your school produces surgeons, moguls and politicians."

"Not lately," Chester said. "Since 2004, most of our graduates matriculate into Magnet Springs High and then into Lanagan County Tech. The girl who cuts my hair went to Bentwood."

"You get a hundred-dollar haircut," I reminded Chester. "Anyway, that won't be your story. Where do you want to go to high school?"

His cherubic face darkened. "Cassina thinks I should go to boarding school. She believes in the value of going away."

Out of sight, out of mind. That was more Cassina's parenting style than her educational philosophy.

Chester continued, "But I might not have to leave. She wanted me to go away for elementary school, and I won that battle."

"How?"

"I didn't leave. For almost six months Cassina thought I was at Cranbrook in Bloomfield Hills when I had actually enrolled myself at The Bentwood School."

"Wait. How could you do that?"

Chester rolled his eyes. "Sometimes, Whiskey, you are so naïve. But I find it refreshing."

"Answer my question."

He rubbed his second and third finger against his thumb in the universal sign for filthy lucre.

"You bribed your way into The Bentwood School?"

"No. I hired somebody to impersonate Cassina and forge my paperwork. Way easy."

"But didn't your mother notice you hadn't left home?"

As soon as I spoke, I realized how ridiculous I sounded. Cassina toured often to promote her latest CD, leaving her son in the care of an ever-changing household staff. Even when she was in residence at her twenty-thousand-square-foot Castle, Cassina routinely ignored or forgot about Chester. That accounted for his frequent presence at my house.

"Never mind," I revised. "So where will you go to high school?"

"I'll probably go where my friends go."

"You have friends?"

Chester's only known playmates were assorted canines.

He shrugged. "I have acquaintances, and I'm an optimist. Now that Mr. Vreelander is in charge, the school has a new admissions policy. They're accepting intelligent, motivated kids only. I'm about to meet my own kind."

I was genuinely happy for him.

"Prince Harry and I have to run back to The Castle now," he reminded me.

The dog had fallen asleep, his fuzzy yellow head resting on Chester's left foot. Apparently the cheese-flavored pedometer had lost its power. When I mentioned that, Chester assured me I was wrong.

"As soon as my body temperature rises from strenuous activity, the pedometer smells and tastes like cheese again. That's the beauty of this thing. Prince Harry will be trying to lick my ankle all the way home. It's a motivator for dog and boy."

After giving them a head start, I slowly followed for a quarter mile. Chester giggled and accelerated whenever Prince Harry's tongue tickled his ankle. Was there a device for sale that would keep Abra at home? Or motivate me to want to keep her there? I had mentioned to Chester that she was gone again. As usual, he promised to watch for her. But we both knew that Abra would come home when Abra was good and ready. Generally, that was only after she had inflicted mayhem on our community. I tried not to wonder what kind of mischief she was up to this time, and how soon the police would be involved.

I didn't have to wonder for long. Approaching Vestige, I couldn't help but notice a Magnet Springs Police cruiser parked in my driveway. Fortunately the flasher wasn't on, and there were no ambulances in the vicinity. Our local police force was, frankly, kind of a joke. Now if it had been a Lanagan County Sheriff or State Police cruiser—as it too often was—I would have been concerned. This was, most likely, either an informative social call or a nuisance report.

As I pulled into my driveway, Police Chief Judith "Jenx" Jenkins hove into view. I honked and leaned out the window. She failed to acknowledge me, appearing intent on casing my house.

"Looking for clues? Or planning a break-in?" I shouted by way of greeting.

Jenx and I shared a long history that predated Abra's criminal record. We were classmates in the Magnet Springs school system, and she hated her given name as much as I hated mine. Jenx was more a Jude than a Judith. Openly lesbian since about age ten, she helped her partner Henrietta operate the best B&B in Magnet Springs—when we weren't in the grip of a crime wave. That is, when Abra wasn't on the loose.

"Where's your dog?" Jenx said, not yet turning in my direction. She seemed to be tracing the foundation of my house.

"Ha, ha. What did she do this time? And what's so interesting about my foundation?"

Finally Jenx gave me her full attention. "It's too early in Abra's crime spree to know the extent of her destruction, but it looks like somebody forced their way in through your basement window."

That got me out of my vehicle in a hurry.

"Did my alarm system go off?"

I was going to say that but didn't. Of course my alarm system hadn't gone off. I rarely remembered to set it.

"I came by to talk to you about Abra," Jenx said. "Being a highly trained professional, I naturally took a look around. This was the first thing I saw."

With the toe of her steel-toe boot, she indicated the place where a pane of glass used to be. Now there was only air.

"I've been meaning to install glass block windows," I mumbled.

Jenx drew her sidearm. "Get back in your car, Whiskey. I'm going in."

"Is that wise? I mean, what if someone's still in there?"

"I'm armed. I also phoned for back-up."

"You called County?" I asked, knowing full well she hadn't. Unless absolutely forced to—as in the case of a violent crime—Jenx eschewed the assistance of larger law enforcement agencies. They tended to make fun of her.

"I called Brady," Jenx replied. "He and Roscoe are en route."

Officer Brady Swancott and K-9 sidekick Roscoe comprised the rest of the Magnet Springs police force. Brady worked part-time, but Roscoe was in line for a pension. Trained by the best police-dog handlers in Lansing, Roscoe could resist even Abra's charms.

Secretly I suspected that Chester might have removed the basement window days or even weeks ago, and I simply never noticed. If I remembered to lock my doors, my neighbor usually let himself in through the window above my kitchen sink, but if that were jammed, he would try others. It wasn't like Chester not to replace the window, though.

I gave Jenx the key so she could let herself into the house, but she didn't need it; I had left the front door unlocked. Impatiently, I waited in my car. Five minutes passed. Ten minutes. Jenx hadn't yet re-emerged when I detected the unmistakable wail of a police siren. Damn. I'd forgotten to ask Jenx to tell Brady not to use that thing. It wasn't that I feared the siren would disturb my neighbors. This was about my own sensibilities. I preferred to pretend that I had a life rarely visited by the men and women in blue.

Brady had barely screeched to a stop behind my car when Roscoe leapt out the passenger side window and bolted past me, slipping neatly through the spot where my basement window pane had been. Brady took his time exiting the vehicle. Lots of time. When, three minutes later, he hadn't yet appeared, I got out of my car and walked back to his.

Whiskey and Soda

I found him chatting on his cell phone. Catching my hostile gaze, he raised a hand to signal that he was nearly finished. I reached in through the open window and seized his phone.

"Officer Swancott is on duty now," I told the caller. "He'll have to get back to you after he responds to my B&E."

"We don't know that this is a B&E," Brady said calmly.

"Then why the siren?"

"I need to test it once in a while."

He motioned for me to step back so that he could open his door and perform his official duties. Brady unfolded his gangly form from the cruiser.

"Who was on the phone?" I said, handing it back to him.

"My wife. She wanted to know what's for dinner."

When not on police duty, Brady functioned as a stay-at-home dad and an online grad student. On the days when he donned a uniform, he often started dinner in the police station kitchen so that he could bring it home hot to his family.

"What's for dinner?" I asked, as we both walked up my driveway.

"I've got chicken and saffron rice in the station crockpot and a lemon pound cake in the oven." He checked his watch. "The cake is my wife's favorite. Let's hope we can wrap this up fast."

As we approached my front porch, the door flew open. Jenx appeared with her sidearm resting in its holster. She was accompanied by Roscoe, who cleared the doorway and stood at attention.

"Hey, Brady," she said, ignoring me. "Think the siren is set loud enough? I couldn't hear it 'til you got real close."

"Want me to test it again?" he said.

"No," I said. "Test it on your own time and property. We're here about my B&E."

"There was no B&E," Jenx said. "Or, if there was, I didn't notice anything missing. Except your dog, and we know nobody took her. You'll have to check for yourself, Whiskey, but it looks status quo to me. Whoever came in left the window pane on the basement floor."

"Broken?" I asked.

"Nope," Jenx said.

"You're saying nothing was stolen? Or broken? That's

weird."

"Shit happens. Or doesn't," Jenx said, yawning.

"Maybe you should get more sleep," I commented.

"That won't happen tonight unless Abra comes home. How long has she been gone?"

"Just since this morning. Why?"

"There are Abra sightings all along Uphill and Downhill Roads."

"Really? People called the police just to report seeing my dog? I didn't think anybody cared."

"Nobody 'cares,' Whiskey. People are scared she'll steal their shit."

Abra did have a reputation. She had been known to steal anything from designer purses to priceless jewels to fellow four-legged creatures.

Jenx shook her head in disgust. "Half the calls are coming from folks who think they saw a crazed long-haired goat."

That would have been Abra. Afghan hounds are a fairly rare breed. From a distance, most people wouldn't know what they were looking at, especially if they saw one running free in the countryside, unless, of course, they'd already had a traumatic encounter with mine. When Abra ran amok, she teased farm animals. Or worse.

"What's she done so far?" I asked with dread.

"Mr. Venable, the dairy farmer, says she startled his cows so bad they didn't make milk today. And Mr. Anderson, the chicken farmer, says his chickens won't lay. Apparently Abra got in the coop this morning and traumatized 'em all."

I closed my eyes, imagining the mayhem.

"On the bright side," Jenx said, "she didn't eat any chickens."

"No worries," Brady piped up. "Cows and chickens have short memories. By the next milking and laying cycles, they'll forget they ever saw a 'goat.'"

"Assuming the 'goat' doesn't intrude again," I said.

"She probably won't," Jenx said. "The last reported sighting had her heading toward town."

"Where she can harass humans," I said.

"She probably won't," Jenx repeated. "We got no tourists and our locals know enough to run when they see Abra coming."

5

K9 Officer Roscoe sighed. Although he maintained his military bearing, no doubt the mere mention of Abra's name tested his resolve. My dog was a wanton hussy who never tired of trying to seduce Roscoe. He had successfully resisted her advances so far.

Brady offered to walk around my yard with Roscoe, just in case the trained member of their team could pick up any clues. Since it hadn't rained lately, the intruder's scent might remain.

"We have time to check it out," Brady assured me. "My lemon pound cake needs to bake another thirty-five minutes."

Roscoe put his nose to the ground, and the human officer followed.

"Making any progress with Noonan?" Jenx asked.

"What do you mean?" I said.

"Seven Suns of Solace counseling. Hey, it worked for Hen and me."

"I'm not doing Seven Suns of Solace. I'm just asking Noonan for advice."

Seven Suns of Solace was a New Age belief system invented by Noonan's estranged husband and "permanent spouse," Fenton Flagg. It was way too full of mumbo jumbo for me. I reminded Jenx of that.

"Whatever. Everybody in town knows you need all the help you can get. Things will be better when Jeb comes home."

"Home? You mean, here?"

"This is where you live, isn't it?" Jenx said.

"This is where I live. I'm not sure where Jeb calls home."

Jenx rolled her eyes. "What the hell is your problem? And don't start that crap about how Jeb likes to stray."

"If he hadn't strayed, we never would have got divorced."

"Yeah, you would have. You both had lessons to learn."

"Now you sound like Noonan."

"Thanks." Jenx beamed at me. "Anyhow, we all know you and Jeb are permanent spouses."

I cringed at the Seven Suns of Solace jargon referring to soul mates stuck together forever.

Jenx continued, "Like Noonan and Fenton—and Hen and me."

"Yeah, well the jury's still out on Jeb and me," I said. "It didn't work the first time we tried it, and I can't go through that mess again."

"Hell, Whiskey, you were kids back then. Now you're gonna have a kid, so this time you gotta get it right."

I sighed. "It feels like I'm in this all alone."

"Try checking your voicemail. Jeb texted me this morning, said you won't take his calls or return his messages. So I'm delivering this one. He's coming home tonight."

"What?"

"You heard me. And don't try changing the locks. You know Larry the Locksmith doesn't like you."

She was right. About Larry.

"Jeb's on the road hawking his new CD," I protested. "Last I heard he was in California."

"He canceled the rest of his concert dates," Jenx said. "You and the baby are way more important than Canine Christmas Carols."

That wasn't as weird as it sounded. Okay, maybe it was. Jeb, whose singing career had gone in every direction except toward success, recently stumbled into an untapped market, crooning tunes to soothe four-legged creatures. Now Jeb was a star, at least in select circles. Overpaid people with over-bred pets eagerly shelled out their shekels for a few hours of peace.

But I couldn't quite picture his concert venues. Dog parks? Animal shelters? Pet Smart?

"Where does Fleggers send him?" I asked Jenx, referring to Four Legs Good, the radical animal-rights advocacy that had discovered and underwritten Jeb's special talent.

"Ask him yourself tonight. Speaking as local law enforcement, I'm relieved he's coming home. Jeb locks the doors."

Jeb even remembered to set the alarm system, but I didn't mention that.

"He should have asked me if I wanted him to come home," I groused.

"Check your voicemail," Jenx said.

After she left, I did. My voicemail box was full and probably had been for days. Almost every single message was from Jeb. I didn't bother to play more than nine or ten of them because they all said basically the same thing. "Whiskey, I love you. We need to talk. In person. Please."

I was sitting on my favorite sofa clearing my voicemail cache when the doorbell rang. Officers Swancott and Roscoe, whom I had completely forgotten, were ready to report the results of their search so that one of them could get back to his pound cake.

"Roscoe definitely smelled something," Brady said.

"Yeah? Something like wildlife? Or something like a human?"

"Wildlife, for sure. You live in the country. But Roscoe gave an indication of smelling humans, too. I just can't tell who. Or how many."

"That's helpful."

"Speaking professionally," Brady said although we both knew this was not his profession, "I'd say we're looking at one person working alone, probably a prankster. But we can't be sure because we don't have footprints. The ground's too dry. So it could have been one guy or a few guys."

For the first time since Jenx had shown me the missing window, I felt a wave of fear. Automatically my hand covered my belly. I looked down and back up at Brady.

"That's normal," he said.

"What is?"

"Protecting your child. You're becoming maternal, Whiskey."

"I'm not the least bit maternal."

Brady sighed, and I could have sworn that Roscoe did, too. They headed back to the station to retrieve a pound cake.

Moments later my doorbell rang again. This time it was my jogging neighbor and his dog, one sweating, the other panting.

"I'll get you water," I offered, heading to the kitchen for a glass and a bowl.

"That would be nice," Chester said, "but we have bigger issues. We need you to ride your bike."

I indicated where my waistline used to be.

"If this is a fitness intervention, I already told you, that's a baby and not body fat."

Chester jumped in frustration. Prince Harry did the same.

"This is not about fitness," Chester cried. "The headmaster's in trouble and we need to warn him!"

"Warn him about what?"

"I got a text from Kimmi's son, Raphael Ramirez," Chester said. "The PTO set up a blockade at the end of the Rail Trail. They're going to mob Mr. Vreelander!"

"Doesn't he have a cell phone?"

"He never takes it with him when he rides. Mr. Vreelander says he's 'in the zone' when he's on his bike."

"I'm sure he can handle anything that happens. Didn't you say he was ex-Army?"

"That's no match for the PTO!"

"Chester—they're mothers."

"Yes. Mothers like Kimmi. Do you have any idea what they're capable of?"

Instinctively my hand had moved to cover my belly again.

"All right. We'll put Blitzen in my car and drive to the access point closest to the trail end."

Blitzen was my nickname for the deluxe touring bicycle Leo had given me for my thirty-third birthday, just a few weeks before he died. I rode it to relax, to keep in shape, and—just

Whiskey and Soda

once—to kill a man. In self-defense. I had no intention of using Blitzen as a weapon again. Truth be told, I hadn't even ridden since I'd figured out I was pregnant.

Now duty called. Sure, my center of gravity was lower, but I was pretty sure I could make the adjustment. Especially if it would calm Chester and his Golden-Af, both of whom were now whirling like dervishes. I asked them nicely to stop.

"We can't," Chester gasped. "When I get excited the pedometer gets cheesy. When that happens, Prince Harry starts licking my ankle and I've got nowhere to run!"

Fortunately, I was wearing bootcut chinos and loafers, acceptable cycle wear for anyone not into Spandex. Grabbing my car keys and my phone, I motioned for Chester and his dog to follow me into the garage. The spinning duo was no help heaving Blitzen into my car. I managed on my own, however. Moments later we were headed toward town, boy in front seat and dog in back, at least until the cheese factor eased.

"Mr. Vreelander must be close to the trail end by now," Chester said. "Better use the parking lot off Orion Road."

Having ridden the Rail Trail myself, I knew the location he meant. I also knew I had to hurry if I hoped to head off the demon moms.

Attempting to lighten the moment, I said, "So Kimmi's son texted you? That was nice."

"Ha," Chester said. "Raphael is as mean as his mom. He was trying to torture me."

"Torture you? Let's cut the drama."

"Raphael and his buddies are bullies. They cause me pain every day."

"So does my mother, Chester, but I know, deep down, she loves me."

"Did your mother steal your blazer and stuff you in a trashcan?"

"No. But she sang 'Born Free' until her voice gave out."

"'Born Free'? I love that song."

Whereupon Chester commenced to sing it. He didn't know the lyrics any better than Mom did, but that didn't stop him, either. Blessedly, we soon arrived at Orion Road, where I quickly found the Rail Trail access and parked my car.

"Listen," I said, signaling for the song to stop. "I don't like leaving you alone here, but—"

"We're not staying in the car," Chester said. "Prince Harry and I are going to jog alongside you."

"No, you're not. I'm the adult and I'm going to handle this. You are going to wait here with the doors locked."

I marveled at how sure my voice sounded. Boy and dog immediately sat down. I reminded Chester that I had my cell phone.

"But don't call unless it's an emergency. I'm too out of shape to talk while I pedal."

Allowing ten minutes to intercept Vreelander before he reached the trail end, five minutes to speak with him, and ten minutes to pedal back, I expected to be gone no more than a half-hour. Chester would pass the time reading a book on his smartphone, and Prince Harry, like any dog, would sleep.

Built of super-light alloy, Blitzen required almost no muscle to hoist out my hatchback. I was soon flying along the paved Rail Trail, marveling at my bike's favorable gear ratio and the fact that nobody else was out riding on this mild December late afternoon. As much as I had griped about our un-Christmassy weather, I had to admit that it gave the gift of easy cycling.

I rode in a tipped-forward posture that inclined me to glance often at the ground. Looking up again, I spied a rider coming around the bend about fifty feet in front of me. It had to be the headmaster as I recognized not only the yellow and white Spandex shirt but also the muscles underneath it. How odd that he was heading in my direction. Had he got wind of the PTO's plot and turned around? Or had he already confronted the mothers, dismissed them and embarked on his return loop?

Vreelander straightened suddenly in his seat, both arms lifting from the handlebar. I smiled, thinking this was his version of a casual wave to a fellow rider—until I noticed he had stopped pedaling. His body hung suspended for a few seconds as the bike continued to roll. His back arched, and his mouth formed a perfect "O." I watched, stunned, as he tipped to his right, arms still raised, mouth open. The bicycle followed his lead, curving and crashing sideways onto the trail.

Heart thudding, I accelerated. When I reached him, he lay motionless on his right side, eyes and mouth wide in an expression of shock or pain. The front wheel of his gleaming blue touring bike still spun silently, but I knew the headmaster would never move again. Protruding from his upper back was the feathered shaft of an arrow.

6

Alternately swearing and moaning, I fumbled my phone out of my pants pocket. It took my shuddering fingers three tries to dial 9-1-1.

Our Chief of Police answered personally, a sure sign that crime was low in Magnet Springs, until now.

"The headmaster of Chester's school is dead!" I screamed. "He's on the Rail Trail and he's got an arrow in his back!"

"Where are you?" Jenx demanded.

"With the dead guy. How else could I know this? I have no intuition!"

"True," Jenx said. She ordered me to breathe before I continued.

"Chester's in my car in the Rail Trail parking lot off Orion Road," I said. "I'm here because Chester got a text message that the PTO set a trap for Vreelander at the end of the trail. Chester wanted me to warn him."

"A trap? What are you talking about?"

"Homework, jogging and *A Christmas Carol*. I'll explain later. The headmaster was coming around the bend in my direction, and then he—then he—"

After I took another breathing break, I managed to finish that sentence. Jenx told me to stay on the line while she dispatched Brady, who was feeding his family, the Lanagan County Sheriff's office, and the Michigan State Police. The state boys always bumped Jenx off the case, or tried to.

"Listen, Whiskey," our police chief said. "A sheriff's deputy will take care of Chester. They're sending a car to get him from your car. You sure you didn't see anybody but Vreelander on the trail?"

"Positive."

"Somebody with a lethal weapon can't be far away, so you gotta take cover."

"What about the—"

"You're sure he's dead, right?"

"He's dead all right."

"You're surviving for two now!" Jenx boomed. "So get the hell off the trail and behind a tree. A whole bunch of trees. And don't hang up! I'm staying on the line with you 'til somebody in a uniform gets there."

"Okay, but what about Blitzen?"

"It's a bike."

"I know it's a bike, but anybody who sees it will know there's another person around."

"They'll know there *was* another person around. Help me save your ass, Whiskey. Run into the woods. Now!"

I scrambled like a spastic person into the rapidly darkening forest that edged the trail.

Since the leaves were off the trees, I didn't think anybody could surprise me. On the other hand, the leaves were off the trees, making me a clear target for anybody with a bow and arrow.

"It's December in Michigan," I reminded Jenx.

"It feels like December in Florida," she replied.

"My point," I panted, "is there's no foliage to hide behind."

"Find an evergreen."

I continued crashing through the naked underbrush. When I glanced back toward the trail, I saw something that dropped me to my knees.

"There's a woman on a bike, riding straight toward the headmaster. She's got a bow on her back—and I don't mean the kind made from ribbon!"

Jenx asked if I recognized her. I didn't.

"She's got one of those things you keep arrows in."

"A quiver?"

"A quiver," I confirmed. "A full quiver."

"Can she see you?" Jenx demanded.

"Uh-oh," I said.

"Can she see you?"

"She rode past me already, right up to the dead guy," I whispered. "Now she's getting off her bike. She's looking real close at the body."

My beige wardrobe afforded the best camouflage I could hope for this time of year. The sun had dropped behind the trees, filling the woods with shadow and chill. I shuddered as the woman bent low over the headmaster's body to scrutinize the arrow in his back. From where I crouched, she seemed unafraid, even unsurprised. After a long moment, she turned her attention to my bike.

"She's checking out Blitzen," I whispered. "Shit. Now she's looking around for the person who dropped the bike."

The woman had straightened and was making a slow, deliberate circle as she studied the surrounding woods. I felt her gaze brush over me, but she gave no sign of seeing anything but darkness.

"Don't move!" Jenx bellowed in my ear. "Don't even breathe."

After a moment, the woman returned her attention to the corpse. Only now she was yelling at it. Suddenly animated, she gestured with both hands as she released a stream of impassioned verbiage. But the words made no sense, and I knew why. The words were French. I told Jenx.

"That makes sense," the chief said.

"It does?"

"She's speaking French—and she's got a bow and arrow, right?"

"Lots of arrows," I said.

"There's a French Archery Club near the trail end. It's called *Tir à l'Arc.*"

"'Teer-ah-lark?'" I repeated. "Does that mean she's the

killer?"

"You're the one looking at her," Jenx said. "Do you think she killed him?"

I studied the woman, who was still shouting at the dead man on the pavement.

"I'm not sure if she's the killer," I told Jenx. "But I'm positive she's French. No American could do drama like that."

"Is she scolding him, or crying over him, or what?" Now Jenx sounded way more impatient than concerned for my safety.

I squinted through the bare branches of the thicket I had crouched behind.

"She's not crying. And she's not what I'd call angry. More like frustrated. Definitely not pissed off like the PTO moms. This is weird. Like watching a foreign film without subtitles."

Jenx huffed into the phone. "Can you at least describe her?"

"Black hair cut short. She's . . . not tall. Maybe five-foot four or five. Slim but muscular. Compact. She's built kind of like a former gymnast."

"How old?"

"From here it's hard to say. Not real young."

"What does that mean?"

"Older than me, for sure. Maybe ten years older. Maybe more. She's wearing dark green work-out clothes and a glove on one hand. There's a leather band on her forearm and some kind of shield-thing on her chest—"

"A bracer and plastron," Jenx said.

"Say what?"

"Arm-guard and breast-guard. Standard archery stuff, like the glove."

"You know about archery?"

"I bow-hunt. If that arrow killed Vreelander, it's gotta be a broadhead."

"Are broadhead arrows legal?" I asked.

"Hell, yes. And not just for hunting. There are broadhead archery leagues."

"Leagues? Like for bowling?"

"Yup. But it's easier to make a fatal mistake with a broadhead than a bowling ball."

"You think this could have been an accident?" I asked.

"Can't tell yet. *Tir à l'Arc* has competitive target archery year-round. If Vreelander was near enough to the range, it might be possible for—"

"Jenx, hold on. She stopped yelling. She's dialing her phone now. Maybe she's dialing 9-1-1."

But she wasn't. No call rang through to Jenx's office.

"She finds a corpse and makes a personal call?" I wondered aloud. "Looks like the person on the other end is asking for details. The woman is checking his body and his bike—and my bike, too. Okay, the call is over. Oh my god. I don't believe it."

"What?" Jenx said.

"Now she's taking pictures. With her camera phone. She's getting shots of Vreelander's body. And Blitzen. The light's kind of low."

Nonetheless the woman continued to click away from several angles.

"Now it looks like she's sending them," I said.

"*Incroyable,*" Jenx said.

"You're speaking French?"

"I said, 'Unbelievable.' You should remember that one. We both took French in high school."

"Yeah, but the only thing I can say is 'Where's the post office?'"

I held my breath, listening.

"Jenx, I hear sirens. Finally. Uh-oh. The woman hears them, too. She's getting back on her bike. She's riding away!"

"Which direction?"

"She's going the way she was heading in the first place. In the direction I came from."

"Okay. Hold on, Whiskey, I gotta talk to Brady—and to County."

With my battery down to 12%, I could only hope the cavalry—in the form of Roscoe and Brady—was coming 'round the bend. The sun had vanished, and I was alone in a dark woods way too close to a corpse. I had witnessed a murder. And if the French woman were the killer, I could have been her second victim.

My whole body trembled so hard I expected to hear it rattle. I wondered if I were about to be sick. Although this wasn't the first time I had seen someone die, it was the first time I had been pregnant when that happened, the first time I might have endangered a precious brand-new life. Hands shaking violently, I managed to close the connection to Jenx and speed-dial the father of my unborn child.

7

Jeb picked up on the first ring. "Hey, Sunshine. Did Jenx tell you I'm coming home?"

So help me, months of frost melted as if lasered away.

"Jeb, I need you. We need you."

I could tell he was driving. I also knew, as surely as I knew my own habits, that he was switching the phone to his other ear.

"What is it, baby? What happened?"

First, I sobbed incoherently. Then I told him, or tried to. My phone battery died, but I wasn't scared anymore even though I was still alone in the dark near a dead man. Jeb was on his way home. Equally important at that moment, Roscoe's bark was growing closer. The baby and I would be fine.

"I'm here! Hey! Over here! Whiskey Mattimoe—I'm over here!" I shouted, willing to yell myself hoarse rather than attempt to stumble blindly through the underbrush. As Jenx had said, I was surviving for two now. Let Brady and Roscoe come save me.

They did, of course, although the process took a little longer than I would have preferred, mainly because Roscoe got distracted by the corpse. But he'd been trained that way. The sweeping beam of Brady's flashlight instantly eased my mind, as did the sound of his voice.

The Lanagan County sheriff's deputies figured out how to drive their cars down the Rail Trail, so they arrived with more manpower and equipment, including blankets. A female deputy draped me in fleeces and offered me a folding canvas chair. I asked her to face it away from the crime scene, which was now floodlit like a movie set.

"We'll have to get Blitzen later," Brady said, squatting alongside me. "After County gets their crime scene shots."

"Blitzen wasn't part of the crime," I said, my teeth still chattering.

"No, but it's here, so it's part of the record."

"I'm here, too, but nobody's taking my picture. I'm going home."

Brady sighed. "Nobody's going to take your picture, Whiskey, because you can talk. Somebody's going to ask you questions any minute now. Probably that guy."

He pointed toward a deputy standing in the spill of the crime scene team's light, making notes in a pad. The man looked up, locked eyes with me, and ambled over.

"I told him you're pregnant in case he can't tell in the dark," Brady said. "He shouldn't detain you for long."

"You're Whitney Mattimoe?" the deputy asked.

"Whiskey," I said.

"You'll have to get that on your own time. I understand you saw Vreelander die."

"She doesn't want whiskey," Brady interjected. "That's her nickname."

"Why would a pregnant woman want to be called Whiskey?" the deputy asked.

"I'm right here," I reminded them.

The nice female deputy returned with a bottle of water. I hadn't realized how parched I was until I started sipping. I answered the male deputy's questions, some of which he asked twice, as if I were dense in addition to pregnant. Finally, he told Brady he could take me home.

"Did somebody from your department take care of the kid in my car?" I asked.

The deputy stared at me like I was an unfit mother.

"A kid and a dog. But not my kid and dog," I said quickly. "Just a kid and a dog I take care of, sometimes. Except for today.

Whiskey and Soda

Today I left them in my car."

This wasn't going well, so Brady translated. We had to find the female deputy again in order to get an answer. She was able to assure us that Chester and Prince Harry were now safely back at The Castle.

"Do they know about the headmaster?" I asked her.

She couldn't vouch for what Prince Harry knew, but Chester was aware there had been an "incident" involving Mr. Vreelander. The deputy told me that Vreelander's first name was Mark, he had no children, but he did have a wife who was now a widow. She didn't live here but the authorities had contacted her.

"Were they separated?"

I recalled the agitated French woman on the trail and wondered if she were Vreelander's lover.

"I don't know," the deputy said. "Mrs. Vreelander directs a school, too. In Dallas, I think."

With a little help from his trusty magnum flashlight and his K9 officer, Brady guided me to the patrol car and helped me into the back seat. Watching Roscoe leap into the front seat, I couldn't help but think of my own big dog, disobedient though she was. Where on earth would she spend the night? I mentioned that to Brady as he started the engine.

"I wouldn't worry about Abra," he said.

"She's alone in the cold and dark."

"Is she, Whiskey?"

I understood his point. By now Abra had probably seduced another furry body to snuggle with.

"Tonight you need to take care of yourself," Brady said. "I hear Jeb's coming home."

For the first time in months, I would have a warm body to snuggle with, too. Jeb would steel me against whatever tomorrow might bring—even if tomorrow included news of more crimes, and even if those crimes involved Abra. I closed my eyes, imagining the warmth of Jeb's embrace. He was due at my house within an hour. I couldn't wait to let him lead me upstairs to bed; I planned to fall into his arms and let fate take care of everything at least until morning, when somebody or something was sure to interrupt our fun.

Vestige glowed warm and welcoming as we approached. Somebody had turned on the porch light. I recognized Jeb's new car in the driveway. He had only recently replaced his ancient Nissan Van Wagon with a neat little leased Beamer, thanks to a cash infusion from his canine-crooning career. As Brady applied the brakes, the front door opened, and Jeb stepped out, a lank, grinning figure in the porch halo. Tears sprang to my eyes, and I did my best imitation of leaping from the vehicle. Not even close to graceful, at least I was relatively fast.

Until I tripped over a dog. A small dog that had no business being in my driveway. Brady shone his flashlight on the ugliest canine I had seen since meeting Mooney, a Rottweiler-bloodhound mix owned by our local judge. This dog was a stocky, short-legged model with a Winston Churchill-like face and wide-set very large erect ears.

"Whiskey, my love," Jeb said, rushing from the porch to help me to my feet. Or so I thought. He paused first to scoop up the pooch and kiss the top of its head; Brady assisted me to a standing position.

"Meet Sandra Bullock," my ex-husband said, holding out the dog to me.

"Sandra? You know this mutt?"

"Know her? I rescued her. Only she's not a mutt. She's a purebred French bulldog."

Jeb squeezed me to him, but the embrace wasn't what I had hoped for. He still clutched the dog in one arm.

"Wait. Go back," I said. "I had a big shock tonight, and I'm not sure I'm tracking this. You're talking about Sandra Bullock?"

Jeb had lusted after the movie star since seeing her in The Vanishing. Or was it Demolition Man?

"Right," he said, kissing my forehead—with lips that had just kissed a dog. "I named this little doll after her. Baby, you're gonna love Sandra as much as I do. And she's fantastic with kids."

"I already have a dog," I reminded him. "And I've successfully given away several."

Jeb whispered, "I heard Abra's gone again. Of course, I hope she comes back, but if she doesn't—"

"Abra always comes back," I said through clenched teeth. "Often with a police escort. What were you thinking? I don't want another dog. Besides, that one is butt ugly."

"Oh, come on. Sandra's a little cutie and a real comedienne, just like her namesake. Give her a chance, Whiskey."

I stepped back abruptly. "I thought you came home because you wanted to be here for me and the baby."

"I do."

"Why on earth would you bring a dog?"

Suddenly Brady cleared his throat and Roscoe made a similar sound. I had forgotten about the police presence in my dark driveway. The two officers stepped forward into the spill of yellow light from my porch.

"Good to see you, Jeb. Glad you're back," Brady said, and the two men shook hands. Roscoe introduced himself to Sandra Bullock by rising to his hind feet and performing an agile dance, one that exposed a certain extension.

"What the—" I began. "Brady, I thought Roscoe was fixed."

"He is," Brady said. "I've never seen that before, either. Wow. She must turn him on."

Jeb said, "All the boys love Sandra."

My own slut hound had never had that effect on the canine officer. How could the dumpy dog with the ugly mug succeed where Abra had failed? At least the Affie knew how to flirt.

"She's not even trying," I pointed out.

In fact, the French bulldog appeared to have dozed off in Jeb's arms.

He whispered, "That's the secret to her success."

Roscoe, who was still dancing, moaned obscenely. So help me, I couldn't take my eyes off him.

Brady cleared his throat. "If you're all right, Whiskey, I'm heading home. Gonna have a little lemon pound cake with my wife."

Jeb chuckled in a way that made me wonder if "lemon pound cake" was guy code for what Roscoe was doing. Brady led the German shepherd, still walking on two legs, back to the squad car.

8

Jeb wanted Sandra Bullock to share our bed, but I wouldn't hear of it. While my preference was to leave her on the porch, Jeb insisted she was an indoor dog who required comfort. We compromised. She would spend the night in Abra's room. The Affie wouldn't need it tonight. Better yet, the door boasted a double lock, and I had no plans to share the key. Although Abra could escape that space, such a feat required physical skills I was sure no French bulldog possessed.

As he laid Sandra down, I saw tenderness in Jeb's face that should have been reserved for our first child. Sure, he had always been nice to animals, but I'd never known him to be a "dog person." Why start now? Once we were out in the hall, I tested the latch with more force than necessary.

"Easy, baby," Jeb whispered.

"Since when do you rescue dogs?" I demanded.

Belatedly he folded me against him the way I had wanted him to do outside. Only now I was too annoyed to melt at his touch. I softened a little...okay, a lot. But it took a minute. He did smell wonderful, and he did remember how to hold me. I inhaled the faintly woodsy fragrance that was uniquely Jeb and tried to pretend there were no dogs in the world, let alone in my house. He tenderly kissed my hair, then my forehead, my eyes, my cheeks, and finally my mouth. We were linked again, at last. I had almost fallen all the way into the moment when he paused to answer my question.

"You can't expect me to make a living crooning for canines and not care about them, can you?"

I had to think about that one.

"Jeb, caring about your job is one thing. Bringing it home is something else altogether."

He sighed and pulled me closer.

"I'm sorry, babe. But I had to save Sandra. I nearly ran her over."

I groaned. "Please don't tell me this is about karma."

"Isn't everything about karma?"

"In Magnet Springs, yes, which is why I'm proud to live in denial."

It galled me that we were wasting precious moments talking when we should have been kissing and cuddling. Talking about dogs and karma was completely unacceptable.

"We can talk later," I said, pulling Jeb toward my bedroom. "Though not about this. Never about this. Tonight we are done talking. Tonight we—"

Jeb took his cue, turning my unfinished sentence into a long sweet kiss, which quickly gave way to groping and other good things. Moments later we were two warm nonverbal bodies pressed together under my quilt. Connection complete.

The real world intruded far too early, poisoning my dreams. I was riding Blitzen along the Rail Trail, alone, when I spotted Jeb riding toward me on a shiny blue bicycle. He wore yellow and white Spandex, exactly like the headmaster. Only Jeb looked goofy in Spandex, and he knew it. He was making a silly face.

I laughed out loud as I waved at him.

Without warning, Jeb did exactly what the headmaster had done. He raised his hands as if to wave back and toppled off his bicycle, an arrow protruding from his back.

My laughter morphed into a scream, but it was so hard to make sound come out. The louder I tried to scream, the less noise I could make. Jeb shook me awake.

"Babe. Wake up. You're having a bad dream."

I was so relieved to find him in my bed next to me, wearing neither Spandex nor an arrow, that I didn't half mind when the phone rang minutes later. Jeb passed it to me.

"Abra's at it again," our tireless police chief began. "I got a report last night of a missing poodle, a champion, very valuable. A family member saw him run off with a long-haired goat. This morning two folks saw a goat and a poodle in Vanderzee Park, doing what animals from two different species aren't meant to do."

"Maybe it really is a goat," I mumbled. "A kinky goat."

"Name one goat in Lanagan County," Jenx said.

"Maybe it's Satan, in the form of a goat."

"It's Satan, all right, in the form of your dog."

I rolled onto my back and tried to focus on the ceiling. My bedroom was still semi-dark.

"What do you want from me, Jenx?"

"I got quite a list. Are you awake enough to listen, or should I tell Jeb, and he can tell you?"

Jeb's grinning face, topped by tousled hair, filled my field of vision once again. Jenx's voice had been loud enough for him to hear, so I passed the phone back to him. Propped up on one elbow, he proceeded to make all those noises that signal agreement. I could only hope he was agreeing to handle everything without involving me.

"I'll get Whiskey up and at it," he concluded and hung up the phone.

"No," I cried, squeezing my eyes shut. "No, no, no."

"Come on," he cajoled. "You know you want to help Chester."

"Chester? What happened to Chester?" I was wide awake now.

"He's fine. He's on his way over. Jenx says his school is holding an assembly this morning to announce the headmaster's death. She's going to be there to address parents and students, and she thinks you should be there with Chester."

Before I could comment, the phone rang again. Jeb passed it to me. I heard heavy breathing.

"It's a little early for a crank call," I snarled at the receiver.

"Whiskey, it's me," Chester panted. "Prince Harry and I are jogging to Vestige."

"Uh, I think that assignment is over," I said as delicately as

I could. "No more homework at your school."

"I'm going to keep it up, anyway," Chester vowed, "as an homage to Mr. Vreelander."

"Okay, but don't tell your classmates or their moms."

"No problem, Whiskey. They don't know what 'homage' means."

In vain I tried to convince Chester that jogging to my house would only make him sweaty. He countered that I had three available showers, and Prince Harry was carrying his school clothes.

"Aha," I said, inspired. "That's another issue. What are we going to do with Prince Harry? He can't go to school with you, and he can't stay here."

"Sure he can. He can play with Sandra Bullock all day."

"How do you know about Sandra Bullock?"

I glared at Jeb, who shrugged.

Chester said, "I talk to Jenx. She tells me everything."

Boy and dog were at my door before the sun was all the way up. Fortunately, Jeb was up and making coffee in my kitchen. In a perfect world, he would have been up to something else in my bedroom, something sexy and fun. But we didn't live in a perfect world. We lived in Magnet Springs, a town steeped in karma. And dogs.

Speaking of dogs, I didn't hear a peep from Jeb's, even when Chester rang the doorbell. Granted, I hadn't known a lot of canines, but every single one I'd ever met went gonzo when there was someone at the door. What was up with this French bulldog? If the doorbell rang, and Abra didn't make a sound, I knew she was gone. Wait a damn minute. Could I have been wrong about Sandra Bullock's ability to escape a locked room?

Wrapping my robe around me—and noticing that I no longer had enough sash to make my preferred double-knot—I peered down the hall. The door to Abra's room was still shut tight. I hadn't heard Jeb open it when he shuffled off to start the coffee. From downstairs came his voice mixed with Chester's and the occasional happy yip of Prince Harry. Still no sound from Sandra.

Then I heard it, the distinct roar of snoring emanating from that room. Not soft snoring like you might expect from a creature who weighed less than twenty-five pounds. This snoring was loud enough to come from a teenage boy, a really large teenage boy, like the fullback on our local high school football team.

I moved to the door, listening in morbid fascination.

"Whiskey!" Jeb stage-whispered from the foot of the stairs.

"What?"

In response he pressed his index finger to his lips. Chester appeared alongside him, making the same sign. I wanted to protest that no amount of beauty sleep could help the dog on the other side of that door until I realized that as long as Sandra Bullock was unconscious, I wouldn't have to deal with her. I gave the okay sign and dashed to the bathroom before Chester could use all the hot water.

Sex with Jeb would have been better, but the steamy leisure of my Roman shower was seductive. I took my sweet time, letting the hot mists envelop me and erase thoughts of a hectic world waiting out there for my contributions. I didn't hear him enter my bathroom, probably because I was running the water at full force. Finally Jeb's melodic voice reached me, singing a silly Barenaked Ladies tune from way back when.

"That would have been more fun with you in it," I said after turning off the shower.

He handed me an oversized towel, first, and a mug of hot coffee, second.

"Wish I could have joined you, babe, but somebody had to make breakfast."

"Chester is really good at that," I pointed out.

"Right. But he has a tough day ahead of him, and school starts at eight. He's counting on you to walk in with him, so you need to hurry. I laid out your clothes on the bed."

It wasn't like Jeb to be well-organized. I wanted cuddly disorganized Jeb, and I wanted him to fawn all over me. Now.

"I've had a trauma, too, you know," I whined.

"I know, but you're a big girl—"

Defensively I folded my arms over my belly.

"A big beautiful girl," Jeb amended, "with a beautiful baby in there."

He planted a kiss on my still-damp tummy. Blame it on hormones, but suddenly I went all weak and weepy.

"What's the matter?" Jeb looked confused.

"What happened on the Rail Trail yesterday really happened," I insisted. "You can't pretend that it didn't."

"I'm not pretending anything," Jeb said. "I was just trying to make you feel better."

"By being more concerned about Chester than you are about me?"

"Time out."

Jeb laid his hands on my shoulders and peered directly in my eyes.

"This morning we're helping Chester. When you get home, we'll focus on you. Promise. That's why I'm here, Whiskey. I came home to be with you and our baby. Last night you didn't want to talk—"

"I didn't want to talk about dogs last night, especially that dog down the hall. Tonight we'll talk about what happened and about what's going to happen with us."

I let the sentence hang there in the warm moist air until Jeb put a period on it with a kiss. It might have turned into a really nice kiss if Chester hadn't interrupted it with a knock.

"Ready for school when you are, Whiskey. Here's a suggestion. The PTO likes people who look good, so you might want to comb your hair."

9

It's not that I failed to make a habit of combing my hair. It's just that my hair didn't look combed. Or stay combed. I had radically recalcitrant hair—thick, coarse and curly. My hair was a triple threat to cosmetologists everywhere, and a daily source of chagrin to me.

Nonetheless, out of respect for Chester, I spent a few extra minutes wrestling with my mane before we left for The Brentwood School. He gave me an "E" for effort, adding that most of the mothers would probably be too worked up about the headmaster to give me more than a passing glance. I could only hope. Waving good-bye to Jeb and Prince Harry, I wondered how Abra's son would get along with the new rescue dog. Silly question. Prince Harry was half-Golden, and Goldens love everybody.

The Bentwood School was situated on an impressive piece of real estate, the kind that nobody with any business sense wants to see wasted on academics. Although I respected education as much as the next citizen, the seasoned Realtor in me couldn't resist estimating the commercial value of the property as Chester and I cruised down its long tree-fringed driveway. Granted, real estate was temporarily in the toilet. Even so, the school's twenty acres of playing fields, woods, meadows, parking lots and tasteful Victorian-style buildings had to be worth three million. In recent better days, they could have commanded five.

Chester pointed to the main building, a sprawling gothic mansion that still boasted a widow's walk with a clear view of

Lake Michigan. I knew that no member of the Bentwood family had ever plied the waves for anything other than pleasure. They made their considerable fortune building and running the local railroad.

"Well, the private school biz must be good," I said. "The parking lots are beyond full."

Traffic had ground to a standstill, giving Chester ample time to fill me in on The Bentwood School's history.

"The original railroad tycoon had only one child," he began, as if reciting an oft-told tale. "At a tender age, that son was sent off to Exeter Academy and from there, to Yale University. After graduation, he returned home with a Vassar-educated wife. Catherine Ormond Bentwood bore him three sons, but she was appalled by the lack of private education available in West Michigan."

"Don't tell me," I said. "She sent their sons to Exeter and Yale."

"Right," Chester said. "But when Catherine's husband died, she devoted herself to founding the kind of academy she had wished were available for their children."

"Sweet," I said. "Do all your fellow students know that story?"

Chester shrugged. "Most of them don't know much."

I watched a uniformed security guard as he directed drivers, one by one, to park their vehicles in overflow locations on the school lawn. He seemed to recognize most folks, acknowledging them with a friendly nod.

"Enrollment is high," Chester said, "but the parking lots weren't built to accommodate all the parents at once. Usually, they drop off their kids and drive on. Today everybody's coming in to hear Mr. Bentwood's announcement."

"How do they know about it? Was it on the news?"

"Social media," Chester replied.

"Social what?"

Distracted, I inched my car forward, impatient for the rent-a-cop to show me where I should park.

"Social media," Chester repeated. "You know—sites where people post photos and updates about every single thing they think or do."

"Oh. Right."

"You should try it."

"I keep meaning to. Then I get busy having a life."

"Mattimoe Realty needs a social media presence," Chester insisted as the security guard signaled for me to follow a white Lincoln Navigator. "Maybe you should hire Avery to create it for you."

"Say what?" The mere mention of my ex-stepdaughter's name was guaranteed to grab my instant attention. And spike my blood pressure. "Why would I hire Avery to do anything? Besides, I thought she worked for your mother."

"She does," Chester said, bouncing emphatically in his seat. "Cassina hires her to manage her social networks. Avery posts and tweets all day. She's a buzz-maker, Whiskey. I'm sure she could help you."

Poor Chester, ever the naïf. The day I would trust Avery to broadcast details of my life would be the day when porcine creatures took flight.

"So Avery works online for Cassina?"

As much as I had wondered what the pop diva was paying my lazy ex-step to do, I'd been afraid to ask. Afraid because Avery was chronically inclined to blow every opportunity and come crawling back to my place, her twins in tow. Out of self-defense I had adopted a "Don't Ask, Don't Tell" policy, wanting to believe that if I didn't inquire, she couldn't possibly fail and need my help. Pathetic? Yes, yet oddly optimistic at the same time.

Our weather continued to be unseasonably balmy. Neither Chester nor I had even bothered to wear a winter coat. We followed the stream of jacket-free pedestrians flowing into the main building, which looked up close like a cheerful Disney version of a Victorian house. Painted pale yellow with sky-blue shutters, doors, and ornate trim, it boasted windows that were surely twice as large as the originals must have been. Someone had wisely chosen to infuse the narrow, high-ceilinged converted classrooms inside with as much light as possible for the sake of the children.

"Uh-oh," Chester said, suddenly slowing his pace. "They're all here, and they're organized. That can't be good."

I followed his gaze to what could only be called a mob of moms. Kimmi Kellum-Ramirez, once again wearing stiletto heels, energetically distributed bright red handouts to a rapidly swelling group of women. Robin Wardrip, looking plain but purposeful in head-to-toe camouflage gear, assisted her. So did another mother, a short but athletic-looking golden-haired woman with a heart-shaped face. She wore a feminine dress with a floral print, but she moved more like a spry young boy than a grown woman.

On a December morning outside any other elementary school, I would have assumed that the pages promoted a Christmas bazaar or contained the lyrics to a favorite carol. Here, though, I knew they had something to do with a dead headmaster, and the moms weren't collecting for his funeral flowers. The grim intensity with which they moved reminded me of soldiers preparing for battle.

"They want to get everybody on the same page," Chester said. "Literally."

"What page is that?"

"I'm pretty sure they're going to demand that Mr. Bentwood take over as headmaster. Again."

"Well, that makes sense. I mean, he's a member of the founding family."

Chester peered up at me with an expression that said I didn't have a clue what I was talking about. "He's not a natural educator, Whiskey."

"Not a chip off his grandmother's block."

The second comment didn't come from Chester. It came from our chief of police, who joined us on the school lawn. She was flipping through a small well-worn spiral notebook, the kind used by responding officers at crime scenes.

"Bentwood's strength is politics," Jenx added.

Chester said, "The art of the possible. The PTO gets what they want when Mr. Bentwood gets what he wants."

"What more does he want?" I asked. "He's already got a school with his name on it, plus inherited wealth."

Jenx shrugged. "More power. More prestige. More . . ."

She mimed a third word after making sure that Chester wasn't reading her lips.

"Sex?" I asked out loud. My bad.

"Yes," Chester confirmed. "Mr. Bentwood has a reputation

with the ladies."

"Really?"

I had met George Bentwood years earlier at a local fundraiser I'd attended with Leo, my late husband.

"Bentwood's married, isn't he? And he's not young."

"What's your point?" Jenx said.

"Well, he didn't strike me as all that attractive."

"Me, neither," the chief conceded. "But I'm a dyke. Lots of straight chicks seem to think he's got something. Maybe it's the twinkle."

"The what?"

"Twinkle. That's what Noonan calls it. She believes there's a gleam some guys get in their eyes that makes them irresistible. She says Fenton's got it. Jeb does, too."

I understood. Some men gave off a vibe that drew women. No question Jeb had it; I'd seen it in Fenton, too. It was one of Noonan's problems with her "permanent spouse" and my whole issue with my ex.

"There's Bentwood," Jenx said, indicating a tall white-haired man with impeccable posture. He motioned for the mothers to follow him inside, presumably so that he could start the meeting.

"They're trailing him like baby ducklings," Chester observed.

To me they looked like cats in heat.

10

Jenx sent Chester ahead with the crowd that was flowing in through the pale blue double front doors of the Victorian home that housed The Bentwood School. Our Chief of Police wanted to bring me up to speed on what she'd learned since last night.

"Chester got it wrong," Jenx said. "The PTO was waiting for Vreelander at the trail head, not the trail end."

"Maybe Raphael Ramirez got it wrong. He's the one who texted Chester."

"Maybe. Or maybe he was supposed to give Chester the wrong information. He's Kimmi's kid, right?"

"Right. Is she a suspect?"

I wanted her to be. Everything about Kimmi Kellum-Ramirez offended me, from her fake tits to her FM pumps. Or maybe she just rattled my green-eyed monster. Kimmi reminded me of all the hot, sexy chicks I would never resemble. The girls who had always caught Jeb's eye and got his free autographed CDs. And more.

"All the mothers could be suspects," Jenx said. "If they have means and motive, plus archery skill. We know they had time. If they'd met him at the trail end, they wouldn't have been able to get to the archery range before Vreelander rode past, but they met him at the trail head. After that, any of them could have driven to the range and got in position before he turned around at the trail end and started back."

"I like Kimmi for the crime," I declared.

"Yeah, well, I got a witness who says she made a real spectacle of herself at the trail head," Jenx said. "She screamed and cried and threw her kid's homework assignments in the headmaster's face."

"Yup. Kimmi killed him."

"Robin Wardrip looks good for it, too. My witness says she took a swing at Vreelander. He deflected the blow, but Robin's got a left hook that could knock out a middleweight. She told him to go fuck himself, and she spat at him."

"I still like Kimmi for it," I said.

"And then there's Loralee Lowe," Jenx said. "She's a mom and a teacher here, and also one of Bentwood's lovers."

"One of—?"

Jenx shrugged. "He's got the twinkle. You saw Loralee this morning. Wavy gold-blonde hair? Dress with flowers all over it? Rumor has it Bentwood's the father of her child."

"Seriously? How old's the kid?"

"Three, I think. She's in Preschool."

"Is Loralee single?"

"She is now. Her ex is her daughter's legal father. But my source tells me the kid looks like Bentwood. Loralee's ex thought so, too. He ordered DNA testing before he walked out. Now Loralee's pushing Bentwood to leave his wife."

"Loralee didn't like the headmaster?" I asked.

"She hated him," Jenx said.

"Why?"

"He was planning to fire her."

"For an ethics violation?"

"Nope. She's a lousy teacher."

Jenx checked the heavy masculine watch on her wrist. "Eight o'clock sharp. We'd better make our entrance."

"We? I'm here to stand by Chester. Now I've got to find him in that crowd."

"Like he could blend in?" Jenx was moving fast toward the school entrance, and I kept pace. "Chester will feel your support, Whiskey. I'm gonna need you up on stage with me."

"Why? I'm just a witness."

"You're the only witness. I want to watch this crowd closely when you tell them what you saw. There's an excellent chance the killer will be in that room."

"What about the French archer? She had the murder weapon, and she was in the right place at the right time. I was an eye witness to that."

"We're looking into her," Jenx said noncommittally as we stepped into the foyer of The Bentwood School. "By the way, the arrow that killed Vreelander was a mechanical broadhead, as opposed to a fixed broadhead."

"What's the difference?" I asked, not at all sure I wanted to know.

"Mechanicals open up inside the victim, deploying blades on contact. They may not penetrate as deep as fixed broadheads, but they're more streamlined as they fly. So they're easier to control over distance, and they cause a lot of internal bleeding."

I shuddered and willed myself to think about Victorian mansions instead. Despite the larger-than-traditional replacement windows and doors, I had expected this one to be dense and shadowy. Not the case at all. Whoever oversaw the renovations had created a sunny, wide open space partitioned into modular rooms with movable dividers and recessed lighting. Every original non-load-bearing wall must have been removed, along with every interior door. The resulting ambience was modern and cheerful with just the right quixotic touches of Victorianism in the arched oversized replacement windows, ornate cornices and molding, and gleaming dark oak floors.

I was so taken by the ambience that I must have stopped in my tracks. Jenx nudged me in the direction of a murmuring crowd we could hear but not see beyond the first-floor classrooms. The meeting place featured a modest-sized stage framed by theatrical lighting fixtures and fronted by moveable stack chairs rather than permanent theater seats. Between the chairs and the stage was a twenty-foot-deep space filled with children sitting Indian style, if one could still use that non-P.C. phrase. The children on the floor ranged in age from about eight years to three years; behind them in chairs sat the rest of the student body. And behind them were the parents who had arrived early enough to get seats. Another thirty adults stood lining the walls.

"No press?" I asked Jenx, noting the absence of TV cameras. Now that I thought about it, I hadn't spotted any news vans outside.

"Bentwood agreed to give them a statement after the assembly. At ten o'clock. I'll talk to reporters at the same time."

Jenx gave me a gentle shove down the center aisle. Heads snapped in our direction and the room's collective voices became a low buzz. School President George Bentwood stood center stage watching our approach. Without a podium he seemed totally at ease in the spotlight. Technically, since all the lights in the room were on, there was no spotlight; still, I felt the heat of everyone's curiosity as I followed Jenx up the three steps to the stage. The whole room fell silent. Bentwood greeted us, an agile man three inches taller than I was, and I stood just shy of six foot-one. He wore a tailored charcoal-gray blazer with European-cut pants and black Italian loafers. His thick white hair and neatly trimmed mustache suggested meticulous grooming as well as enormous vanity. He acknowledged first Jenx, then me, with a warm handshake and a cordial nod. Clearly the occasion disallowed smiles.

"Ms. Mattimoe," he said in a deep fuzzy voice designed to draw others close. "We are grateful that you're here. So sorry for the circumstances."

As his astonishingly bright blue eyes met mine, I spotted it—the twinkle. He gave my hand an extra squeeze and leaned closer.

"We've met before. You are a stunning woman."

The twinkle, for sure. He added a winning grin that his larger audience couldn't see. This was a man whom women would remember even if he didn't inspire them to leap directly into his bed. Yet he hadn't lingered in my mind after that long-ago charity fundraiser. How had I missed his appeal? I could chock that up to only one possible excuse. I'd been completely smitten with my then-new hubby Leo.

Now I faced my audience, row after row of bright-eyed children eager to hear what I'd come to say. I glanced at Jenx, willing her to, if at all possible, read my thoughts. This was a horrible idea. How could I recount my grisly experience to these innocents?

Although psychic powers, or what passed for them, seemed to abound in Magnet Springs, telepathy was not among Jenx's arsenal of strange talents. Hers involved rattling our local geomagnetic fields when she herself felt rattled. Nonetheless, she turned to me now and said, "No worries, Whiskey. Your

Whiskey and Soda

story is for the adults in this audience only. Mr. Bentwood just wants to say a few words first to the student body."

"Ladies and gentlemen, girls and boys," he began. "As you may know, The Bentwood School has suffered a tragic loss. This morning we gather as a family gripped by shock and grief at the news that our headmaster, Mark Vreelander, passed away suddenly last night."

Passed away suddenly? That was one way to put it, although not the accurate way. I glanced at Jenx who was busy scanning the crowd.

Bentwood continued, "Whenever a healthy, relatively young person dies unexpectedly, there are, of course, questions. I've invited two people to help us answer those questions—Magnet Springs Police Chief Judith Jenkins and Whitney Mattimoe, broker and owner of Mattimoe Realty. Chief Jenkins will offer professional insights, while Ms. Mattimoe will speak as an ordinary citizen who happened to witness a tragic event."

Tragic? More like violent and probably criminal. As in murder.

I cleared my throat loudly to cue Jenx that this was not going in a direction I liked. Hell, I was already in therapy for my inability to relate well to children. The last experience I needed as a wary expectant mother was the traumatic memory of making hundreds of them simultaneously cry. With all those cherubic faces blinking up at me, I couldn't imagine a single reassuring remark. Mine was not a family-friendly story. There was no G-rated version of death by broadhead arrow on a public bicycle trail, and Bentwood must have known that.

As if reading my mind—and maybe, in fact, she could—Jenx signaled for the School President to lean down to her level. Jenx is only five-foot-five, so Bentwood had to bend. Listening intently, he frowned before straightening and returning his attention to his audience.

"I'd like you to please give your full attention to Chief Jenkins," he said, and gave her the floor.

The younger children applauded until the older children hushed them. Jenx took a small step closer to the edge of the stage.

"Good morning," she said loudly.

"Good morning!" all the kids replied.

"I'm here because sometimes part of my job is passing

along important information."

A boy who looked younger than Chester shot his hand into the air. Jenx paused for a nanosecond, apparently weighing her options.

"I'll take one question now, and we'll save the rest later," she said, pointing to the kid.

"That's what TV is for," the boy blurted.

Jenx looked confused.

"Passing along important information," he reminded her.

"True," Jenx said, "but sometimes the police are the first to know, and so they're the first to tell you, like I'm going to do now."

I could feel everybody in the room lean toward Jenx.

"But even before I do that, I want to remind you about another part of my job, the most important part," she said.

"Getting the bad guys!" the same little boy called out.

A woman hurried down the aisle, presumably to manage or remove the audience participant. I recognized her as Loralee Lowe, the teacher and PTO mother in the flowery dress who had been passing out red papers before the meeting.

Smiling like a good cop, Jenx said, "I do my best to stop the bad guys before they can do anything bad. My main job is keeping people safe. That means I try to prevent bad stuff from happening, including accidents."

Accidents? Was Jenx going to tell the students and parents of The Bentwood School that their headmaster had died as the result of an accident?

The chief of police drew herself to her full height and cleared her throat.

"Mr. Vreelander was riding his bike last night, and something went wrong. We don't know exactly what happened yet, but we do know for sure he didn't suffer. Ms. Mattimoe was out riding her bike, too, and she is absolutely sure that Mr. Vreelander had no pain at all. Right, Ms. Mattimoe?"

All eyes shifted to me. All horrified eyes.

"Uh—right. Definitely no pain," I lied, straining to blot out the memory of Vreelander's stricken expression.

Dozens of little hands now waved frantically for attention.

Whiskey and Soda

Jenx selected a worried-looking girl about four, who pointed straight at me.

"Did she push him off his bike?"

"Of course not," I cried. "I was riding in the opposite direction."

"Were you playing chicken with him?" a boy demanded.

"Whiskey—I mean Ms. Mattimoe—was not playing chicken," Jenx said. "She was just out riding, minding her own business."

Children are not fools. I could see that most of them no longer trusted me.

"Was she drunk?" a boy asked Jenx.

"No," Jenx said. "Ms. Mattimoe doesn't drink. She's going to have a baby."

"The cop said 'whiskey.' That lady was drunk!'" an older boy informed the crowd.

Jenx gave the universal signal for time-out, which might have worked if Kimmi Kellum-Ramirez had not selected that moment to rush the stage on her rat-a-tat-tat five-inch heels. Stilettos make an alarming noise on solid hardwood. We all shuddered, but I shuddered more than most. Kimmi held a poster-size photo of Blitzen lying on the Rail Trail next to Vreelander's corpse.

"That's Mattimoe's bike, isn't it?" Kimmi cried. "Lots of people have seen her riding it. You expect us to believe she just happened to be on the Rail Trail when the headmaster died? Two years ago she killed a man with that bike!"

"In self-defense," I said.

"I'm talking to the cop," Kimmi snapped. "And I demand an explanation."

"Yeah, we want an explanation. These are posted all over town!" Robin Wardrip shouted. Thumping toward the stage in combat boots that complemented her camouflage gear, Wardrip held up at least a half-dozen copies of the same poster. Under the photo the caption read

**DO YOU RECOGNIZE THIS BIKE?
CONTACT THE LANAGAN COUNTY SHERIFF**

followed by a phone number that looked even to my mind like somebody's cell.

"That is not an official poster," Jenx barked as she seized the papers. "And that's not the County Sheriff's phone number. Now step back. Way back. I'm talking to the children. You'll get your turn later."

Both Kimmi and Wardrip appealed to Bentwood for support, but Jenx cut them off. They huffed away, one stomping, the other clomping. Bentwood had said nothing. In fact, he had retreated a few steps during the brief confrontation, slipping into the shadows near the back of the shallow stage as if to remove himself from the conflict. Coward.

In a carefully modulated voice, Jenx was once again addressing the children.

"As I was saying, Mr. Vreelander died suddenly yesterday while he was out riding his bike. The good news is that he had no pain. That's all we know right now," she summarized.

"Do you mean he fell off his bike and then he died?" a small girl asked tremulously. "Can falling off your bike kill you?"

"No," Jenx said. "Mr. Vreelander fell off his bike because he was already dead."

Lots of little children wailed. The same older boy who spoke earlier didn't wait to be called on this time, either.

"So the only reason it didn't hurt when he fell was because he was already dead?"

"Yes," Jenx said.

More children burst into sobs.

"I mean, no," Jenx said. "That's not why it didn't hurt. It just plain didn't hurt. Nothing hurt the headmaster. Right, Whiskey? I mean, Ms. Mattimoe?"

"Right," I said, but I couldn't hear myself above the crying children.

The older boy with the big mouth now stood on his chair as if commanding a mutiny. He addressed the whole room.

"You heard her. She said 'whiskey' again!" Turning on Jenx, he demanded, "What can kill you without hurting you? Unless you're drunk?"

"You don't have to be drunk," Jenx fumed. "Lots of things can kill you without hurting at all."

Whiskey and Soda

That response unhinged almost every kid not already bawling, and a few adults, too. By the time I signaled Jenx to shut it, her wine-red face was gleaming with flop sweat. Uh-oh. We were about to witness something that might hurt, Jenx's special electrical talent. Unless School President Bentwood intervened, the chaos was about to intensify. Jenx and other members of her family had the gift—or curse—of geomagnetic agitation. When their anger spiked, so did electrical currents. One stage light was already flickering.

I turned to Bentwood, who stood in the shadows, arms crossed over his chest. Was he a master of detachment, an icon of calm, or a complete waste of skin? This was his student body. High time he manned up and started acting presidential. But before he could or would, someone else did. A plus-sized woman wearing an expensive suit the same color as Bentwood's blazer heaved herself onto the stage, instantly slicing the noise quotient in half.

"I'll handle it, George," she announced.

I detected the distinct leer of cynicism in those few words. A resonant contralto, the woman's voice was the tool of a seasoned school principal. Facing her audience she said, "Most of you don't know me although I know about most of you. I am Pauline Vreelander."

Gasps issued from a few adults, and the widow smiled. My first impression? Although ten years older than her husband and not the least bit buff, she was every inch the polished administrator. Her neatly coiffed brown hair was streaked with gray; she wore tasteful designer eyeglasses and minimal make-up. I could see no sign that she had recently wept.

"I thank Chief Jenkins for being the first to contact me last night," she said, and I continued to marvel at the mellifluous quality of her voice. "I believe the chief when she says that my husband did not suffer. So you should believe her, too. Now, on his behalf, I have a few words for the students of The Bentwood School."

She scanned the rows of silent youngsters before her.

"You know your headmaster always wanted you to be brave and strong and do the right thing, don't you?"

Hundreds of small heads bobbed in agreement.

"So take a deep breath."

The whole student body did.

"And now, in an orderly fashion, stand up, go back to your classrooms, and get on with your work. Mr. Vreelander would be very proud of you today."

As if under a sedative spell, three hundred children who had been hysterical only moments earlier rose as one and calmly filed out of the auditorium. Mrs. Vreelander watched them go. When the School President finally stepped forward, she snapped, "Later, George," without removing her eyes from the students. Only after every child had quietly departed did she turn her attention to the adults in the room.

"I'm glad you're here. Even though we haven't met, I feel I know most of you. Despite the miles between us, Mark and I were very close. He told me everything."

She beamed a chilly smile at her audience.

"As Chief Jenkins knows, I've arranged to take a leave from my position at Tree Hill Academy in Dallas. I plan to stay in Magnet Springs until I get the answers I need."

11

The assembly should have ended with Mrs. Vreelander's stunning announcement, but George Bentwood officiously hastened to add that he had nothing to add. He urged parents to watch the school's social media for updates, and he, Vreelander's widow and Jenx exited stage left. A teacher's aide ushered the rest of us from the meeting room out to the school foyer. The parents dispersed although I noticed quite a few lingering on the school lawn to gossip. About "drunken" me and my bicycle? Or about Mrs. Vreelander and her doomed husband?

Frankly, I was relieved and impressed that the widow had arrived and taken control of that scene. I couldn't blame Jenx for not knowing what she was walking into; it was almost as if Bentwood had set her up. Why would the school president want to make the police look bad? Surely he knew, as most folks in Magnet Springs did, that if Jenx lost her temper, a geomagnetic firestorm could follow.

"A force to be reckoned with, wouldn't you say?"

I glanced around to see who was speaking. A shapely auburn-haired woman close to age fifty smiled at me conspiratorially. She wore a simple black suit with reasonable heels.

"Pauline Vreelander, I mean," the woman said. "Although Chief Jenkins is no doubt a force to be reckoned with, in her own way. I'm sorry, I should introduce myself. Stevie McCoy, Admissions Director of The Bentwood School."

She extended a slim cool hand.

"Whiskey Mattimoe," I offered in case she hadn't witnessed the entire fracas on the stage.

Stevie McCoy nodded. "You didn't expect the mothers to come forward with that poster, did you? You looked surprised."

"Don't you mean horrified?"

We shared a grin.

"Well," Stevie said, "sometimes our PTO can be a little. . . "

Her voice trailed off, and her brow furrowed as she searched for just the right word. I tried to help.

"Excitable? Overzealous?"

"Out of their freaking minds," Stevie concluded. She lowered her voice. "I work with those wingnuts every day. Putting up with their melodramas is one of my job requirements. I acknowledge their emotional roller coaster, but I refuse to ride it."

I liked this woman. She expressed my sentiments exactly.

"I sell high-end real estate, so we serve pretty much the same market," I said. "But your PTO is like a mob of my worst clients overdosed on caffeine and estrogen."

"That's exactly who they are," Stevie agreed. "It's all about their egos and their kids, in that order. They're vain, possessive and most of all, entitled, and it's my job to keep 'em happy. Or at least keep 'em enrolled."

"You said you're the Admissions Director, so isn't your job to bring 'em in?"

She laughed ruefully. "In a small private school, we all wear more than one hat. My real job is recruitment, retention, marketing, public relations and media relations. So, yes, first I have to bring 'em in, but then I have to make sure they don't leave. That's the hard part."

"Really? Why?"

She laughed again. I was beginning to think it was some kind of defense mechanism.

"Because once they write that tuition check, they think they own the place, and when every little thing doesn't go exactly the way they want it to, they threaten to go somewhere else. Half my parents are 'shoppers,' Whiskey. They change schools every couple years, if not more often. I'm supposed to keep that from happening, however."

When she brushed a strand of dark red hair from her forehead, I realized that Stevie McCoy was probably older than I had thought, a little past the mid-century mark. She obviously took good care of herself. I noticed that she wore no wedding ring although she did have a tasteful gold necklace and matching earrings.

"How long have you worked here?"

"Since I had to," she replied. That could have been the start of an amusing story except we were interrupted by one of Stevie's un-amusing moms.

"What the hell is he telling Vreelander's widow?" Robin Wardrip demanded. She stood in a defensive posture, feet planted wide apart, arms akimbo. Maybe it was the camo gear and combat boots, but that woman made me wish I was armed.

Stevie straightened her posture and flicked on a cool professional smile.

"I'm sorry, Robin. Who are you talking about?"

"You know damn well who I'm talking about. Bentwood, that horse's ass. He can't even control a school assembly. If he wasn't such a wuss, we wouldn't have had to hire Vreelander in the first place, and none of this shit would have happened."

Stevie's face darkened, but her smile never faltered.

"Come on. Let's go grab a cup of coffee."

"Do I look like I need coffee?" Wardrip asked.

"Decaf, then," Stevie said. "Or something else. Let's see what I can find for us in my office."

I wondered if she meant alcohol. Or maybe horse tranquilizers? Considering it was barely nine A.M., and this was an elementary school, neither seemed likely, although Wardrip definitely required taming. With nary a backward glance, Stevie guided the disgruntled mother away from me and up an airy staircase that presumably led to second-floor offices. Wardrip's rant, punctuated by what sounded like consoling mews from Stevie, continued long after they were out of sight. Maybe real estate wasn't the toughest sell in town.

"Madame Mattimoe?"

The French woman from the Rail Trail was standing close to me, unnaturally close according to the culture I'd been raised in. Staring up at me with a concerned expression on her fine-lined face, she had to be at least as old as Stevie. Her short-cropped black hair sported cardinal red highlights that I had missed in the fading light.

"My name is Anouk Gagné," she continued, her accent thick. "I believe I found your bicycle."

"My bicycle wasn't lost."

"Well, I think you left it somewhere."

"I think you put up 'wanted' posters all over town."

Her frown gave way to an amused smile. "'Wanted' posters? This is not the Wild West."

"Then why do you ride around with a bow and arrow? Make that lots of arrows."

"I am an *archère,* Madame."

"Yeah? Well, last night you looked like a killer."

Her smile evaporated. "I do not know why you would say that. Last night I found my friend dead on the Rail Trail. If only he had listened—"

"Mark Vreelander was your friend?"

"Yes."

"Why did you yell at his dead body? Why did you message pictures of it to somebody instead of dialing 9-1-1?"

As I spoke, Gagné's face morphed into an expression of revulsion.

"You were watching me? Spying on me? Why would you do that?"

"Why would I do that? Because there was a dead body on the Rail Trail, and you looked like a crazed killer. I was trying to save myself. In case you haven't noticed, I'm pregnant, which means I'm surviving for two now."

"Anouk! How are you, *cherie*?"

I recognized Bentwood's voice although I hadn't heard much of it that morning. He, Jenx, and Pauline Vreelander must have adjourned their meeting, for they now stood in the school foyer, possibly en route to offices upstairs.

"George," Anouk Gagné cried, giving his name its purred French pronunciation.

She babbled something in her native language, and he responded in kind. They embraced with a passion I considered inappropriate for public viewing, especially in a private grade school. The foot of difference between their heights may have contributed to the hug's intense groping quality, but it didn't explain or excuse the prolonged kiss. Didn't Europeans peck both cheeks and move on? I sneaked a peek at the other two onlookers. Mrs. Vreelander watched the smooching duo impassively. Jenx yawned, either because she'd had a late night or because heterosexual mating rituals bored her.

When Gagné and Bentwood finally peeled themselves apart, the school president summoned the presence of mind to introduce her. He started with Pauline Vreelander, who briskly interrupted him to complete the social amenities—in French. Within seconds, the new widow and the archer were exchanging musical nasal sounds, which is how I hear French. Pauline seemed to speak like a native. When it was Jenx's turn, the conversation reverted to English although she demonstrated a little residual high-school learning by adding, *"Enchantée,* Madame."

Show-off.

"I think we met a long time ago," the chief told Anouk. "I used to date a girl who was into archery."

"Very likely," Anouk agreed.

To me Jenx added, "Madame and her husband own *Tir à l'Arc.*"

"We divorced," Anouk interjected. "I am now sole proprietor. I instruct archers, coach the leagues, and manage the club."

She gave me a sideways gaze. "Madame Mattimoe seems to think that I put up those posters with her bicycle."

"Of course you did," I said. "I saw you take and send that photo instead of calling 9-1-1."

"I did take the photo," she admitted. "But I did not make the posters."

"Who did? Who did you send the photo to?"

"I sent the photo to every archer I know."

"Because you knew that one of them had killed him?"

"Au contraire. I knew that none of them could have killed him. He was one of us."

"What? Are you saying that Mark Vreelander was an archer?"

"An extraordinary archer," Anouk said.

Pauline nodded. "My husband was an alternate on the 1984 Olympic team. That's where he met Anouk. She was one of the trainers."

The widow and the archer smiled at Jenx, Bentwood and me, no doubt enjoying our stunned expressions.

"One reason Mark took this position was so that he could work with Anouk again," Pauline continued. "He hoped to convince her to teach an archery seminar at the school."

Bentwood's momentary blankness suggested that he hadn't been privy to any of that. But he recovered smoothly by contributing a fact he did know.

"We're always delighted to see Anouk at the school. She sent her son and daughter here, Class of '05 and Class of '07."

Recalling Chester's comment about the school's steep academic decline, I did some hasty mental math. "Are they in college now?"

That hit a nerve. Bentwood coughed softly, and Anouk averted her eyes.

"My daughter is a manicurist, and my son is a professional recycler."

I felt my customary compulsion to babble whenever I put my foot in it.

"How nice for you. My cuticles just scream 'Help!' And as a Realtor, I can tell you there will always be a need to get rid of trash."

I wasn't sure who I felt embarrassed for. Maybe it was Chester since we were discussing his future fellow alumni. Or maybe I just felt bad because my mother had raised me not to point out other people's failures. My mother. I suddenly remembered that she was bearing down on Magnet Springs.

Jenx said, "Mrs. Gagné, I'm gonna have to question you formally about what happened last night. We can do that down at the station, but I'm on the same page as Ms. Mattimoe. Why the hell didn't you call 9-1-1?"

"Excuse me, Chief Jenkins," Bentwood interrupted. "Shouldn't Mrs. Gagné have her attorney present?"

Jenx shrugged. "She can if she wants to. I'm not treating her as a suspect; I'm interviewing her for information. Mrs. Gagné was the second person at the crime scene. Ms. Mattimoe got there first, and she called 9-1-1 before she took cover, as I instructed her to do. Moments later, Mrs. Gagné arrived to find a dead body and an abandoned bicycle. I want to know why she only phoned her friends."

"I assume," Bentwood said officiously, "that when she saw Mrs. Mattimoe's bicycle, Mrs. Gagné assumed that someone else had already been there and called the authorities."

"With all due respect, sir," Jenx said, "what you assume doesn't mean squat."

"You called someone," I told Anouk. "I saw you dial and heard you speak French, very excited French."

All eyes moved to the archer.

"I phoned a friend," she said as if that fact were obvious. "Like Mr. Bentwood says, I assumed the rider of the bicycle had already called the police, and they were *en route.*"

She lent the original French pronunciation to those last two words, making them sound ever so nice.

Jenx cleared her throat. "We can discuss that later. What I'd like to know now is whose phone number's on the posters."

"That would be Mark's cell phone number," Pauline Vreelander volunteered.

12

Anouk Gagné said, "I think someone I sent the photo to either made the poster or forwarded the photo to someone who did, and that person knew Mark's phone number."

"Obviously," Jenx growled.

"Perhaps using Mark's cell phone number on the poster was someone's idea of a joke," Pauline Vreelander said. "Though it's not funny."

We all nodded our heads in agreement.

"Who knew your husband's cell number?" Jenx said.

"Everyone affiliated with the school."

"Did he use that phone for school business only?"

"Oh, no. It was his personal phone, but he shared the number with everyone—pupils, parents, teachers, staff. Mark and I disagreed about that. . . ." Pauline's voice trailed off.

"You don't share your personal number with everyone at your school?" Jenx asked.

"Absolutely not," Pauline said. "I check my office voicemail each evening and respond to calls that qualify as urgent. Mark responded to everyone, every time."

I piped up. "My neighbor Chester told me that the headmaster didn't take his cell phone when he rode his bike."

"That was his quiet time," Pauline agreed. "But he always checked his phone after his ride and responded to calls then."

"Where is his cell phone?" Jenx said.

Everyone looked questioningly at Pauline, who said, "I don't know where he put it when he went for his ride."

"I imagine it's either in his office or at his home," Bentwood said, trying to sound certain about something.

"Or in his car," Pauline said. "I know that he sometimes drove his car to a point on the Rail Trail and rode from there."

"Did he take certain routes on certain days of the week?" Jenx said.

"He had several favorite routes, but he liked to make spontaneous choices based on weather and his mood."

"He bicycled down Broken Arrow Highway yesterday," I said.

When Pauline raised her eyebrows, I added, "I didn't know him, but I was talking to Chester, my neighbor, when he rode by. He told Chester to carry on with his two-mile jog."

Pauline and Anouk smiled knowingly, but the school president didn't look at all pleased.

"He probably rode from either school or home," Pauline concluded.

"Can you provide your husband's cell phone?" Jenx said. "Or will I need a warrant?"

Damn, she was good at bluffing. I happened to know that the case was now in County's hands, if it hadn't already been passed on to the State boys. No way Jenx could leverage a warrant, at least no strictly legal way.

"I'll be happy to help you locate Mark's cell phone," Pauline said. "Are you curious about who responded to the poster?"

Jenx nodded. I was curious, too, about who had tried to finger me as the killer based on Anouk's inflammatory photo combined with Blitzen's unfortunate reputation as a murder weapon. Her antagonizing heels, boobs and attitude notwithstanding, Kimmi Kellum-Ramirez was no longer my favorite suspect. Now I liked Anouk for liking me. Translating TV cop lingo, we didn't personally like each other at all; I figured Anouk was trying to frame me for something she had either done herself or conspired to do.

"This is a deflection," I blurted. "Whoever made that poster and put Vreelander's number on it was playing a sick game or worse."

"Trying to distract people from the real crime," Jenx agreed. "Or, at the very least, they were playing a schoolboy prank by routing the calls to the victim's own phone."

She faced Bentwood. "Can you think of anyone who would do that?"

Once again, the school president had nothing. After a pause followed by a dramatic throat clearing, he said, "I can't imagine anyone making light of Mark's demise, let alone taking Mark's life. Frankly, every aspect of this tragedy exceeds my comprehension."

Anouk squeezed his arm, a gesture that seemed almost as intimate as their earlier kiss.

"I'm all right," he said although no one had asked. "But I do think I need a short break before the press arrives."

"Go ahead," Jenx said. She checked her watch. "You got twenty minutes, and if you oversleep, I got it covered."

"I hardly expect to sleep," the school president said. "Anouk, did you wish to see me privately?"

The question sounded vaguely like a proposition. Did he need a nap-mate?

"No, no," Anouk said, waving him away. "I came to see Chief Jenkins."

She faced Jenx. "I did call the police station this morning. They said that you were here."

"You came to see me about the murder?" Jenx asked.

I noticed that Bentwood wasn't leaving, after all.

"Not about that, no. Although I will answer your questions, of course. I phoned your office this morning because I recovered my dog."

"Your dog?" Jenx said, baffled.

"My poodle is the one who went missing yesterday," Anouk said.

"The champion stud dog? You called that in?"

"My daughter phoned it in. She reported seeing Napoleon run off with a long-haired goat."

I coughed.

"A long-haired goat?" Pauline interjected. "Those are quite rare, and most dogs don't like them."

"That's true. But my daughter heard that a long-haired goat was terrorizing farm animals in this area," Anouk said. "And then she saw it at my house."

"What time was that?" I asked, keeping my tone neutral.

"Around three. I was still at the archery range giving lessons. My daughter was alone. She saw the goat leap the fence into our backyard. It flirted with my dog, then Napoleon followed the goat over the fence. Amazing."

"Amazing," I agreed, studying the dark oak floor.

"Napoleon had never jumped that fence before, but he was scratching at the back door early this morning. I wanted you to know that, Chief Jenkins."

"Was he all right?" Jenx said. Although she was talking to Anouk, I could feel the chief's eyes boring into my skull.

"He was fine. Fatigued and in need of grooming, but otherwise fine. He was not alone, however."

I glanced up. "The goat came back?"

Anouk smiled cagily. "There never was a goat, Madame Mattimoe. Only an Afghan hound. Your Afghan hound, I believe."

"We haven't determined that," I said, trying to sound like the last lawyer who defended my canine in court.

"Now we can," Anouk said. "The bitch is in my car."

13

I stared at her. "You left Abra in your car?"

"It's not hot outside," Anouk said. "I'm not worried about the dog. I'm thinking about your upholstery. She eats that stuff."

"I crated her."

"Yeah, well she eats metal, too, especially if it's shiny."

I took a reluctant step toward the door and paused.

"How did you know she was my dog?"

"Please, Madame. Everyone knows."

Again Anouk was violating my comfort zone, standing closer than anyone not in love with me should. Smiling, she added, "Abra has a certain, shall we say, reputation."

Everyone in the rarified world of well-bred dogs knew too much about my canine. Abra had recently won worst-in-show at the Midwest Afghan Hound Specialty, a nightmare I would never live down.

"Why bring her here?"

"I knew the chief of police was here. The bitch is a convicted felon, so I'm doing my civic duty by turning her in."

"She's not a felon this time." I turned to Jenx. "Is she?"

The chief assured me that there were no warrants pending for Abra's arrest. However, the dairy and chicken farmers hadn't yet decided whether to file civil suits. Against me.

That was how it worked. Abra was the felon, yet I was legally responsible. Go figure. The law, I had learned, had little to do with fairness. How could a human be held responsible for a hound that no human could contain or track? And to think that Four Legs Good, the animal rights activists responsible for Jeb's canine-crooning career, believed our pets needed more rights than they already had.

"No legal threats this time, Whiskey," Jenx summarized. "Unless, of course, Mrs. Gagné wants to sue."

On her behalf George Bentwood said, "She'll want to see her lawyer before she decides."

"No," Anouk said. "I have decided already. Napoleon had a life-changing experience with that Afghan hound. He is now fixated on her. Madame Mattimoe and I will have to arrange play-dates."

She meant sex-dates. I did not want to picture a poodle "fixated" on my hound, let alone my hound's role in encouraging that. Before I could be expected to comment, my cell phone rang. I gave silent thanks that I hadn't done the right thing by turning if off.

Seeing that the call was from Jeb, I removed myself to the far end of the foyer.

"Hey. What's up?"

"Lots of stuff," he replied cheerfully. "How's it going there?"

I informed him that my oversexed Affie was in the car of the French woman I had seen last night.

"She hooked up with a standard poodle named Napoleon, who's now addicted to her love."

"So everything's back to normal," Jeb concluded. "Odette has been texting you. She phoned me when you didn't text her back."

I hadn't checked my phone since leaving home. "Problem at the office?"

"You might say that."

Before I could reply, my phone signaled another incoming call.

"Odette's on the line now," I told Jeb.

"Better take that," he said. "Then call me back."

"Your mother has arrived from the Sunshine State," my best salesperson announced in her rich Tongan accent. "Please remove her from the premises."

"She's at the office?"

"She's running the office. Your mother has appointed herself our new receptionist and office manager."

I should have known. Irene Houston was a chronic early arriver and lifelong subscriber to the fallacious notion that everyone loved a surprise. Naturally, she had reached Magnet Springs ahead of schedule and decided that nothing would delight her daughter more than a drop-in visit at work.

My mother had built a career running the office of a small insurance firm. I could only imagine her reaction upon arriving at Mattimoe Realty to discover that I had no office manager because the woman who used to hold that job was now running from the law. Business being as bad as it was, and my swollen belly making me look as bad as it did, Odette and I had agreed that we could get by with my doing the behind-the-scenes work, but Irene Houston had other ideas.

"Your mother is sitting at the front desk, answering our phone," Odette hissed.

"Our phone is ringing?"

"That's not the point."

Odette Mutombo is brilliant at selling real estate for one reason only. She refuses to take no for an answer, so I couldn't argue with her now. Secretly, though, I was excited by two developments. First, that our office phone had rung, and, second, that I had stumbled upon a way to distract my mother during her visit. Irene Houston needed to keep busy. As a result, the minute she got on my nerves, I would put her to work. Of course, I'd have to ease that past Odette, but I knew something my best agent didn't. My mother was relentless. Given that real estate success depends mainly on persistence, I suddenly had a winning team, and half of it would probably work for free for as long as she was determined to pester me.

I promised Odette that I would come straight to the office. As soon as I hung up, however, I remembered that Abra lurked in Anouk's car. Like a ticking time bomb. Before I could decide what to do, Jeb phoned again.

"I figured you'd get distracted and forget to call me back."

The man knew me too well. I was about to ask him to come

Whiskey and Soda

fetch Abra so that I could handle matters at the office when he said, "I just took Sandra Bullock for a walk and saw something you're not going to like."

"The dog at the end of your leash?"

"No. Sandra heels perfectly."

"Great. Will she get her own apartment?"

"Whiskey, listen. Somebody smashed open the door on Leo's workshop. I can't see that anything's missing, but the door is history."

I groaned and told Jeb about the missing basement window pane that Jenx had detected.

"Could it be the same person?" I wondered aloud. "Why would they come back, especially if they don't steal stuff?"

Jeb had no answer, but he offered to report the incident to Jenx. I said I'd tell her myself since she was standing a few feet away.

"Sorry to give you bad news," Jeb said.

"It's not all bad," I said. "Between Abra and my mom, I've got two excuses to get out of here."

However, I was too intrigued by what was happening in front of me to bolt just yet. Stevie McCoy—Director of Admissions, Recruitment, Retention, Marketing, Public Relations and Media Relations—had returned with Robin Wardrip. In the close quarters of the school foyer, Camo-Mom and Jenx were straining not to acknowledge each other. The air was suddenly thick with unspoken personal history and something that felt distinctly like sexual tension. Unless I was wildly mistaken, Anouk Gagné was enjoying the game. She slipped sidelong knowing glances at both women, amusement dancing in her dark eyes.

The press arrived at that moment in the form of three eager and attractive young field reporters with their camera crews. The lobby was now wall-to-wall humans, which was my cue to go fetch my dog. Camo-Mom seemed to be in an even bigger rush than I was to exit the building. She pushed past the press and out the door, red hot face clashing with her olive drab ensemble. I glanced at Jenx, who was in high color herself. She stared after the fleeing PTO member, an expression in her eyes that I would have described as longing, if we weren't talking about Jenx, who was totally committed to Henrietta and had been for years. Meanwhile, Stevie was organizing the press as Bentwood whispered to Pauline, who seemed to be taking it all in stride.

"One of my former protégées," Anouk said, following my gaze in Robin Wardrip's direction.

I couldn't imagine Camo-Mom loving French poodles, so I tried another direction. "Archery?"

Anouk nodded. "Her anger issues were a liability at the range. Speaking of liability, may I show you to your hound?"

Resignedly I let the energetic French woman lead me to her SUV, which I could have identified without assistance. It was the only rocking vehicle in the parking lot. Frantically jumping from one side of the crate to the other, Abra set up her spine-tingling howl. I slowed my pace, knowing full well that the instant I opened the car door, she would launch like a rocket right past me. We needed a strategy to manage the transition.

"I have a strategy," Anouk announced. "Walk to your vehicle, and I will take it from here."

For a second, I thought she meant I could get in my car and drive away. Alone. Then I realized that she planned to bring the bitch to my car. That was probably the next best option.

I fully expected Anouk to pull her battered Ford Explorer alongside my vehicle so that we could team-wrestle Abra from her crate into my backseat. Although we're talking about a distance of less than four feet and a dog who weighed less than fifty pounds, lightning quick reflexes and ample upper-body strength would be required. But that was not what went down. Drawing her front bumper up to mine, Anouk signaled for me to stay in my car. She got out, disappeared around the back of her Explorer, and returned with Abra calmly heeling.

No leash and no agitation. When Anouk opened my passenger-side door, Abra entered like a lady. She even lay down in the backseat.

"How—?" I began.

Anouk handed me a green business card featuring a bow and arrow, the same logo I had noticed on the side of her green SUV. The card read:

Tir à l'Arc
Archery Instruction and Competitive Leagues
~We win~

followed by a phone number and email address.

"Other side," she said.

Flipping the card, I found a whimsical sketch of a standard poodle with an amazing pompadour haircut.

Gagné Standard Poodles
Bred, Trained, Shown
~We win~

The text included the same phone number and email address listed on the other side.

High-school French flashback: gagné is the past tense of gagner, which is the verb "to win." I said this aloud to Anouk.

"But of course," she said impatiently. "I am an experienced trainer and handler of large dogs. It is only natural that Abra would respond well to my methods."

I thought it more likely that this wasn't my dog. Inspecting her closely, however, I recognized the mischievous glint in her eyes. The instant that Anouk vanished, all hell would break loose. I noticed something else, too.

"You groomed her."

"But of course," Anouk said again. "Do you give gifts that are in poor condition?"

I could have pointed out that Abra was no gift, but that would have been petty. Although Anouk had returned a dog I wasn't sure I wanted, she had brought her back safe, calm and clean. That never happened. Abra, the chronic runaway, always came home a complete mess.

"So, you also train and groom dogs that aren't standard poodles?" I asked.

Anouk pursed her lips as if tasting something sour. "I can train and groom other dogs. However, I choose not to."

I knew it was too good to be true.

"In this particular case," she continued, "I may be willing to make an exception. I may agree to work with Abra if she continues to make Napoleon happy."

Did Napoleon need a playmate? A hooker? A dominatrix? Anouk seemed to read my mind.

"Napoleon is the best dog I've ever bred or shown. His conformation is superb, and he enjoys competition. Alas, he has been deeply depressed for months, ever since I sold Josephine."

"Josephine? Was she his doggie girlfriend?"

"She was his mate and also his soul mate." Anouk sighed. "I had my reasons for selling her, but I regret them now. Or I did until Abra came along. Your girl amuses Napoleon in a way I didn't think any bitch ever could again. The light is back in his eyes."

The twinkle. Apparently even poodles had it.

14

My first choice would have been to drive straight to Vestige, drop off Abra and then go deal with my mother. No sooner had I pulled out of The Bentwood School parking lot than I remembered that a French bulldog named Sandra Bullock was now in residence at my house, hopefully for the short term only. But I couldn't just dump Abra and run. To be fair to Jeb, I should be there when we introduced one bitch to another, and I figured the process might take a few minutes if we were going to do it right.

That meant Abra had won a free trip to my office. Sure, I could have planned to leave her in the car while I confronted—I mean, greeted—my mother. Except that I didn't have a crate in the car, and I valued my leather upholstery.

Suddenly, I saw a way to turn the whole situation to my advantage. If, as Odette had said, Irene Houston were determined to assume a position at Mattimoe Realty, all I'd have to do is let her believe that every day was Bring Your Dog to Work Day. Abra and real estate were a lethal combination. She automatically aligned herself with my most sinister clients. Add the fact that my mother was deathly afraid of being knocked down by a big jumping dog. Hello, solution to my problem.

Periodically checking Abra's status in the backseat, I was amazed to find her still resting. She looked serene, like Sarah Jessica Parker napping in her trailer on the set of the latest *Sex in the City* movie. How long could this unnatural behavior last?

My plan for my mother depended on Abra's returning to her normal spastic self.

I dialed Odette's cell.

"Are you on your way?" she hissed, sounding more impatient than happy to hear from me.

"Yes, and I'm armed with Abra."

I filled Odette in on my scheme to scare off my mother with my dog, adding, "The only glitch will be getting her settled down again and back in my car. My dog, I mean. Not my mom. I've got no leash and no crate."

"Do you have a stun gun?"

"No. Maybe we'll get lucky and a muscular male tourist will happen by to assist us."

Odette made her famous raspberry sound, confirming that downtown Magnet Springs was still deserted.

"We'll think of something," I muttered.

"You'll think of something. That's your dog, and the other one is your mother."

Moments later, I parked my car in the lot behind my office, next to a bright blue Chevy Volt with a Florida plate. Checking the rearview mirror, I held my breath. Abra still hadn't twitched so much as an eyelid, which set up the question I'd never been able to solve. How to wake her without exciting her? Sure, I wanted her to be frenzied inside my office, but I needed to get her there first without a leash.

I imagined carrying the sleeping bitch inside, but that didn't seem a promising start to the wild scenario I needed. Also, at six months pregnant, I probably shouldn't lift an Affie. At least not in front of my mother, who would surely see it as an opening for strident advice.

Tap-tap-tap.

The sudden sound on my windshield made me jump, and Abra, too.

"Yoo-hoo! Odette said you were on your way so I came out to greet you."

A deeply tanned version of my seventy-year-old mother stood smiling and waving. What had become of her tightly permed gray hair? For the first time in her long life, Irene Houston was a strawberry blonde. I would never have recognized

Whiskey and Soda

her wardrobe, either. Mom wore skintight black Capri pants and a stylish peasant blouse that revealed cleavage. Before today, I would have sworn that cleavage was something my mother did not have.

"Get out of the car, Whitney. I want to give you and my future grandbaby a great big hug."

I glanced into the backseat where Abra now stood growling, hackles raised.

"Um, I can't predict what that dog will do if I open the door," I said with total honesty.

"Oh, she'll settle right down," Mom said. "Come on out."

Abra's growl intensified, and she leaned back into her haunches like a coil preparing to spring.

"She's getting crazy, Mom."

"Tell her to relax. Who's the pack leader, you or her?"

Apparently, Mom had forgotten every story she'd ever heard about Abra.

"Sorry, but I don't think I dare open the door 'til we—"

Mom opened the door for me.

"Down, girl!" she barked.

The command worked. Instantly. I wouldn't have believed it if I hadn't seen it, but my Afghan hound stopped growling and lay down, her tail thumping.

"How did you do that?" I said.

"Same way I handled you when you threw a tantrum. You gotta learn to be firm, Whitney."

We hugged but only for second. The Houston clan are neither clingers nor coddlers. We don't frighten easily, either. Therein lay the fatal flaw of my Bring Your Dog to Work plan. Mom would get a leash and a crate, and—unlike me—she would use them efficiently.

"Good news," Mom announced. "I'm here to help you with your business. And I've already figured out what you need."

"A vacation?"

"An experienced office manager and receptionist who works for free. In other words, me."

"You can't work for free."

"I've already started. Ask Odette."

"Odette called me, Mom. She's not happy—"

"I'm not happy letting Irene work without compensation."

Someone with a richly syncopated voice was speaking. Someone who sounded remarkably like Odette.

"Whitney, you have to pay your mother, and you have to pay her a fair wage."

"Well, I don't need much," Mom said. "I get social security."

I wasn't listening. I was gaping at Odette.

"Something remarkable happened in there," my best agent whispered.

"Your body was inhabited by aliens?"

"Your mother balanced our books. Then she took a phone call from a prospective tourist and convinced him to rent a cabin for two weeks."

We both regarded my mom, who cocked her head distractedly.

"Phone's ringing," she said and trotted back inside to answer it.

"You wanted her out of here," I reminded Odette.

"That was before I realized she was competent."

"She's my mother. She'll make us crazy."

"She'll make you crazy. Other people's mothers have no effect on me."

Odette smoothed her gleaming black marcelled hair with a perfectly manicured hand. She was always impeccably dressed and coiffed, yet she deigned to work here.

"I feel commissions coming on," she cooed and followed my mother.

I peeked into the backseat of my car, where Abra had fallen asleep again. Between Anouk and my mom, my dog might actually be manageable. I wasn't ready to say that out loud, though.

Call me superstitious. I mean, realistic.

15

With Abra dozing in my car, my mother managing my office, and Odette making me money, I decided to go home.

My goal was to devote the rest of the day to Jeb. Almost three months had passed since we parted company in a confusion of jealousy and insecurity. Okay, we broke up because of my jealousy and insecurity, but Jeb hadn't helped the situation by being so eager to hit the road to promote his new CD. Although last night's reunion had been passionate, it was overshadowed by a murder and a rescue dog.

As for the latter, I didn't want to believe that Jeb's saving Sandra Bullock was more than an isolated good deed. He couldn't possibly plan to keep her, especially now that Abra was back. Today I would help him find Sandra's "forever home." We just had to figure out who was in the market for a boxy little dog that snored and snorted.

When my phone rang, I was pleasantly surprised to discover that the caller was Stevie McCoy.

"May I call you Whiskey?" she began.

"Everybody does."

"Everybody thinks Stevie is short for Stephanie, but it's not. It's my real name." She laughed. "Listen, I might be in the market for a Realtor. Would you have time to talk with me after work today?"

Another prospect? *Ka-ching.* Then I remembered that I had just vowed to devote the rest of the day to Jeb. Oh well, he didn't know that, and we couldn't raise a kid on music royalties alone. I agreed to meet Stevie wherever she wanted.

"How about Mother Tucker's Bar and Grill?" she suggested.

I never turned down an opportunity to visit my favorite local tavern even though I was temporarily off my favorite beverage, Pinot Noir. We agreed to meet at the bar at five. That would give me enough time for a second installment in my reunion with Jeb. We could get the doggie introductions out of the way. Secretly, I doubted that Abra would even acknowledge Sandra, and who cared, anyway, since Sandra was a short-term guest.

I remembered that I was temporarily banned from meeting real estate prospects in public. Odette had ordered me to remain behind the scenes until I recovered whatever limited physical appeal I had once had before my body swelled and I lost my tenuous grip on fashion. This case should qualify as an exception. After all, Stevie had chosen me. For the first time in months, the adrenalizing juice of professional ambition surged through my veins. I could still make magic, even while pregnant and even in a down market.

I checked my dashboard clock. It was just past eleven. Jeb and I should be able to dispatch with the doggie hellos by noon. We could grab ourselves a tasty lunch—or a tasty substitute for lunch—and spend the next three hours sorting out our own hellos, to be continued after my meeting with Stevie.

It occurred to me that we might be able to shave time off the canine meet-and-greet if Jeb had Sandra Bullock standing by when Abra and I rolled into the driveway. I'd never introduced the Affie to a female dog before, but how different could it be? Abra would let the French bulldog know that she could visit for a few days, provided the sight hound didn't have to look at her.

When I phoned Jeb, he was less certain that we could rush the process. I chose not to challenge him or even mention that he would need to find another home for Sandra. If he didn't already grasp that, we would sort it out soon enough.

My man followed my request to the letter. He and Sandra Bullock were standing side by side in the driveway when I pulled in. It had been too dark the night before to discern Sandra's true color. By daylight I saw that she was a wrinkled and stocky ash-blonde, the canine equivalent of a career barmaid. She wore a leash and collar, both made of gold lamé with too many faux emeralds. Please. That was like dressing an elephant in a tutu. I saw Jeb's expression as he gazed at her. It proclaimed, "I can't do enough for this dog."

When I hit the brakes, Jeb waved at me. He used his other hand to produce from behind his back a sparkly green hat with a wide floppy brim, which he placed on Sandra Bullock's square head, securing the chin strap. She wagged her stubby tail.

The car windows were closed tight, which should have blocked the scent of French bulldog but didn't. Suddenly wide awake and on her feet, Abra sniffed the air noisily. When she spotted Sandra, or more likely Sandra's shiny hat, the howling began. Afghan hounds are relatively quiet compared to, say, scent hounds. When they do set up a racket, it is of the ghostly "rhoo-rhoo" variety guaranteed to prickle your nerves. Add to that Abra's tendency to leap and lunge. Before I could turn off the engine, she was performing a ballet solo using the entire car interior as her stage.

Of course Sandra heard Abra's reaction. Even tucked under a chapeau, those oversized bat ears were probably keen enough to detect my innermost thoughts. What was the French bulldog's response to Abra's frenzy? She transitioned from standing next to Jeb to lying demurely at his feet, blinking up at him with long-lashed black-button eyes. Jeb blew her a kiss. Gag me. It was time to end that six-legged love fest.

I rolled down my window with the intention of saying something unflattering about Sandra's hat. The comment died in my mind the instant Abra escaped my vehicle. Still "rhoo-rhoo"-ing, she sailed above my belly and the steering wheel straight out the window, landing squarely on Sandra's head. Clearly the hat offended her.

The Frenchie had astonishingly quick reflexes, not to mention survival instincts. What ensued was a blur of noise and motion as the two blondes spun themselves into a whirring ball of spit, fur, and fury. Jeb knew better than to try to physically separate them. He shouted for me to lay on the car horn, which I did, and they shot apart just long enough for Jeb to snatch Sandra's leash and scoop her into his arms. Grabbing a crazed, snorting dog should have been a bad idea except that Sandra settled down instantly, tucking herself neatly into his embrace. Jeb slipped into the house and secured the front door.

My bitch had scored the hat. As she celebrated her victory by dashing up and down the driveway, I cowered in the car, wondering what to do next. Abra's trophy notwithstanding, this didn't feel like a win. The other team was in the house; we were in the driveway.

Abra slowed her pace, no doubt frustrated by lack of audience response. I cracked open the passenger door, and she jumped back in, depositing the slimy accessory on the passenger seat. Warily we eyed each other and the hat.

My phone rang.

"You okay?" Jeb said.

"I'm not sure."

"How's Abra?"

"Why don't you ask her yourself? Better yet, put Sandra on. Maybe they can talk it out."

"Whiskey—"

"What's up with the costume for your little girlfriend? I think the hat was what set Abra off. She's a sight hound, you know."

"Abra attacked Sandra," Jeb said.

"Sandra provoked her."

"How? She was lying by my feet."

"Sandra was lounging in Abra's driveway wearing a big hat and bling. Way too much bling, by the way, for her figure."

"What?" Jeb was laughing, and that pissed me off.

"Abra's a prideful beauty," I barked. "And she's drawn to shiny things. She's also an alpha dog. She came home to find a tacky French bitch wearing cheap jewelry and acting like she owned the place. You're lucky Abra didn't kill her."

"Sandra's an alpha, too," Jeb said. "She doesn't care if Abra has the home field advantage and twenty more pounds."

"She'd better care."

"May the best bitch win."

"My bitch lives here."

"When she's not on the lam."

"Cheap shot," I cried. "Your bitch is just visiting."

Thunderous silence.

"Hello?" I said finally.

"Hello," Jeb said.

"You do understand that Sandra can't stay, don't you?"

"No. Explain it to me."

Whiskey and Soda

I tried. I really did. Yet Jeb managed to gently turn each of my objections into a reasonable alternative, reasonable, that is, to anyone who adored or collected dogs and wasn't expecting her first baby.

"I don't want a dog," I explained. "Yet I have a dog. One dog. That's the max. Besides, these two dogs hate each other, and I don't do doggie drama."

Well, I did, of course, but not on purpose.

"Let's give them time to cool off," Jeb said. "Then we'll try it again, and we'll do it differently."

"Without Sandra?"

"That's funny, Whiskey."

I was serious, deadly serious, and ready to weep from frustration. Abra had crawled into the backseat and fallen asleep again. I had to give her credit for compartmentalizing her life.

Reminding Jeb that I had taken the afternoon off to spend with him, I asked what he proposed to do now.

"How about I stay here and make sure Sandra feels secure while you take Abra for a long, relaxing walk?"

It was my turn to apply the silent treatment.

"Whiskey? I know you're there. I can hear you breathing, and I can see you through the front window."

I could see him, too. He was holding the phone and Sandra Bullock. I forced myself to do the less immature thing. I waved instead of giving him the finger. Finally, he set Sandra down and walked out to talk to me in person. I continued to let my best self shine by cracking open the window so he wouldn't have to shout through the glass.

Damn. After all these years, I still loved the sight of him leaning against my car, trying to coax me out of it. His casual, earnest, sexy way—the same approach he'd used in high school—still lit something inside me. Until he mentioned Sandra's name again.

"Jeb, I'm having a baby! I can't have another dog, too."

"I hear you," he replied. "But I need you to hear me. Sandra's my first dog. I rescued her. I can't give her away."

When I didn't respond, he said, "Peaceful coexistence is possible. Look at Iran and Iraq."

"Bad example."

88

"Okay. South Korea and North Korea."

"Seriously?"

"Can we just try again?" Jeb said.

"Are you talking about us, personally, or Abra and Sandra?"

"We don't have to try, Whiskey. We are solid. It's the dogs that need work."

I didn't want to work with dogs or even hang out with them. I wanted to curl up with Jeb and make the bad parts of the world go away for a while. Jeb helped me sneak out of the car and into the house without waking Abra. We secured Sandra again in Abra's bedroom.

I had to give the little gargoyle credit for going quietly although I detected a definite fart, a real stinker, ominous coming from a dog that small. I hoped Jeb had fed her the wrong food because that could mean flatulence was an accident and not a permanent condition.

Too late I realized that Abra would go wild when she whiffed the Frenchie's odor in her boudoir. We would deal with that later, much later. Now Jeb was leading me to our boudoir, which fortunately didn't smell like dogs or farts.

16

After we made love, ate, slept and made love again, I reluctantly broke the cycle, informing Jeb that I had to go back to work. First, though, we had to let Abra out of my car and figure out how to avoid another dogfight. Jeb and I strategized, dividing the chores. I would feed and walk Abra while he dispatched Sandra to the exercise pen. He would disinfect Abra's room afterward.

Although I doubted that erasing the French bulldog's scent was possible, I had a bigger worry, that Abra and Sandra would fly at each every time their eyes met. Oh, I still believed that Sandra would have to leave, later if not sooner. I didn't need to talk about it, though. All that good sex had suffused me with optimism, or maybe just more denial.

Around my house, leashes vanished like potato chips, but I needed leashes more. The one I grabbed from a wall peg near the back door was basic black leather. Strictly functional, unlike the gold-lamé-and-faux-emerald number Jeb had bought for Sandra Bullock. Granted, Abra wore a rhinestone-studded collar, but that was a nod to Leo's belief that every female needed at least one piece of nice jewelry.

I gave silent thanks that Abra had not gnawed my car's upholstery during my absence. In fact, she was still dozing when I opened the door. Once on the leash and out of the vehicle, she gobbled the kibble that I offered. Not that Abra was usually a dainty eater, but she was used to being fed indoors. I could tell that she was suspicious; she eyed me sideways as she chewed.

Jeb had requested thirty minutes to vacuum the house and sanitize Abra's room. Since that would include a change of linens, I was glad I had a back-up comforter for her bed. Sure, Abra preferred her plum-tone Calvin Klein Madeira duvet, but the alternate—her sky-blue IZOD Calypso comforter—bore no trace of Sandra's DNA. I just hoped Jeb could rid the rest of the house of alien dog dander before I brought Abra inside.

Twenty minutes passed. The Affie and I were on our third vigorous pull around my property when my phone rang. The caller had a 469 area code and a melodious female voice.

"Ms. Mattimoe, this is Pauline Vreelander. We met this morning."

"Yes, Mrs. Vreelander. How can I help you?"

"I'm calling because I'm going to need a Realtor. I want to sell our home here as soon as I possibly can."

So help me, I stumbled, and it had very little to do with Abra's pace. After months of trying to jump-start my business in a stalled real estate market, I suddenly had two requests for my professional services within a single day. Ironically, both were new contacts developed as a result of a tragedy that I had just happened to witness.

"Are you ready to list the property for sale?" I said.

"Almost. I'd like to show you the house and discuss my options first. I know this is short notice, Ms. Mattimoe, but could you possibly stop by today?"

It was already after three, which meant I was meeting Stevie McCoy in less than two hours. Before that, I not only needed to make myself presentable, I also needed to tame two wild dogs. Maybe Jeb would be willing to handle the hounds solo.

I told Pauline I'd try to rearrange a couple meetings already on today's docket and call her back. Immediately I dialed Jeb. He answered, panting. I was panting, too.

"We shouldn't be breathing this hard unless we're doing something wickedly good to each other," Jeb said.

"Abra's dragging me in circles. What's your excuse?"

"I'm running your vacuum cleaner at record speed up and down the stairs."

Quickly I filled Jeb in on Pauline Vreelander's call.

Whiskey and Soda

"Do what you need to do, Whiskey. Chester's stopping by on his way home from school. You know he'll want to help me with the hounds."

Whatever Chester lacked in size and strength, he more than made up for in good will and animal magnetism. The kid could talk to most dogs and some cats. I couldn't explain it, yet I had seen it. Even more amazing, Abra adored him. I wondered what that felt like.

Another call was coming through, this one from Jenx.

"You left the Bentwood School just in time," she said. "The press conference wasn't pretty."

"Neither was the student assembly. You're saying the press conference was worse?"

"Way worse. A couple PTO moms barged in. They asked more questions than the press, and they heckled me."

"Why?"

"Guess they didn't like my answers. Or maybe they don't like lesbians."

If that were true, then Camo-Mom hadn't been in attendance.

"Who showed up?" I asked.

"Kimmi Kellum-Ramirez. So did Loralee Lowe."

"Lowe's a teacher. How could she leave her class?"

"She brought her class. The kids bawled all over again when I said the headmaster was dead. Geez. You'd think I killed him."

"Maybe that is what they think."

"Nah. They think whiskey killed him, and I don't mean you. They're still confused."

"I still like Kimmi for the murder," I said.

"Any of those PTO moms had time to scream at Vreelander and then head over to *Tir à l'Arc*. The killer fired from there, or near there. We're waiting for the State Boys to complete a trajectory report."

"How far can an arrow fly?"

"Depends on the archer and the arrow," Jenx said. "And the bow."

"And the bow?" I asked.

"Sure. How many pounds of pull the bow has. If we like a

PTO mom for this, she's gotta have skill and strength."

I pictured Kimmi drawing back the bow. Her augmented anatomy would interfere, not to mention all that dangly gold jewelry.

"You didn't answer my question," I said. "How far can an arrow fly?"

Jenx sniffed. "Up to forty yards."

"How far was Vreelander from the range?"

"About thirty yards. This was a clean kill. The shooter struck the upper center of a man's back as he moved away, probably traveling close to fifteen miles an hour. I'm no trajectory expert, but I'd say we're looking at a champion archer. Male or female."

I replayed the mental image of Vreelander coming toward me around the bend, raising his hands and falling down dead. For the first time I wondered what might have happened if I'd started sooner or traveled faster and encountered Vreelander earlier in his ride. If the would-be killer had seen me first, the headmaster might still be doing twenty miles a day. I said so to Jenx.

"Yup, and you might be dead. Don't make yourself crazy with 'what-ifs.'"

"But isn't it true that most murders are crimes of opportunity?"

"Passion and opportunity," Jenx said. "Somebody hates somebody else so much they figure out a way to whack 'em."

"So there's no way this was an accident? A shot on the range that went out of control?"

"Not this kill. Somebody who wanted Mark Vreelander dead was armed and ready when he rode by."

"Maybe an employee at the range?"

"Anouk's the only employee," Jenx said. "But archery clubs have lots of skilled shooters. The killer could be somebody who competes in a league, or who joined the club just to keep their skills sharp."

"Will you subpoena the club roster?" I said.

"The State Boys will, probably, if Anouk doesn't hand it over. But the killer's name might not be on it. He, or she, could have been a guest or a trespasser."

I noticed that Jenx hadn't mentioned a certain PTO mom

who knew archery and the chief herself, Robin Wardrip, so I opened that door.

"Did Camo-Mom storm the press conference, too?"

"Who?"

"Robin Wardrip."

I listened to the silence on the line. When it dragged on, I decided to make life easier for my old schoolmate. "Jenx, Anouk Gagné told me that Robin knows archery. I think she also knows you."

"Used to know me. A long time ago. Way before Hen."

The words were clipped and defensive.

"So, did Robin come back for the press conference?"

"Nope."

"She could have killed Vreelander. She was part of the angry PTO mob on the Rail Trail, and she fits the profile."

"We don't have a profile," Jenx huffed.

"You liked Robin for the crime before we saw her at the school. Something happened when you two made eye contact—"

"Nothing happened."

"This morning you said she was a suspect. Now that you've seen her again, you've changed your mind."

"Bullshit. My history with Robin doesn't affect the way I do my job. Anyone who'd be better off with Vreelander dead is a suspect. It's too early to have a profile."

"Robin took a swing at Vreelander a half-hour before he died," I reminded Jenx. "Plus, she had the skill to kill him, and the strength, too."

"I'll remember that," the chief said.

I didn't enjoy sparring with Jenx. Besides, all this talk about murder made me queasy, and I'd had enough of that just being pregnant. I switched subjects, mentioning my two new real estate prospects, both involved with the Bentwood School.

"Do me a favor, Whiskey, and take a real close look at Vreelander's house."

"What am I looking for?"

"Anything that helps you understand the headmaster," Jenx said.

"You're authorizing me to snoop?"

"Since when do you wait for my okay?"

She was right. Curiosity was my primary reason for becoming a Realtor. I followed the code of ethics, mostly, but I sure did love to snoop. It didn't hurt that Jenx often appointed me temporary volunteer deputy. I even had a badge. On close inspection though, it looked like a booby prize.

"You think something's not right with Pauline Vreelander?" I asked.

"I didn't say that. She never lived in that house. I understand she has a condo in Dallas. Find out if they ever shared an address. See if Vreelander has a PC. Look around."

"What about his office at the school? Who's searching that?"

"The State Boys," Jenx snorted. "I sneaked in for a minute this morning. Vreelander kept a clean desk. No stray papers. All his pencils were sharpened and lined up straight. Only personal artifacts were a couple framed photos of him and his wife. Everything else looked professional. I didn't have time to check his computer. If Brady could get his hands on that hard drive—"

"Any chance of that?"

"Nah. Let me know what you see at the house. Be a good volunteer deputy."

17

I handed Abra off to Jeb as soon as he'd removed the most offensive traces of Sandra Bullock from the house. From the most sensitive area of the house, that is. Our meekest hope was that Abra might tolerate the Frenchie's scent if it were limited to a respectful distance from her boudoir.

Jeb agreed to trot Abra around the property a few more times, evading views of the doggie exercise pen, where he'd temporarily stowed Sandra. The plan was to simultaneously tire the Affie and give me dog-free time to dress for my Realtor gig.

Rifling through my closet with exceedingly low expectations, I spotted a beige corduroy jumper I could not remember acquiring. The label read "Maternal America" size XL. I wore size 8, max. Correction: I used to wear size 8, max, when I wasn't in my current condition.

A lifelong anti-shopper, I had committed zero time and energy to purchasing maternity-wear. The jumper, therefore, was the work of closet gremlins. Underneath I wore a long-sleeved tan T-shirt that was obscenely tight, which didn't matter since it was covered by the surprise jumper.

I now had a reasonably attractive clothing item that fit. However, I could not explain its existence in my wardrobe. Nor did I want to think what size I would be by my due date if at six months I was already wearing maternity-size XL.

Happily for me, denial was my best-developed skill. Flushing the worries, I grabbed my briefcase, phone and keys, and exited through the front door, close to where I had parked my car. Jeb jogged past, pulled by Abra. He held up four fingers.

"Four what?" I asked.

"I think I can last maybe four more laps," he panted. "Will she be tired by then?"

"Not a chance."

"The relief team's here!" announced a high-pitched voice punctuated by two kinds of barks.

Up the driveway jogged Chester accompanied not only by Prince Harry but also by Velcro, the teacup-sized shitzapoo I'd re-gifted him six months earlier. Chester was carrying Velcro because the pooch's legs were too short and his joints were too weak making Velcro the neediest, noisiest, most annoying canine alive. If another dog that shrill and manipulative ever entered my life, I would have to . . . give it to Chester. I shuddered, remembering Velcro's ruining a romantic relationship and fraying my last nerve. Abra had been indifferent to Velcro, but the micro-beast had driven me nearly mad.

Now I was off to make money, which is what I was trained to do. Suddenly, I had two prospects in a single afternoon making this my best shot in months at showing that I still had the right stuff. Waving good-bye to Chester and Jeb, I vowed not to check my phone for their progress reports. Hear no doggie, see no doggie, know no doggie.

The Vreelander home was located on Fresno Avenue, about a mile from The Bentwood School. Frankly, I had assumed that housing would be part of the headmaster's compensation. Most private-school employees couldn't afford to buy a home in a tourist town, but until I met with Pauline, I wouldn't know the Vreelanders' situation.

Their house was a red-roofed, wood-shingled white Craftsman bungalow, a low-slung story-and-a-half structure, built circa 1920 during the Arts and Crafts movement. A small dormer covered a modest-sized off-center front porch; wide horizontal windows flanked the red front door.

I parked on the street and studied the house. Its curb appeal was high. The lawn, still green in December, was uniformly thick and trim. Aggressively manicured yews lined the foundation. A wide brick path led straight from the sidewalk to the steps. Shades were down on both front windows making it impossible to tell whether anyone stirred inside. There was no driveway because the detached garage of this and all other homes on the block faced an alley running parallel to the street. Similarly styled bungalows lined both sides of Fresno Avenue. At 3:30 on a bizarrely mild December day, I almost expected to see kids in the street playing baseball, but the neighborhood was perfectly still.

Pauline Vreelander had changed out of the business suit she'd worn that morning. She answered the door in a navy blue boatneck sweater with ivory wool pants. I saw no trace of tears or stress.

"How are you, Ms. Mattimoe?"

"I'm fine, but please call me Whiskey—unless, of course, my nickname makes you uncomfortable."

She laughed, a short staccato burst that sounded like a much needed stress release.

"Not at all. That confusion at the school this morning was most unfortunate."

I nodded. It was my turn to ask her how she fared.

"I'm all right, thank you. No doubt I'm still in shock. Mark always seemed more alive than most people. To accept that he's dead will require some time."

"If there's anything I can do to make your life less stressful—" I began, but she shook her head.

"I'm hoping you can help me professionally. As you know, I live and work in Dallas. Mark took this position with the intention of spending at least five years at The Bentwood School. That was why we bought, rather than rented, a home. Our plan was for me to retire at the end of this academic year and join Mark here. I was going to start my own educational consulting firm."

"And now?" I asked.

She smiled again, the ghost of old dreams flickering in her face.

"I hope you can help me decide."

"Decide what?"

"Whether to offer the house for sale on the open market or accept George Bentwood's cash offer and close the deal this week."

Pauline produced a business-sized envelope made of heavy

vellum bearing the blue and yellow logo of The Bentwood School. Her full name was handwritten with a flourish in dark-blue ink.

"Open it, please," she said. "His offer is inside."

Without comment, I unfolded the expensive stationery and read the brief memorandum composed on school letterhead using today's date.

TO: *Pauline Vreelander*
FROM: *George Bentwood, President*
RE: *379 Fresno Avenue, Magnet Springs, MI*

Please accept my condolences on the death of your husband. This offer is in addition to and independent of the life insurance policy included in Mark's contract.

On behalf of The Bentwood School, I hereby tender a cash offer, good for three days from the date of this memo, for the purchase of the home and its furnishings at the above-mentioned address. As School President and Chairman of the Board of Directors of The Bentwood School, I am authorized to present this proposal for acquisition of the stipulated Fresno Avenue property as a permanent part of the institution, to be used for the short- and/or long-term residence of future lecturers, guests and/or administrators. Details of said offer are stipulated below.

I wore my poker face as I processed the figure and the terms of Bentwood's proposal, not lifting my eyes from the page until I was ready to meet Pauline's intense gaze.

"His offer is close to current market value," I said. "About what you could reasonably expect to get if you listed now for a quick sale. The 'plus' is that it's a cash offer, which means you can—"

"—be done with all this." She finished the sentence, her voice cold.

"Is the house in both your names?" I said.

She shook her head. "It's in my name only. I understand, though, that it's viewed as marital property."

"That's not an issue at this point if you want to sell. Do you want to sell?"

Whiskey and Soda

"Don't you really mean, do I want to sell to George Bentwood?"

"You'd be selling to The Bentwood School," I pointed out.

"True," Pauline said. "But I'd have to deal with that bastard."

I could feel my eyebrows arch. Nothing in my brief dealings with Pauline Vreelander had suggested that she strongly disliked the school president. My mind flashed back to the chaotic assembly that morning. Pauline had taken over for an utterly ineffective Bentwood when she calmly addressed the student body. Did she dislike him for his lack of leadership, his apparent laziness, or another reason altogether? I decided to tread lightly.

"I can recommend a real estate attorney who could handle this transaction for you. You wouldn't have to deal directly with Bentwood."

"Forgive me," she said. "My remark was inappropriate. I called you, Whiskey, because I like what I've heard about Mattimoe Realty. Also, you inspire trust."

I did? Pauline Vreelander had seen me only amid the post-mortem kiddie chaos at The Bentwood School. I found it hard to believe that, in that setting, I had inspired trust. My name alone had inspired panic.

"You remain calm under pressure," Pauline added. "Chief Jenkins told me you behaved bravely last night."

Ah, last night. I hardly considered my reaction to Mark Vreelander's murder "brave." At least I hadn't peed my pants or turned my bike around and headed for home, screaming at the top of my lungs. I had called the cops like a good citizen and scrambled into the woods to save my life and my baby's. My baby. I had used the possessive form automatically. Like a woman with genuine maternal instincts.

"Whiskey, are you all right?"

Pauline Vreelander studied me with genuine concern.

"Oh. Yes. Sorry. I was just thinking about last night."

"How awful that must have been for you, especially in your condition."

I glanced down to see that both my hands had moved to cover my bump.

"Do you have children?" I asked.

"Like many educators, Mark and I devoted our lives to

other people's children."

"I see."

I didn't, though, at least not completely. "I thought Mark was career Army."

"Mark was a teacher first, a good one and then he went into administration. At the last possible minute he enlisted." She shook her head at the memory. "Mark was determined to serve his country. He built a military career designing training programs. When he retired from active duty, he couldn't wait to get back to his first love, K through 8."

Odd, I thought, but who was I to pass judgment on anyone's career path? I, who had been my ex-husband's part-time roadie and full-time groupie-repellant until I found my calling in real estate, which happened only when I found and married Leo Mattimoe.

"If you don't need or want to sell the house immediately," I said, "we may be able to get you a better offer. It's entirely up to you."

"Would you like a tour?" Pauline asked.

Would I ever. I liked the looks of the living room and what I could see from there of the kitchen, which had been recently updated with stainless steel appliances. The house featured exposed wood ceiling beams, wide wood molding and shiny golden oak floors. Everything on the first floor appeared to be in excellent condition. The furnishings, too, were of high quality and the décor—in warm light gray, dark brown, deep red, and amber—was tasteful and relaxing.

"Did Mark hire a decorator?" I said.

Pauline hesitated before replying, as if deliberately selecting both tone of voice and word choice.

"Loralee Lowe decorated the house when she lived here with her daughter. I understand she trained as an interior designer before becoming a teacher." Pauline scanned the living room. "Perhaps she should have stayed in the design field."

I glanced at the widow, who had affixed a stiff smile to her face. It didn't seem connected to the rest of her.

"This is nice," I agreed neutrally. "So, you and Mark bought it from Loralee and her ex-husband?"

I assumed the teacher and her spouse must have sold the house to arrive at their divorce settlement.

Rather than answer my question, Pauline commented on her own previous remark. "She definitely has a fine eye for color and shape."

I seized the opening she gave me. "You think Loralee is a better designer than teacher?"

"Oh, my, yes," Pauline exclaimed and then tried to backtrack. "But who am I to say? I don't work with her."

"Mark did," I let my voice rise hopefully, cuing her to continue.

She switched the topic to the renovated kitchen. It featured gray and beige granite surfaces, a bright terracotta floor, and lots of sunlight streaming through three windows. From there we checked out the small dining room and the more than adequate master bedroom suite, complete with Jacuzzi tub. Upstairs were another full bath and two relatively small bedrooms, one used as a guest room, the other as an office. The office door was closed.

"I apologize in advance for Mark's mess," Pauline said, her hand on the doorknob. "He was obsessively neat about everything except his office, and I haven't had time, needless to say, to clean it up."

Her remark contradicted Jenx's report about Vreelander's spartan office at The Bentwood School. Was Pauline over-apologizing for a room that needed cleaning?

Not at all. When she swung open the door, I was stunned by the windblown state of the space. Loose papers appeared to have been tossed with notebooks and journals—some cracked open at the spine—across the L-shaped desk, the credenza, the coffee table, the loveseat, the two chairs, and the floor. Some papers were in short messy stacks; others seemed to have fluttered aimlessly to their final resting spot. The room struck me as a private place, the retreat of a person who didn't work seriously there, or who didn't care how it would look to others because others never entered. Could that explain Mark's being a slob at home and a neat freak at work? I wasn't sure if the psychic duality was possible, but how else to explain the contrast, unless Jenx had exaggerated her findings, or someone had straightened Mark's school office before the chief arrived.

"Chaotic, I know," Pauline said. "I, for one, couldn't work like this, but Mark swore he could find anything he needed in two minutes or less."

I chuckled politely. "Did he use the same system at work?"

"It was the system he preferred," Pauline replied. "Mark was extremely self-disciplined in almost every respect. But his approach to office organization? Entirely intuitive and impulsive. He loved being able to run his office the way he wanted to."

"Did he and Bentwood see eye to eye?"

"On what?" Pauline's voice turned sharp.

"The way Mark ran his office and the school."

"If you're asking me whether Mark and George got along, the answer is yes. George was instrumental in hiring Mark. After having been headmaster himself for fifteen years, he was ready to step down, not retire but rather remove himself from the day-to-day running of the school. Oh, there was pressure from the Board and some of the parents to make a change, but I believe that George accepted it. He had met Mark at a couple NAPA conferences—"

"I'm sorry—what's NAPA?"

"National Association of Private Academies. It's an accrediting organization, highly esteemed. I accompanied Mark when he came here for the interview last spring. We discussed the pros and cons of his accepting the position. The salary was less than he could have commanded on either coast, but the cost of living in Michigan is relatively low. We both liked Magnet Springs so much that we imagined retiring here, and we got an excellent price on this house."

When she told me the figure, I nearly swooned.

"Were Loralee and her husband facing foreclosure?"

Pauline frowned. "Loralee's husband never lived here. We bought the house from George Bentwood."

"Was it part of the school?" I asked.

"It was never part of the school. It was George's private love nest."

18

"Love nest?" I stupidly repeated the phrase.

"Let's put it this way," Pauline Vreelander said. "George owned the house and he visited often. Loralee and her daughter Gigi lived here, after Loralee's husband threw them out."

I wanted to hear Pauline's take on the scandal. "George is married, isn't he?"

"In the eyes of the law." Her tone was as dry as the best martini.

"Loralee moved out and your husband moved in?"

"Mark needed to move in before Loralee had found a place. So he worked out an arrangement. Loralee stored her belongings in the basement and moved to a motel until she could find an apartment."

Pauline paused deliberately.

"Mark and I believed that George sold the house because his wife found out about it. We also thought she'd found out about Gigi, who is George's daughter, although George hasn't admitted paternity."

Anyone who works in real estate hears more tales of domestic drama than the average barkeep, but this was shaping up to be a doozy.

"Why does Bentwood's wife put up with him?" I said.

"Who knows? I've never met the woman. They own a second home in Naples, Florida, where she spends most of her time. According to Mark, Mrs. Bentwood has her own money and lots of it. George, of course, has a trust fund. The only career he's ever had has been directing this school in some capacity. He draws a modest salary, yet he lives very well."

"By 'very well' you mean the homes and the mistress?"

I hoped that Pauline would spill every dirty detail she'd ever heard. Although she was a classy lady, rage and resentment simmered beneath her polished surface. I wanted to lift the lid and smell the whole stinky soup.

"When Mark came to work here, he discovered quite a web of intrigue. George Bentwood has his issues, and so does the PTO. It appears that the PTO plays nicely with others only when it suits them to do so."

"And when it doesn't suit them?"

"They do whatever it takes to get what they want."

"What does the PTO want?" I said, truly clueless.

"What does any private school PTO want? Occasionally, it's something that directly benefits the children. Usually, though, it's something that will raise the parents' stock by making them look prestigious."

I recalled Stevie McCoy's comments about the PTO's vanity and possessiveness.

"You're saying that parents at The Bentwood School feel entitled to call the shots?" I asked Pauline.

"You won't find a private school where that isn't at least partly true," she replied. "Here, however, it's completely true."

Her voice was dark with bitterness. I asked my next question cautiously.

"Did the PTO continue trying to run the school after your husband arrived?"

"They didn't try to run it. They absolutely did run it. Mark instituted policies and rules that the mothers subverted at every turn. They went so far as to . . ."

I half-expected her to say "murder him."

" . . . pressure Bentwood into making Mark back down."

"But I thought the PTO didn't like Bentwood. I thought that was why he hired Mark."

Pauline said, "The PTO doesn't like anyone who interferes

with their preferences, whether it's their tradition or their brand-new idea."

"But what leverage do they have?"

She cocked her head as though she couldn't believe my density. "Tuition. If parents stopped sending their children here, the school would cease to exist."

"Isn't that Stevie's job as recruiter, marketer and general go-getter?"

"Stevie can't sell a school that is blackballed in its community."

"The PTO could do that?"

"The PTO would do that if their demands weren't heard. Trading favors is the preferred currency of The Bentwood School. George is open to many options, and so are the other players."

Her choice of the word "players" caught me off guard. I imagined a giant game board with stand-up cardboard cut-out figures that looked like Bentwood, Vreelander and the most aggressive PTO moms.

"How did your husband feel about his job?" I said.

"Mark loved working with children. Their needs always came first. As for dealing with adults, he had the ability to pick his battles, to decide what mattered now, what could wait, and what he could surrender without regret."

"I imagine that's an essential skill set for this job," I commented.

"Mark had an extraordinary ability to read people and, to some extent, to play people. He could make them think they were winning when in fact he was winning. I used to wonder if that were due to his military training or a natural talent."

Suddenly, I had a strikingly different view of Mark Vreelander. Not merely the buff, youthful career Army educator bent on shaping up The Bentwood School, but a canny leader and manipulator keen on subtlety and careful plotting.

I wondered how their marriage worked. They seemed like a "power couple," two professionals pursuing individual goals that required them to live far apart. Mark had looked younger and more attractive than his wife. Did any of the PTO moms try to seduce him? Did anyone succeed?

"It must have been difficult for you to live apart this year,"

I ventured.

"We've lived apart most of our marriage," Pauline said. "Twenty-six years. When Mark was in the Army, I was assistant principal and then principal at three different schools, none of them located near where he was stationed. Fortunately, I had a fairly flexible schedule during summers and holidays, and that's when we spent time together. Otherwise, it was mainly a long-distance marriage."

She inhaled deeply as if to steady herself.

"A challenge, yes, but it worked for us. We talked on the phone every day of our lives. Mark and I are—were—strong individuals. Independent. And yet we loved each other very much. We were looking forward to living together here in Magnet Springs."

For the first time, Pauline's voice cracked and I saw that she was genuinely overcome. This was not a woman who permitted herself to show emotion. She tried to cover the surge by smoothing her hair, which didn't need smoothing. My hair did. I turned away to pat my own unruly curls and give her what privacy I could.

My mind reeled. How could a man as physically attractive and energetic as Mark Vreelander have lived a nearly celibate life? In my experience, a typical guy could sublimate his urges in a gym or on a bike for only so long, and then he needed sex. Live, hot, intense sex. And maybe even companionship, somebody to hang out with. How could daily phone chats and a few in-person visits a year sustain a man with a healthy libido? Even inmates got more conjugal visits than Mark Vreelander. Did he lack a libido? Or was he taking care of his needs in a way that Pauline either didn't know about or didn't want to know about? Maybe Pauline did know, but she didn't want anyone else to.

I had a lot of questions but no graceful way to ask them. I took another approach.

"If you don't mind," I said, "I'd like to know how Bentwood sold this house to you and Mark in the first place. Did he mention it to Mark as soon as he offered him the position?"

"He did," Pauline said. "George made it sound like an offer that was too good to refuse. He encouraged us to look at comparable homes in the area, which we did. George's asking price was well below the competition, and he even included the furnishings. We liked almost everything."

"Loralee is an outstanding designer," I said.

"If only she put that much enthusiasm into her teaching," Pauline said. "Mark wouldn't have had issues with her."

Jenx had remarked that Vreelander was ready to fire Lowe. I asked Pauline if that were true.

"He wasn't going to break her contract, but Mark did warn her that she needed to make definite and specific improvements before the end of this year."

"Such as?"

"Mark was highly skilled at developing training programs. He insisted on working with Loralee to devise one that would shore up her weaknesses as a teacher. She refused, however. I'm sure she thought George would save her."

"What are her weaknesses?"

"Content area, mostly. She's sloppy when she teaches science and history and often doesn't get her facts straight the first time around. If she backpedals to correct herself because somebody points out her errors, she only confuses the students more."

"Do parents complain?"

"Some do, but Loralee has a powerful ally in George, and Kimmi Kellum-Ramirez is her best friend."

Finally, we were talking about my least favorite mom, the one I most relished dishing. I asked Pauline to tell me what she knew about Kimmi.

"What can I say? Every private school has some version of her, the hot nouveau-riche young mother with too much money, estrogen, and time, and absolutely no breeding. Kimmi's the type who has plastic surgery as a hobby."

"Also shoe-shopping," I said, and Pauline smiled.

"Seriously, though, Kimmi knows how to organize her peers. She may lack impulse control, but she's skilled at convincing others to do what she wants them to."

Kimmi was in fact the one who had organized the bike trail blockade. I wasn't sure, though, if she had intended for it to be a stop along Vreelander's last ride.

"Who else caused Mark trouble?" I said.

"Robin Wardrip was a continual thorn in his side."

"Why? What was her issue?"

"Robin disliked George as headmaster because he didn't encourage sports and was too soft with her boys. She thought he was turning them into wimps. Then she disliked Mark because he was too tough, or so she said. The truth is she started working against Mark the minute she realized she couldn't control him any more than she could control George."

"So who killed your husband?"

Talk about popping the question. That came out way more abruptly than I'd intended. I thought about rephrasing, but what was the point? Pauline pursed her lips. I expected her to say she had no idea.

Instead, she said, "Whomever George Bentwood likes best."

19

"Are you saying that Bentwood is connected to your husband's death?"

Pauline Vreelander shrugged.

"Probably not, at least not directly, but I deeply believe that George's life was simplified when Mark's life ended. Anyone who—"

A three-tone chime interrupted her sentence. Someone was at the front door. Pauline excused herself to answer it, leaving me alone in Mark Vreelander's chaotic home office.

What I did next does not comply with my personal moral code, except when I work as a volunteer deputy. Jenx had asked me to do what I could to find out who killed the headmaster. Since there was no time to check the files on his computer, I rifled through whatever I could lay my hands on, starting with the loose papers scattered everywhere. Mostly they were printouts of boring professional articles, on which Vreelander had highlighted passages and made indecipherable margin notes in a cramped hand. With titles like "Strategies for Pooling K-8 Information Streams" and "A Holistic Design Approach to Educational Evolution," the articles appeared unconnected to his death.

Mixed in among those pages were random household bills, advertisements, and lists. I had about as much luck translating Vreelander's to-do lists as I did his article notes, but I did recognize a few phrases, including "put away porch furniture" and "winterize gas grill." I also found bits of scratch paper featuring the kinds of doodles most of us make while chatting on the phone.

In other words, I had nothing.

I moved on to his desk drawers, which were as disorganized as his desktop. Stray rubber bands kept uneasy company with paper clips, pens, highlighters, sticky notes, scissors, rolls of tape, loose staples, cough drops, and chewing gum. What did I hope to find? A flash drive, a checkbook, or an address book would have been helpful.

From downstairs came Pauline Vreelander's voice uncharacteristically raised in anger. I froze. What was she saying? To whom was she saying it? I caught the emphatic phrase "absolutely not" followed by the word "no" repeated several times. I heard another female voice, not as loud or distinct. Pauline talked over much of what the woman tried to say.

"You need to leave, and you need to leave now."

The words were pronounced by Pauline as if for the benefit of someone deaf, senile, or exceedingly stupid. The door slammed. I yanked open the one remaining desk drawer, using more muscle than necessary in my rush to finish. This drawer was so light that I nearly pulled it free. Inside were a broken stapler, some index cards and two flash drives. I popped both drives into my jumper pocket, carefully closed the drawer and listened. No sound came from within the house. Was Pauline calming herself before returning to me?

Outside a car door slammed. Too late, I realized that the headmaster's home office faced the front of the house. Had I been more alert, I might have glimpsed the visitor. Now I scrambled to the dormer window across from the desk, raised the mini-blinds and peered out. A white SUV was peeling away from the curb. I had no clue whether the visitor had been the driver or a passenger.

Still no sound from downstairs. My stomach tightened, not because I feared Pauline Vreelander, but rather because I didn't completely believe her. There was volatility under that steel veneer. I didn't buy her unlikely description of their marriage, and I didn't accept her calm response to her husband's violent end. When my own husband died suddenly—of natural causes—I came unglued and stayed that way for months. Pauline showed neither shock nor grief, at least in front of me. When I did see emotion flicker, it seemed to be resentment that life would no

Whiskey and Soda

longer work out the way the happy couple had planned. But were they a happy couple? Who was the unwelcome woman at the front door? And how did she manage to provoke Pauline?

Footsteps. I resumed the position she had last seen me in and pulled my phone from my purse so that I appeared to be nonchalantly checking text messages when Pauline returned. I didn't even look up until she spoke.

"So sorry about the interruption, Whiskey. Do you have any questions about the house?"

About the house? Pauline the educator was back on task, refocusing us both on the point of our meeting. I clicked off my phone and slipped it back into my bag.

"Before you went to answer the door, you were saying that George Bentwood's life was 'simplified' when Mark died. If you don't think George killed him, who did?"

Pauline stared. "Did I say 'simplified'? I don't recall. This has been a very confusing day, as I'm sure you understand."

"But who would have benefitted by Mark's death?" I said, feeling a twinge of guilt for prodding the freshly widowed.

She sighed, apparently concluding that I was not worth resisting.

"Probably anyone whose life was made harder by Mark's policies. I'm not sure that's a motive for murder. More likely, the killer is someone who deeply needed to please or protect George. For all intents and purposes, he is The Bentwood School."

I felt my eyebrows arch in question, but Pauline had given me what she would.

"Thanks for your time. If you decide to put the house on the market rather than accept Bentwood's offer, let me know. I'd be delighted to be your agent. If you like his offer, I strongly advise you to use a real estate attorney. As I said, I can recommend someone."

Was I imagining it, or did Pauline scan Mark's desk to see whether I had disturbed anything? I had, but how could she tell unless she had memorized the mess? Coolly she thanked me for my time and proceeded to show me out. At the front door we shook hands. Hers was much colder now than it had been when I arrived. Due to stress? Anxiety? Fear? Someone had upset Pauline Vreelander's balance although I expected that she would regain it quickly. She held the door open for me and wished me a good evening. Instead of leaving, I lobbed one more question just to watch her response.

"You sounded distressed when you answered the door. Who stopped by?"

I might as well have barked like a dog.

"Excuse me?"

"Someone upset you, Pauline, and I'm sorry that happened. Who would do such a thing at this difficult time?"

She pressed her thin lips together. For a split second I thought she might order me to leave.

"One of the mothers. She insisted that Mark borrowed a report that the PTO needs back."

"Why would he have that?" I said, when what I meant was why would he have it here?

"Exactly what I told her," Pauline agreed pleasantly.

Only that wasn't what she had said, or all of what she had said, at any rate. I had heard her loudly insist, "No, no, absolutely not."

"It's a trivial matter, I'm sure," Pauline said.

She gestured dismissively with the hand that wasn't on the door. The hand that was on the door opened it wider to ensure an easy exit for the pregnant lady.

I stalled. "Too bad you don't know the mother personally."

"Why?"

"Well, you might have felt more comfortable discussing it."

"Why would I want to discuss a PTO issue?" Pauline snapped.

"Right. I meant to say that you would have felt more comfortable dismissing it."

"I felt just fine dismissing it, and now, regretfully, I must dismiss you. I'm very busy today, Whiskey, as I'm sure you understand."

I concurred and quickly reiterated my condolences as I stepped outside. I wondered, though, how profound a personal loss she had suffered. Legally Mark Vreelander was her husband. In reality, was he also her lover, her soul mate and her best friend? Or was he her "beard"? Jenx used that term for an opposite-gender friend acting as lover to disguise the other person's homosexuality. Was Pauline a lesbian? She didn't seem so to me, and my Gaydar was usually spot-on. It could have been blunted by pregnancy, though.

If she wasn't a lesbian, was Mark gay? As briefly as I had glimpsed the man in his Spandex, he seemed straight to me, but the real question wasn't their sexual orientation or the quality of their marriage. It was who killed the headmaster, and why. If the woman at Pauline's front door were in fact a member of the PTO, I had to wonder why those moms continued to misbehave. Their nemesis was dead. Why pester the widow? Unless they needed something that was in her house.

I paused at the curb. Did Bentwood need something in that house, too? His purchase offer included the furnishings. Was that a tribute to Loralee Lowe's design prowess or an attempt to obtain an item that belonged to the late headmaster? Bentwood had made Pauline an offer she wasn't likely to refuse. Did he hope she would take his check and leave before finding something of value, perhaps something hidden in plain sight?

Fingering the two flash drives in my jumper pocket, I glanced at the house. A heart-shaped face peered down at me from the dormer window in Vreelander's upstairs office. The mini-blinds dropped back into place, but not before I had identified the watcher: Loralee Lowe.

20

Mentally I played back my tour of the Vreelanders' home. I had walked through the entire house without seeing or hearing anyone besides Pauline. Did Loralee enter when the doorbell rang? Was she the verbal combatant whose words I couldn't decipher? Or had she slipped in through the back door during that brief fracas, either with or without Pauline's knowledge? Why would the widow agree to meet in her own home with the woman her late husband had planned to fire?

As I slid less than smoothly into the driver's seat, my phone signaled the arrival of a message. I almost didn't read it when I saw that it was from Jeb. No way was I going to concern myself with updates on the Abra-Sandra situation. That matter needed to be fixed by the time I got home, end of story. Before I could drop the phone back in my bag, up popped a photo of Sandra dressed as one of Santa's elves. Her perky costume was accessorized with large holly-bordered sunglasses and a ridiculous pointy green cap.

Refraining from bouncing my phone off the windshield, I replied: You're supposed to make Abra *like* her.

I dropped the phone into the depths of my big dark bag, took two steadying breaths and checked my watch. One thing was working out just right today, my schedule. I would be on time to meet Stevie McCoy at Mother Tucker's.

Even if Pauline Vreelander wouldn't need my real estate services, Stevie had indicated that she did. An unmarried woman

Whiskey and Soda

working at a private school wasn't likely to be in the market for high-end real estate. But Stevie knew a lot of people who could be. Considering the aggregate wealth of parents at The Bentwood School, the potential for getting referrals made tonight's meeting worthwhile. Not to mention that I enjoyed Stevie's world view, mainly because it mirrored my own.

How I had come to love sipping Pinot Noir at Mother Tucker's carved-oak bar. Naturally I would be sipping something nonalcoholic tonight, but I expected to get high on ambience alone. Since blossoming into an obviously pregnant person, I hadn't done nearly enough socializing. Now I asked myself why. Expectant mothers often led gloriously active lives, at least celebrity expectant mothers did. My social orbit had shrunk in direct proportion to my waistline's expansion.

Truth be told, I had been depressed about my relationship with Jeb, as well as the Michigan economy. Combine personal and professional woes with an unexpected pregnancy, and life could seem less than rosy. Not anymore. Suddenly Jeb was back and business looked brighter than it had in two years. True, there was one more crazed canine than usual at my house, but Jeb and Chester were working on that.

I embraced the mixed odors of booze, food and fresh pine as I pulled open the restaurant's front door. Mother Tucker's proprietors had outdone themselves decorating for the holidays. Live Christmas trees in assorted sizes twinkled from every corner. Smiling, Stevie McCoy waved from the bar, where she was sipping what looked like a cosmopolitan.

"Welcome," she said. "I'm buying the drinks. Soda?"

Feeling uncharacteristically cheerful, I craved something tastier. "How about hot apple cider?"

"With cinnamon," Stevie suggested.

The barkeep said he'd have to check the kitchen, but he thought he could accommodate that request.

"Nutmeg, too?" he suggested. "Or ginger?"

"Throw in both, plus brown sugar. I'm living large these days, literally."

Stevie laughed. Outside The Bentwood School, she looked relaxed and happy. Her wardrobe change enhanced the impression. She wore Ugg boots, skinny-leg jeans and a plush lavender pullover with a plunging neckline. Stevie had a smooth throat and perky breasts for a woman in her fifties. I was the kind of gal who noticed what I wanted to emulate as I aged. If a body that tight had ever produced a child, I would feel heartened.

"You're about, what? Six months?" Stevie asked.

"Exactly," I said.

"Is the baby kicking?"

"Not much."

The truth was not at all. I had felt a few flutters, but nothing that anyone would identify as a foot, elbow or knee, nothing to convince me that there was an active little person in there.

"I carried my son high like that," Stevie was saying. "Not a problem 'til my eighth month. Then breathing became a bit of a challenge. You'll be fine, though, especially since you're not delivering in the height of summer."

"I'm due in April," I said, realizing I hadn't spoken that sentence out loud to anyone except Jeb, Mom and Noonan, and those three had to make me say it.

"The second trimester is the best," Stevie declared. "I felt wonderful, and my tits never looked better."

In fact, Jeb and I were both enjoying my historical first cleavage. Not bad for a girl who had always dreamed of filling a B-cup, and I did feel remarkably better than I had during my first trimester.

"Boy or girl?" Stevie asked.

I shook my head. "I don't want to know the results of my gender scan."

"Neither did I," she exclaimed. "Call me old-fashioned, but I enjoy a good surprise."

Her attitude sounded a tad healthier than mine. I had declined finding out the gender because I didn't want to be responsible for planning the perfect "all-boy" or "all-girl" arrival. Preparing for a generic baby was as much as I thought I could handle. Jeb, however, was eager to create a gender-specific nursery. From now on, I would feed him Stevie's "I enjoy a good surprise" line. Jeb loved surprises. I was sure I could convince him to embrace this one.

Stevie McCoy had the kind of charisma that many sales professionals cultivate: she drew people to her by disclosing personal tidbits that actually revealed very little. By the time we had chatted for a full hour—over two cosmopolitans for her and two spicy hot ciders for me—I knew these facts about her:

- She had a son.
- She was divorced.
- She went to work at The Bentwood School because she needed a job after her divorce.
- She knew how to handle even the most demanding parents.
- She considered Robin Wardrip and Kimmi Kellum-Ramirez to be among the most high-maintenance people on the planet.
- She respected Mark Vreelander although he tried to make too many changes too fast to suit the parents.

The most revelatory aspect of our conversation was what she didn't say. Stevie offered a total of zero responses or comments about George Bentwood. Oh, she made vaguely appropriate noises whenever I brought him up, but she managed to smile, nod, sigh, and shrug her way into the next transition without going on the record about anything to do with the school president. Empowered by all those spices in my cider, I played hardball.

Me: "I hear that Loralee Lowe had George Bentwood's love child."

Stevie: "Who told you that?"

Me: "Oh, several people. I don't know their names."

Stevie: "Hmm." (Silence.)

Me: "I understand that was why Loralee's husband left her."

Stevie: "Really?"

Me: "Was that why Bentwood stepped down from the headmaster position? Because of the scandal with Loralee?"

Stevie: "I'm not aware of any scandal."

Me: "You do PR and marketing for the school, right? You must be aware that there's gossip in Magnet Springs about Bentwood's being a womanizer."

Stevie (shrugging): "Gossip is something I can't control. We do a lot of charitable work in the community. George and the school are mainly known for that. How about ordering some dinner? I have some real estate questions for you."

I agreed to eat something. All that hot cider was making me feel like a beach ball filled with warm surf. For my comfort, Stevie suggested we move from our bar stools to a booth by the window. When I stood up, the contents of my belly sloshed and jumped a little. Either I had taken in way too much fluid, or the inhabitant of my womb was learning the backstroke.

Stevie smiled when I put my hand on my bump and described the sensation.

"Congratulations, Mom. Your baby is saying hello."

My doctor had told me that first babies rarely felt as active in the womb as later ones did. I think she said it had something to do with changes that occur in the uterus after one kid has already stretched it to the max. Since I had no intention of ever going through this again, I let all references to "subsequent pregnancies" zoom right over my head.

"I loved being pregnant," Stevie sighed.

"Seriously?"

"Oh, yes. If I could have had more than one, I would have had three or four, probably."

Her voice and her gaze trailed off nostalgically into the black night outside the restaurant window.

Tempted though I was to probe her personal life, that was not an area in which I excelled. As a sales professional, I had learned to steer clear of all but the most relevant and necessary questions. Stevie had said she was divorced. Why go down that road? In my experience, most people's moods turned sour if you brought up the subject of their ex.

I asked about her kid instead. Every mom I knew thought her offspring hung the moon, at least until they grew up, moved far away and forgot her birthday.

"His name is Tate," Stevie said brightly. "And he's in the eighth grade."

"Eighth?"

I shouldn't have repeated his grade like that, but the number startled me. I had assumed that Stevie was old enough to be a grandma. In fact, I had been toying with asking how many grandbabies she had. If her son was in eighth grade, she must have been near forty when she gave birth.

I suddenly felt much better. My thirty-fifth birthday was coming in late March, and I was due to deliver a week later. If

Whiskey and Soda

Stevie McCoy could get her body back, I had a fighting chance of looking like a slim, trim woman again instead of an egg with legs.

"It's harder when you're older," Stevie said. "It's sweeter, though. I only wish I had started my family when I was young."

She gazed out the window again, sadness settling on her usually cheery features. I wanted to change the subject.

"When you called, you mentioned having a real estate question. What can I help you with?"

Stevie took her time answering, sipping first from the dregs of her second cosmopolitan.

"I may be looking for a new place to live."

"House or condo?" I asked.

"Probably condo. Two bedrooms, two baths."

"Where do you live now?" I asked, wondering at her sudden reticence.

"On campus. Tate and I rent a furnished cottage that used to be reserved for visitors and guest instructors."

Curious, I thought. George Bentwood was offering to buy the Vreelanders' home for that very purpose. If so, why would Stevie need to move out? Or was it her choice? Maybe Bentwood knew nothing of her plans. I decided to go fish.

"Does the school maintain only the one cottage?"

"Currently, yes, although George may convince the board to invest in additional real estate."

I had a lot more questions for Stevie. As a Realtor, I needed to find out what she wanted in a home. As a volunteer deputy, I needed to find out who she thought had killed Mark Vreelander and why. I didn't get what I needed. At that moment, we were interrupted by two folks I had never expected to see together at Mother Tucker's.

"Well, hello there, dear," exclaimed Mom, beaming at me. Her newly tinted red-gold curls glimmered unnaturally.

"I'm treating your mother to drinks and dinner," purred Odette. "After you left, she did amazing things on the telephone. I have a brand new listing."

Odette announced the address, which I recognized as part of a tony subdivision up the coast. Any property there would list for more than a million.

"Nice job, Mom," I said.

"Nice jumper," she replied, studying my outfit. "You look a lot better than usual, Whitney. Is Jeb dressing you?"

Before I could respond, Odette introduced herself to Stevie, slipping her a business card.

"I've heard about you," Stevie said. "You've sold homes to several families at The Bentwood School."

Odette reeled off five or six names. "When you're ready to buy or sell, give me a call."

She walked away. Mom lingered a minute, smiling like a contented flight attendant.

"Odette's the best in the business," she confirmed.

"I was talking to Whiskey about real estate," Stevie said.

"Talk to Odette," Mom said. "She's better at it."

21

My mother was right. Odette was better at selling real estate than I was. But, dammit, I was Odette's boss. Hell, I was my mother's boss, too, as of that afternoon, and I wanted to claim Stevie McCoy as my client.

"Jeb is not dressing me," I hissed at Mom.

Although I couldn't claim credit for buying the jumper, I didn't want her assuming that I needed Jeb in more ways than I actually did. Mom was already following Odette to the corner banquette, arguably the best seat in the house. If either of Mother Tucker's owners had been on duty that evening, they would have given me that table.

Some people liked me at least as well as they liked Odette. Some even liked me better although I couldn't have named anyone specific at that moment, except Jeb. Maybe Stevie would become one of my fans.

I smiled warmly at her, and of course she smiled back. That didn't do a lot to boost my ego because Stevie was a smiler. As soon as I met her at the school that morning, I had noticed that smiling was something she did automatically and often. If she thought smiling would help recruitment, retention, marketing, PR, or whatever else her job entailed, no doubt she smiled, just like she was doing right now.

"How soon would you like to start looking for your next home?" I asked her, sounding like a sales agent on steroids.

"How about tomorrow?" she replied.

I was so excited that I had to fight the urge to shout out the news to Odette and Mom.

Instead, I forced myself to speak quietly. "What time will work for you, Stevie?"

She checked her schedule on her smart phone.

"I can take a long lunch tomorrow," she said. "Could you show me a few places between, say, eleven and one?"

"I can show you a few astonishing places," I said. "Prepare to be amazed."

Even as the words gushed from my mouth, I knew I needed to dial my act back a few notches. Amazement might not be possible on Stevie's budget. Then again, depending on the condition of the furnished cabin where she and her son had been living for five years, even a modest two-bedroom, two-bath condo could be a big step up.

"How much are you prepared to spend?" I asked.

Color rose in Stevie's face, calling attention to her gorgeous bone structure. I could only hope to look that good at fifty-something.

"I'll be honest with you, Whiskey. I haven't qualified for a mortgage yet, but I've done my homework on the subject. Unless I'm sorely mistaken, I should be able to afford something between two-twenty-five and two-fifty."

I exhaled softly, feeling relieved and more than a tad surprised. If I had guessed Stevie's budget—never a wise idea—I would have topped out at one-fifty.

"Excellent," I said. "Do you want to see a mix of condos and houses?"

She did. For a quarter-mil I wouldn't be able to place her anywhere near water, of course, but I was confident I could provide a couple of items from her wish list. It included a fireplace, an attached garage, ample closet space, and a porch or deck. When I asked if she wanted stainless steel appliances in the kitchen, she shrugged.

"I rarely cook, so the kitchen isn't important."

"But you have a teen-age son," I pointed out.

"Tate isn't fussy about food. I raised him to eat what he's given."

Exactly what my kid would learn. I experienced another

micro-panic attack as I realized that I would surely have to start stocking groceries and maybe even learn to cook a few things. No question about it. I was totally and hopelessly unprepared for motherhood.

"Most kids learn to like what you feed them," Stevie added, as if reading my mind. "The secret, of course, is to provide healthy foods and make them attractive."

"Of course." I faked a knowing smile to cover my terror.

"Tate is great about eating fruits and vegetables as long as I let him have a few treats every day," she said.

Idly, I wondered whether I'd laid eyes on Tate that morning. Stevie struck me as a natural redhead—unlike my mom—but I couldn't recall seeing a red-haired teenage boy. I had retained enough of my high school biology to know that red hair in humans is a recessive trait, so Stevie's kid might not have inherited her hair color. He might not resemble her at all.

"What does Tate look like?" I said, hoping to bond with Stevie while also tickling my memory.

"Naturally," she smiled, "I think he's the handsomest boy in the school, but I might be prejudiced. Let's see. How can I describe Tate? Well, he's not tall yet although I know another growth spurt is coming soon. To me, his best feature is probably his eyes. They're bright blue, like a summer sky."

Stevie gazed out the window into a night so black it was almost opaque.

"He's an ambitious boy," she added. "He gets impatient sometimes because he wants more of the world than he's ready to handle, but I tell him he will have everything he needs and wants, in time."

The waiter arrived with our food, Portobello mushroom burgers and steak fries for both of us, plus a side of guacamole with chips for me. Since my morning sickness subsided, I had developed insatiable cravings for certain foods I used to be indifferent to, including avocados. Go figure. Stevie excused herself briefly to use the restroom, instructing me not to wait for her before tucking into my meal. I complied greedily. When she returned, we both devoted more energy to chewing than talking. Even so, those delicious moments were interrupted by the beeps of several incoming texts. If one wishes to make bucks in the real estate biz, one really can't afford to ignore those, no matter how inconvenient the timing. I set my utensils down, rummaged in my bag, and checked the messages. All of them were from Jeb. More photos of Sandra Bullock in costume. Now she was wearing a nurse's uniform complete with an old-fashioned starched white cap perched between her bat ears.

Jeb's message read: How cute is she?

I huffed and texted back: How cute does Abra think she is?

Realizing that Stevie was watching me, I apologized.

"My boyfriend brought home a dog that my dog hates. He's trying to work it out between them, but that's not happening. My dog is an Afghan hound. This is my boyfriend's dog."

I showed Stevie the silly nurse-costume photos, assuming she would side with me.

Instead she exclaimed, "A Frenchie. I love those dogs."

"Seriously? Well, you can have this one."

"I wish. I'm not home enough to take care of a dog, and neither is Tate, so condos that restrict pets are not a problem."

I made the mental note. As I did so, another text arrived from Jeb: Bad news. Another dogfight. Chester taking Abra home 2 his house 2nite.

So help me, I growled.

"Sorry," I told Stevie. "The dogs are still fighting, and that ticks me off because my dog was there first."

I was in the process of texting Jeb a "his-bitch-or-mine" ultimatum when Stevie interrupted.

"Have you considered hiring a pet psychic?"

"A what?"

"A pet psychic. They can be very helpful resolving animal aggression."

I cocked my head the way Prince Harry used to before lifting a leg on my furniture. I wasn't about to pee, but I was confused.

"A pet psychic?"

Stevie nodded. "I know it sounds silly, but a number of our parents have had excellent results."

Now I was even more baffled.

"Parents at your school consulted a pet psychic to work out their aggression?"

Stevie laughed. "To work out aggression between dogs in their household. They swear it works when all else fails."

I wasn't sure we'd tried "all else," but I was absolutely sure I didn't have the time or energy to sort out doggie issues, particularly when they caused issues between Jeb and me. As ambivalent as I felt about Abra, I couldn't bear her being exiled from Vestige while the bat-pig dog posed for the camera-phone in silly costumes. I said as much to Stevie.

"Frenchies do love to dress up," she said. "And everybody loves a Frenchie."

"Not me."

"You will when you get to know her."

"I know myself, and that is never gonna happen."

"I recommend the pet psychic," Stevie said.

"There's one in town?"

"Oh yes."

Why was I surprised? Magnet Springs was a hotbed for New Age mumbo-jumbo.

"She's been here for years, but she's selective about her clientele," Stevie explained.

"You mean, she's pricey."

"Oh, she's not in it for the money. You're right, though, her services aren't cheap. She accepts only those cases where she's sure she can help."

"Where she's sure people can afford her," I translated.

Stevie shrugged.

"Who is she?" I said.

Stevie reached into her handbag and pulled out her wallet. From it, she extracted a business card.

"I keep a supply of business cards for parents who might have issues. Anything I can do to help our families helps our school."

She smiled reflexively. I took the card she offered, which featured a lighthearted line-drawing of two dogs, strikingly different in size and shape. One looked like a stocky little terrier; the other was a long-legged creature with a graceful neck and a dramatic tuck. The card read:

Pet Psychic
Solving Your Animals' Destructive Issues Without Force
~We win~

followed by the same phone number and email address on a business card that was already in my wallet.

"Anouk Gagné is an archer, a breeder and a pet psychic?" I asked. "What credentials can a pet psychic possibly have?"

"Satisfied clients," Stevie said. "I could refer you to several families who were very grateful for her services."

I picked up my phone and reviewed the photos of Sandra Bullock in nurse uniform and elf costume. Since when was Jeb into doggie role-playing? But that was beside the point. The point was that the hound who had a right to live at my house was now boarding at Chester's house because of a usurper dog I didn't even like. Oh, the irony. Chester used to hang out at Vestige because his mother allowed him no pets at home. Tonight he had three dogs at The Castle, and all of them came from Vestige.

"My head hurts," I told Stevie. "What do you do when you have a massive headache, and you're pregnant?"

"Go home and lie down," she said sympathetically. "Have your boyfriend rub your feet."

That sounded like a wonderful plan, provided the Frenchie was down for the night. I reached for the check, but Stevie beat me to it.

"I invited you," she insisted. "And I enjoyed this."

"Me, too," I said. "Tomorrow I buy lunch."

We agreed that I would pick her up in front of The Bentwood School at eleven A. M. sharp. I glanced toward the best booth in the house, where my mother appeared to be regaling my star agent with stories. As I watched, Odette refilled Mom's wine glass. The woman who had raised me almost never drank, at least not while she lived in Michigan. Tonight I hoped she had a designated driver.

Mom paused long enough to take a big sip of the red wine, probably a fine Pinot like I would have been savoring if I weren't in mom-to-be mode, resumed her story, imitating someone inclined to roll her eyes and sigh a lot. Her routine amused Odette to no end. I rolled my eyes and sighed.

Head throbbing, I made my way out of the restaurant into the fresh night air. Almost nothing about the evening smelled like December in Michigan. Except for the faintest trace of wood smoke from someone's distant chimney, it might as well have been late March. I caught the scent of damp earth and old leaves. Even the lake sent up a mossy odor appropriate to warmer months. The air offered nothing crisp or frosty.

As I opened the driver's door, I noticed a folded piece of paper tucked under my left wiper blade. Grunting, I leaned around to pluck it, planning to chuck it when I cleaned out my car. But this was no advertisement. My name was handwritten on the outside below the horizontal fold. I got inside and read the short note inside before fastening my seatbelt.

I have information about what you saw on the bike trail last night. I would prefer to share it with you before I call the police. Phone me at

The writer had provided a local cell phone number but no name.

I locked my doors and clicked off the dome light. I scanned the parking lot, which was devoid of people, or at least people I could see. My headache was gone, replaced by a scalp to sole jolt of fear. I glanced down to see that my left hand, the one not holding the note, covered my bump. While the stress of recent events couldn't be good for my baby, I now believed I had maternal instincts.

Suddenly, Baby kicked hard. No question, there was ferocious life in there and a fearsome killer out there. Whoever left that note had come looking for me. Granted, my personalized license plate **MI HOME** may have simplified the search, but the note-leaver knew where to look. I shivered and not from the cold. We didn't have any of that. What we did have in Magnet Springs was a murderer who knew I had witnessed his—or her—crime.

22

Dialing Jenx's direct line, my hand didn't tremble as much as it had the previous night. Now there was no fresh body in front of me, just an alarming anonymous note.

"Yo," Jenx answered, sounding annoyed, and also like she knew who was calling.

"Do you have Caller ID on this line?" I said.

"What do you think, Whiskey?"

"I think you should know about the note I just found on my windshield."

I read it to her, complete with phone number.

"Can you find out whose phone that is?" I said. "It's the same exchange as Jeb's."

I remembered something.

"It's the same exchange as the cell number on the Blitzen poster."

"It's the same number," Jenx replied. "At least I think it is."

"Yeah? Pauline Vreelander said that was her husband's cell, and she said she'd give it to you as soon as she found it."

"She hasn't got around to that yet," Jenx said. "But I got the number here somewhere."

I pictured Jenx's desk, a mini-version of the Grand Canyon, steep stacks of manila folders with scattered scraps of paper floating between them.

Whiskey and Soda

"If it is the same number, what's going on?" I wondered aloud.

"It could be a prank, or maybe somebody involved in this mess got hold of Vreelander's cell phone. Or—third possibility—Pauline was wrong about her husband's number," Jenx said. "If she speed-dialed him every day, she might have forgotten it or been a digit off. Hang on, I got a call."

Back on the line a minute later, Jenx huffed in my ear.

"Damn. Another report of vandalism. That makes three tonight."

"You think it's the same person who was in my basement and Leo's workshop?"

"Yup. Tonight they're messing with security lamps north of town. Brady and Roscoe were supposed to be off duty, but they're out investigating. Brady doesn't mind. He's got a car payment due."

Jenx said she'd run the phone number on my note as soon as she could, and tomorrow she'd remind Pauline Vreelander to show her Mark's cell. I asked what I should do about the note.

"What do you wanna do?" she said.

"Give it to you so you can use it to catch the killer."

Jenx pointed out that by now my fingerprints were all over it.

"How do you know that?" I said.

"Cuz you never correctly handle evidence."

"If the weather was cold like it's supposed to be in December, I'd have gloves on," I muttered.

"Speaking of evidence," Jenx said, "how about telling me what you found in Vreelander's house?"

"Good news. I stole something from his desk."

"You might wanna rephrase that, Whiskey. You're talking to the chief of police."

"Okay. I 'borrowed' a couple flash drives. Interested? Or should I put them back?"

"Bring 'em to the station. I'm working late."

"I'm going home first. You wanted me to bond with Jeb, remember? By the way, Vreelander's home office is a mess. According to Pauline, that's how he liked to work."

"Not at school, he didn't," Jenx said and hung up.

Surveying the parking lot one more time, I started my car and pulled out. All the way home to Vestige, I made frequent checks in my mirrors. Nothing and nobody the least bit suspicious appeared. To calm myself, I found a Christmas music station on the radio. I had to click it off, though, when they played Jingle Bells performed by barking dogs. It only spiked my annoyance at Jeb for letting Sandra Bullock bully Abra out of her own lodgings. That little flat-faced thespian had better not be in costume when I got home.

Even before I reached my driveway, I sensed that something was off. The security lights. All three of my mercury vapor lamps were out. Had Jeb even noticed? Or was he too busy changing Sandra's outfit? I thought of Jenx's report of new vandalism north of Magnet Springs. As I swung my car into the driveway, my headlights caught a slight black-clad figure dashing behind the clump of tall white spruces in the far corner of my front yard. I hit the brakes and my horn. If I couldn't catch the bastard, at least I'd scare the shit out of him. Was it a "him"? The vandal wore a hoodie and gloves and moved fast. I'd never heard of girls doing this kind of damage, but what did I know? I never used to fear the PTO, either.

I honked again with my left hand as my right hand pawed the contents of my purse for my phone. Got it. I would call Jeb first, then Jenx. Maybe Jeb and Sandra could run out and corner the creep. If I had any luck, the snorting, farting little Frenchie might keep on running and never come back. Nah. That was a sight hound thing.

Before I could dial, the front door flew open, and Jeb emerged with his pooch. Apparently my porch light was broken, too. Both figures stood in silhouette against the warm glow of my living room. I could see that Sandra wore a big hat. It looked like a sombrero.

"Somebody broke my outdoor lights. He's over there, behind the spruce trees!"

Jeb didn't wait for me to finish before he broke into a run. Although Sandra's stubby legs couldn't match his stride, she took off after him, barking energetically. I could almost forgive the sombrero because her voice meant business. That was no high-pitched little-dog yip. There was a distinct trace of English bulldog.

Jenx sounded more alert on this call. She said she'd dispatch

Brady and Roscoe, who were two miles away. I was okay with their using the siren this time, not that she asked my permission. I wanted to scare the perp silly. Also, I was tired of honking.

The chief wasn't thrilled when I told her that Jeb was chasing the bad guy.

"Did it occur to you he might have a weapon?" she said.

"I didn't see a weapon. The guy's all in black."

"Lots of dangerous things are black. Guns and crowbars, for starters. Did you think he broke your lights with his bare hands?"

"He's wearing gloves," I mumbled, but sweat bloomed on my forehead and the nape of my neck.

Jenx disconnected to summon Brady and Roscoe. Although Jeb had disappeared into the trees, I could still see Sandra in my headlights as she bounded clumsily after him. The wail of Brady's siren was so sudden and close that it made me jump, and I had known it was coming. Sandra stopped dead, tipped her head back and yowled. Though not as eerie a sound as a sight hound's howl, it was a big enough noise to scare somebody.

Between the siren and Sandra, the vandal must have had enough. A figure in black bolted from the trees toward the road. My headlights caught him, hoodie down, short light hair exposed.

Several things happened fast. Jeb appeared and tackled the vandal before he could cross the road. Brady pulled his screaming squad car in behind my vehicle, cutting the siren but leaving flasher and headlights on. Sandra Bullock landed on top of the prone intruder, barking her hatted head off. She also displayed a menacing underbite.

I approached the action as soon as Brady and Roscoe had secured the scene. In my opinion, Sandra's threatening act was strictly for Roscoe's benefit. She intended to sexually excite him, this time by showing that she could subdue anybody, even while wearing a sombrero. Her routine had the desired doggie effect, which was not what any human requiring police assistance would desire. Whining, Roscoe danced on his hind legs. He demonstrated a form of ardency not relevant to his profession. Brady led his disabled partner back to the squad car.

Although I never saw Sandra look directly at Roscoe, that didn't mean she'd missed one second of his response. It dawned on me that the little Frenchie might be an amazingly accomplished canine tease.

Jeb had knocked the vandal on his stomach, and Sandra had landed on his back. Thanks to Roscoe's psycho-sexual break, nobody got around to rolling the guy over until Brady returned from the car. While we waited, Jeb and I didn't talk. We studied what appeared to be a delinquent teen-ager. His back heaved under Sandra's wide stance as he tried to catch his breath, but he said nothing and kept his face covered.

When Brady returned, Sandra automatically jumped down on solid ground, seeking Jeb's approval. She got that in the form of a big hug and, gag me, a kiss on her flat muzzle. Hell, Jeb hadn't even gotten around to kissing me yet tonight, and I was carrying his baby. Needless to say, there would be no romance tonight until somebody brushed his teeth.

"Roll over," Brady commanded the kid on the ground.

Nothing happened. The vandal in black continued to lie on his stomach, panting, arms shielding his face.

"I said, roll over!"

As if on cue, Sandra Bullock growled from her perch in Jeb's arms.

"Okay, okay," the kid muttered. "Just keep that creepy little dog with the hat away from me."

He rolled over, like an obedient criminal. Brady shone his magnum torch straight into the kid's face.

"Hey, I can't see," he whined.

I caught a flash of pale skin and bright blue eyes before the kid covered his face again.

"That would be because you broke all the lights, Genius. So now I have to use this," Brady said, fixing the beam in place.

The kid swore, but it was a mild epithet. Even as he tried to shield himself from the glare, I recognized him. It was the obnoxious middle-school agitator from the morning assembly.

23

"How old are you?" I asked even though it probably wasn't my turn.

"Old enough," the kid snapped, peering at me through his fingers. "Hey, I know you. You're the drunk who pushed Vreelander off his bike."

"Am not. Did not," I said.

"Shut up," Brady snarled. "Not you, Whiskey, but you might want to step back."

I did. Brady moved a little closer to the sneering kid on the ground.

"What's your name?"

"I know my rights. I don't have to say anything. I wanna lawyer up."

"You can do that," Brady said reverting to his standard relaxed manner. "But you look like a minor, and in that case, we need to call your parents first."

"He's a student at The Bentwood School," I told Brady.

"I'm not just a student there," the kid said. "I'm president of the Student Council."

I recalled Chester's comment about the spiraling quality of The Bentwood School graduates. They seemed to be on a par with the current PTO. Probably there was a correlation.

"You're the president?" I repeated. "Is that why you hijacked the assembly this morning?"

He grinned. "I hijack every assembly. The kids expect it."

"Mr. Vreelander let you do that?"

"Not so much, but he didn't last long, did he?"

"What's that supposed to mean?" Brady said.

"He's dead, dude. You're a cop. You should know that."

"Stand up," Brady said. "Nice and slow."

"What if I don't feel like it?"

"Cops don't much care what you feel like, dude."

Sandra Bullock, who was ominously close to the kid, chose that moment to let loose another Frenchie howl. He scrambled to his feet.

"You gonna cuff me?"

He was talking to Brady, but his nervous gaze was on Sandra.

"It's what cops do."

Brady told the kid to put his wrists together just so, and he snapped plastic restraints in place. To me, they looked like a garbage bag tie, apt for this piece of trash.

"You work alone?" Brady asked.

"It's hard to get good help," the kid said.

"What are you, twelve?" I interjected.

"Twelve, my ass. I'm fifteen."

"Fifteen's a little old for middle school. What's the matter, can't ya read?"

"I have a learning disability," the kid muttered, sounding defensive.

"Oh. So you're stupid, is that it? Or just lazy? I hear a lot of dumb asses go to your school."

The night was dark, but I could feel Brady and Jeb staring at me. I wasn't done.

"What's a loser like you plan to do in high school? Let me guess. A lot of remedial work, right? And of course you'll have truancy issues. Followed by a career in—oh, I don't know—fast food? Or maybe drug dealing? Yeah, that one pays better. Until you land in jail, which is where you're headin' tonight, dude. Great job. You get to see your future."

The kid was whimpering. Jeb cleared his throat and touched my arm.

"Uh, Whiskey, how about we let Brady finish up?"

"Oh. Sure." But I had one more remark for the kid. "The dog in the sombrero should scare you. If you can't do the time, don't piss off the canine. We got lots of crazy dogs in this town, and they bring boys down."

By now the kid was sobbing. Brady led him without resistance to the squad car, where Officer Roscoe had set up a howl for his beloved Frenchie.

"What the hell got into you?" Jeb asked. "You made that kid piss his pants."

"I did?"

Jeb nodded. Sandra probably deserved a share of the credit although I had done my part. Back on the ground, the Frenchie trotted along on Jeb's other side. We headed into the house, where lights were still working.

"Pregnancy brings out my 'bad cop,'" I said. "When Jenx hears what happened, she'll respect me as a volunteer deputy."

"No she won't," Jeb said. "You still leave fingerprints. She called me about the note on your windshield."

He started to kiss me, but I remembered the dog germs in time to duck. I promised he could have his way with me as soon as Sandra was in lockdown and he was sanitized for human contact.

"This has been a rough week for ya, babe," Jeb said. "But you're not alone anymore."

I nodded. "You're back, and so's my mother. Unfortunately, you came with a dog, and my mom got a job at my office."

The doorbell rang. It wasn't late, but after the dog traumas, the anonymous note, and the vandalism, I didn't feel like entertaining. Jeb promised to get rid of whoever was there. As Sandra padded after him toward the door, I counted on her to discourage company unless it was someone who fancied odd dogs.

I did know a few folks like that, and one of them was at the door, Chester. Prince Harry was at his side, cautiously sniffing Sandra's sombrero. Chester held Velcro, the teacup shitzapoo, who trembled like a tuning fork. Velcro usually trembled, so it probably wasn't about Sandra or her hat.

136

"Where's Abra?" I said cautiously.

"That's why I'm here, Whiskey. I am very, very sorry to inform you that she ran away. Again."

It was only then that I realized Chester was crying. His cheeks were streaked with tears, which Velcro now licked.

"How'd she get away this time?" I said as calmly as possible.

"When I took Prince Harry and Velcro out to pee, she pushed past me and kept on going. I thought she was asleep on my bed."

"Oldest trick in her book," I mumbled. "Don't beat yourself up, Chester."

"I guess I'm not used to managing three dogs at a time."

"You mean two dogs plus an Afghan hound," I corrected him.

As I spoke, I glanced over Chester's head into the night beyond, where Brady's squad car had stopped in the street, flasher still flashing. I had assumed he'd be en route back to the station by now.

"What's going on out there?" I wondered aloud.

"Look!"

Chester pointed, but we would have seen it anyway. In the headlights of the squad car, Abra leapt and pirouetted, no doubt for Officer Roscoe's benefit. No way she would voluntarily turn herself in so soon after escaping The Castle.

I had a theory. "Chester, did you hear sirens just before Abra fled?"

"Yes," he said, pushing his glasses back up on his nose. "I did hear them when I opened the door to let out the dogs. The next thing I knew, Abra knocked me down and zoomed away."

As we three humans dashed toward the dog by the cop car, we were accompanied by three more canines. Brady stepped out of the vehicle when he saw us approach.

"Whiskey, can you contain Abra?"

"I think you know the answer to that question," I replied.

At the very least I should have made the effort to grab a leash before leaving home, but I could rarely put my hands on one. Besides, we all knew how these things ended. Abra would bolt again, and we would wait for sightings, followed by criminal charges.

We watched as Abra performed some kind of erotic doggie dance that involved flashing her ass at the same time she jumped straight into the air. I had never seen that one before.

"She's trying too hard," Chester commented. "She's desperate to get her man."

I could relate. Wincing, I watched Abra leap onto the hood of the car and press her best parts against the windshield. At least I'd never done that.

As if to prove that one bitch at this address knew how to get her man, Sandra strutted over to the squad car, and gently pawed the rear passenger door. In the window above her hatted head, Roscoe's leering face appeared. His eyes goggled as his wet tongue slimed the glass.

"Wait!" Chester cried.

He wasn't commanding a canine. He had just remembered that there was a leash in his pocket. Holding it out, he started toward Abra, who had paused her performance to see what Sandra was up to. Uh-oh. We were about to witness another girl-fight.

"Chester—" I began, foreseeing chaos. Both my hands jumped to cover my baby bump. "Abra's going to—"

I was poised to say "go bonkers," but I didn't have to. Flaring out her full coat and tail, she flew at Sandra Bullock, biting the sombrero, and letting the momentum send them into a spinning roll along the road. Prince Harry ran alongside like a color commentator, punctuating the action with woofs and jumps. While he might have been cheering for his mom, I thought it more probable he just liked to bark and leap.

If I hadn't been sure that my Affie would best the Frenchie, I would have screamed like a girl for people to pull them apart. Two people did pull them apart, the man in uniform and the man I loved. Meanwhile, I claimed whatever self-protection privileges came with pregnancy by moving quickly in the opposite direction. Brady and Jeb sorted it out fast; the snarls and snorts lasted only moments. Neither dog whimpered or howled in pain. Neither man did, either.

"You can turn around now, Whiskey," Chester shouted.

He was holding Velcro in one hand and a leash attached to Abra in the other. Bedraggled but self-satisfied, Abra chomped on Sandra's sombrero. I could only hope that the taste of victory was sweeter than the taste of whatever that hideous accessory was made of.

"Abra scored two hats today," I announced. "I declare her the winner."

Prince Harry panted and grinned as if his team had just won a national championship. Jeb was busy comforting Sandra Bullock. Again. Except for losing another hat, she seemed none the worse for wear. Any excuse to cuddle with her man was probably her definition of triumph.

Brady opened the squad car door, presumably to reassure his K9 partner. The vandal cowered in the backseat. Under the dome light, his face shone ghostly white, and his eyes were a dark shadow. Suddenly he cried out, sounding more like a frightened child than a delinquent teenager.

"You got crazy dogs in the car, on the car, and around the car. I want my mom! Somebody call my mom!"

When the kid collapsed in a wracking sob, Chester stepped forward for a better look.

He said, "Tate?"

24

I turned to Chester. "Please tell me that's not Ms. McCoy's son."

"Well, I could tell you that," Chester said. "But I'd be lying."

The one and only person I liked at The Bentwood School—other than Chester, of course—was the mother of a juvenile delinquent, the very vandal who had damaged my property and been a royal pain during the morning assembly.

Where did Stevie think her son was tonight? Do kids that age still need a sitter, I wondered. I felt sick because I didn't know. Would my child turn out to be a criminal, too, because I was clueless about parenting?

Fortunately, Chester interrupted that trainwreck of thought.

"Tate's got issues, but he's great at stand-up."

"He ran like a rat," I said.

"Stand-up comedy," Chester clarified. "Tate loves the spotlight."

I pictured the kid in a police helicopter searchlight. Where was Tate's dad? If Stevie was the only parent, did she want it that way?

I swallowed hard, recalling that I had briefly thought Jeb didn't deserve to know I was pregnant since he hadn't seemed totally committed to me. After my anger receded and I did tell him, I still felt entitled to handle everything my own way. Now I shuddered at my selfishness and ignorance. Good parenting, I realized in a white-bright epiphany, wasn't about being right; it was about trying to do right. Maybe that was what Noonan and my mother had been telling me for months. I asked Chester if he had a pen; I wanted to write it down in case I got confused again.

"There's a pen in my shirt pocket," he said. "But I don't have a free hand to grab it."

Of course, he didn't. In one hand, he was holding a quaking teacup dog, and in the other he was holding the leash of a recidivist-felon dog. Chester was a loving, caring kid, yet his father had been strictly a sperm donor and his messed-up celebrity mom had provided little more than a womb, followed by a large household staff. Hmm. Maybe there was hope for my kid.

As I extracted the pen from his pocket, Chester said, "I meant to tell you, Whiskey, you look lovely in that jumper."

"I'm six months pregnant. I look fat."

He shook his head. "You look nice. I'm glad Jeb went shopping for you."

So my mother had been right. Jeb was dressing me. When had he found time to go shopping? And how did Chester know about it?

"We discussed your wardrobe on the phone last week," Chester explained. Translation: Chester had told Jeb I looked horrible. "I recommended Curvy Mommy, an online clothing retailer for expectant mothers. You're going to find more surprises in your closet."

"Curvy Mommy?" My toes curled in revulsion. "How would you know about a fashion website for pregnant women?"

"I know how to do research, thanks to my tutors."

Thanks to Tate's crime, the only source of illumination in my yard was a sliver of moon, but I could see Chester beaming.

"We have a few good teachers at The Bentwood School," he said. "I think Ms. McCoy is good at her job, too. It's probably not her fault that Tate's a criminal."

I wanted to believe that for two reasons: to forgive myself in advance for not being a perfect parent and to excuse Stevie because I liked her.

After using Chester's pen to scrawl "do the right thing" on my palm, I invited Abra back to her own bedroom. Chester agreed that the original bad dog shouldn't be shipped off just because a new naughty girl had arrived on the scene. Sandra Bullock could spend tonight at The Castle with Velcro and Prince

Whiskey and Soda

Harry. Jeb resisted at first, offering a series of increasingly lame excuses for why Sandra needed him close by. When he argued that she would pine for him, Chester chimed in.

"No worries, Jeb. Frenchies aren't choosy about the human company they keep, just as long as they keep human company, and they like most other dogs although Frenchie females often fight other females."

"As we have clearly seen," I agreed. To Chester I whispered, "Did you read that somewhere? Or did you make it up?"

"My brain is so full I can't always remember how I know what I know, but I know I know Frenchies."

Jeb's last objection to Sandra's spending the night at The Castle was that she might unintentionally seduce the dog-boys. I pointed out that Velcro was too fragile to engage her, and Prince Harry was too young to stand still.

Chester handed me Abra's leash. She gazed affectionately at him for a long moment before sighing and consenting to come with me. She came with me because I dragged her. When Chester summoned Sandra, she trotted toward him with Frenchie zest and nary a glance back at Jeb. Later my guy and I would admit to each other what we'd felt at that moment. I wished my dog would come when I called, and Jeb wished his dog would come only to him.

We watched the boy who loved dogs run off with three of them into the darkness separating Vestige from The Castle. Jeb had offered to drive them all, but Chester wanted to jog in honor of the dead headmaster.

Aware that she was getting her own bedroom back, Abra did a happy dance and swallowed more of Sandra's hat. En route to the house, she found the Frenchie's semi-chewed afternoon-fight hat, and added it to what was left in her jaws. She bounded up the stairs, sailed onto her bed, made the usual pointless doggie circle, flopped down on her pillows and promptly fell asleep. Gotta love a dog with no guilt.

In my house, all dogs get equal treatment at night. It's called lockdown.

Jeb embraced me from behind as I secured Abra's door.

"Amazing," he whispered. "You can make a boy and three dogs disappear."

"Four dogs, if you count the one who's unconscious," I whispered back.

He closed my mouth with a kiss before I could finish.

25

If only I could report that every part of my night with Jeb was as deliciously romantic as that first deep kiss. In the beginning everything was sweet and sexy. We stood in the hall kissing and molding our bodies to each other. Jeb led me to my bedroom—our bedroom—where he undressed me slowly, caressing every newly exposed inch of skin. He paused when he reached the palm of my left hand, where I had scrawled the Chester-inspired morality note to myself.

"What's this?" Jeb strained to decipher my blurred script. "'Do the right thing?'"

"Forget about it," I whispered. "Let's keep doing the other thing."

"Why did you write this?"

The hormones flooding my brain wouldn't let me remember. They were screaming, "Take me. Take me now."

So I passed that message along to Jeb. He kissed me but without the desperate passion I craved.

"Seriously, babe," he said, "what's this about?"

He was holding up my left palm so that I could reread what I had written.

"Not now," I moaned. "Later. Much later. Kiss me."

Jeb complied, but his ardor had declined. While we made love, I could tell that his mind kept circling back to the note on my palm, which I couldn't wait to wash off, proving that my mind veered there, too. Did he think I wrote the note because I had done something awful? Or because I was tempted to? Did he think I had cheated on him? Did he—horror of horrors—suspect that the baby wasn't his?

The instant that fear slammed my brain, I jackknifed into a sitting position.

"Did I hurt you?" Jeb said, rolling away.

"No, and I didn't hurt you. Honest. I've always been faithful."

"Sure you have," he said, suddenly sounding sleepy.

I shoved my left palm in his face, using the index finger of my right hand to tap what was now a black smear.

"This is about our future. This is about being good parents. Together."

"Got it," he yawned. "When I saw it, I thought maybe you were thinking of Sandra."

"Huh?"

"I hoped it meant you were going to be fair to her."

Uh-oh.

"Fair?" I said warily.

Jeb slid a pillow under his right shoulder so that his face was close to mine.

"You know, treat Sandra like she's your dog, too."

"I already have a dog. We have a dog. Her name is Abra."

"No, babe," Jeb said. "Abra is the dog you got with Leo. She's always going to be part of him."

"Why can't you adopt her?" I almost shouted in frustration.

"I already have, but I also want a dog that's ours. Yours and mine."

"Sandra Bullock is your dog," I said.

"I found Sandra, but she's yours, too. She will love you, Whiskey. Sandra loves everybody."

I didn't hear a compliment in that line. I knew it was true, however. Sandra wagged her stubby stump of a tail at everyone she met.

Suddenly, I understood why Abra hated her. Sandra was an

automatic tail-wagger, much as Stevie McCoy was an automatic smiler. Sandra wagged because she was built that way, whereas Stevie smiled to advance her sales career. Like Abra, I didn't have much truck with naturally friendly types, but I could empathize with those who feigned friendliness to earn a living. I'd been known to do it myself.

Sandra's easy gregariousness was the antithesis of Abra's basic nature, which was to remain aloof and unattainable. Therein lay the seed of the two canines' conflict. If only the bitches could talk it out. I said as much to Jeb.

"Maybe Chester can help," he mused. "The kid's been known to speak a little canine. Remember how he translated for Abra last summer?"

Jeb was referring to Abra's experience as sole witness to a heinous act. Whereas Chester's translated account of her doggie narrative wasn't admissible in court, it did lead authorities to make an arrest.

"These dogs need counseling," I said, trying to work up the courage to mention Anouk Gagné, Pet Psychic.

"You mean, like a pet psychic?" Jeb said.

"You know about pet psychics?"

"I know about one. The woman you saw on the Rail Trail. What's her name? The one whose poodle's hot for Abra. Lots of people take their dogs to her. Hey, aren't you supposed to take Abra over there for a play date this week?"

I demanded to know how Jeb had heard about Anouk's pet psychic biz before I did. After all, I sold real estate in this town while he spent half his time on the road.

"It's that denial thing you got going on, babe. If you don't want to know about it, you don't know about it."

Jeb caressed my belly just as our baby kicked. Hard.

"That is so cool. You got a boy in there, for sure."

"Could be a girl," I said. "A strong-willed girl who wants out."

Jeb chuckled. "Just like her mom."

We kissed again. And again. As usual, my guy plucked the sweetest strings within me, and the rest just happened naturally. After our lovemaking, I dreamt about Jeb, and my dreams felt almost as fine as the real thing until they moved to a view of the Rail Trail on a warm sunny day. I was riding alone on Blitzen,

Whiskey and Soda

working up a sweat. Suddenly I spotted Jeb riding toward me, wearing yellow and white Spandex.

"You look like the headmaster," I called out.

Jeb raised his hands, just as the headmaster had done.

"Don't do that!" I screamed, but it was too late.

Like the headmaster, Jeb rolled off his bike. I squeezed my eyes shut, but not fast enough to block the sight of an arrow sticking out of his back.

"Nooooo," I cried. "This can't be happening!"

"Whiskey, wake up. You're having a nightmare."

I blinked at him in the blackness of our bedroom.

"I was having the dream again. You were riding on the Rail Trail. Like the headmaster, and you got killed just like he did."

"Don't worry, babe. I got no plans to ride a bike on the Rail Trail. Besides, nobody wants to kill me."

"I'll bet that's what Mark Vreelander thought," I said, wiping tears from my eyes. "Look at me. I'm crying."

Jeb chuckled. "You must really love me."

"This isn't funny," I said. "I'm really upset."

"I know you are, babe, and it makes me love you even more than I already do."

He drew me close and gave me a comforting kiss just as my phone rang. Jeb took his time completing the kiss before grabbing the phone from the nightstand and passing it to me.

"What time is it?" I barked into the phone without bothering to check Caller ID. I could guess who was on the other end.

"Seven twenty-nine," Jenx said. "I worked an all-nighter."

"Not my problem. You need to respect people's schedules."

"And you need to respect the commitments you make," she retorted. "You promised to deliver two flash drives to the station."

"Yeah, well, a bad bout of vandalism can mess things up."

That reminded me of my lunch-hour appointment with the little criminal's mom. Were we still on? Or was Stevie due down at Juvie Court with her kid? I asked Jenx what went down after Tate arrived at the station last night.

"He lawyered up, just like he told Brady he would. Ronald

Kittler is representing him."

"Seriously?"

Ronald Kittler was the priciest criminal defense attorney in Lanagan County. I suspected that Stevie's real-estate nest egg was now her son's legal defense fund.

Jenx said, "The good counselor showed up with Mom less than an hour after Brady brought Tate in."

"Now that's what I call customer service. Have charges been filed?"

"Not yet."

"Any chance you'll drop the charges?" I let my voice rise in childish hopefulness.

"You want me to drop the charges?" Jenx said. "Tate McCoy vandalized Vestige, among other properties."

"I know, I know. Could you require restitution without litigation?"

"Restitution plus community service," Jenx huffed. "You'd better tell me why you think that little shithead deserves a break."

"He's a nice enough kid."

"He's a prick," Jenx said.

"He's fifteen," I protested.

"In addition to being a vandal, he's got a raging case of P.O.P."

Jenx was referring to his talent for pissing off police. She continued, "I was ready to pitch him through the plate-glass window just as his mom and attorney walked in."

"Tate was contrite by the time he left Vestige," I said. "He was so scared he peed himself."

"Correction: he was so scared of you and the dogs he peed himself. Brady told me what happened."

"Okay. So the kid's a jerk," I conceded. "But his mom's nice. She's the only sane person at The Bentwood School."

"You want to sell her a house."

"Well, yeah. That, too. I don't how she can afford Ronald Kittler."

"That's not our business. Lots of people work out deals with their attorneys."

Was Jenx hinting at something sexual? I had met Kittler several times. He was twenty years older than Stevie, divorced and not attractive in any way that I defined the term.

"Are you saying that Stevie and Kittler are an item?"

"No. I'm saying lots of people have unexpected resources. My guess is that Boss Man's covering part of this bill."

"Boss Man?"

"Tate's only phone call last night was to George Bentwood."

I blinked. How many kids would call the head of their school if they got busted?

"Tate called George, and George probably called Kittler," Jenx said. "Who knows? Maybe legal fees are included in the tuition."

"Maybe they should be," I mused. "Bentwood probably called Kittler because he doesn't want more bad press for the school, but why didn't Tate phone his mom?"

"Maybe George is a father figure," Jenx offered. "Somebody Tate confides in. Or maybe he was afraid his mom would go ballistic."

"Stevie seems like one of the 'cool' moms," I said. "Bentwood seems way too detached to be fatherly. Does he even have children?"

"Officially? Nope. But Loralee Lowe is pressuring him to admit that Gigi's his. She's got the DNA tests—and the pissed-off ex—to prove it. From what I hear, she's playing nice so far, hoping Bentwood will step up and do the right thing."

I didn't see how admitting illicit paternity would be the "right thing" for George, given that his distinguished family had founded The Bentwood School, and he was the school president as well as Loralee's employer.

"Who told you Loralee's plan?" I said.

"It's a rumor."

"Come on. Who told you?"

"You know I can't divulge sources."

"Bullshit. This isn't even your investigation. The State Boys have it."

"Which is why you gotta bring me the flash drives," she growled before clicking off.

26

When I returned my phone to the nightstand, I realized that my man was no longer warming the sheets.

"Jeb?" I asked the air.

No reply. Unless you counted a flying Affie answering to someone else's name.

Abra the Afghan hound bounded across my bed en route to my bathroom. Seconds later, I heard her lapping out of the toilet like a common cur. She was probably not to blame for her lack of decorum as I couldn't recall when I'd last refilled her water bowl. Munching Sandra's hats had made her thirsty.

"Pancakes or oatmeal?" Jeb shouted from downstairs.

"For breakfast?" I inquired hopefully.

"I'm not taking a survey," he replied.

"In that case I'll have both."

Momentarily overwhelmed with joy, I let myself sink back into my pillows. Not only was I getting a hot breakfast cooked by someone else, but that "someone else" happened to be the cheery father of my child. A man who now seemed more attentive—and attractive—than ever before in our long history. I was beginning to believe, finally, that Jeb just might be the loving and loyal partner I needed him to be.

Absentmindedly, I glanced at the gray smear on the palm of my left hand. Even though I could no longer read it, I remembered what I'd written, and what Jeb had said about it. He was correct, as usual. Doing the right thing would have to include Sandra Bullock.

After eating pancakes and oatmeal and offering Abra clean water and maybe, just maybe, enjoying dessert-in-bed with Jeb, I would call Anouk Gagné. I would take a deep breath and ask her to please, please apply her pet psychic skills to Abra and Sandra so that Jeb and I and our baby could live happily ever after.

Abra interrupted my reverie by leaping onto my bed and doing something she almost never did. She licked my face. I hate dog spit. Especially in the vicinity of my own spit, and extra especially when that dog spit just came from the toilet.

"Yuck. Ick. Arrgh."

"She's trying to kiss you, Whiskey," Jeb said, laughing as he entered our bedroom with two steaming mugs.

"Slime me, you mean. Don't even ask where her mouth has been."

"I never ask that question," he said, deftly delivering his own kiss along with the coffee.

It was the kind of kiss that renders breakfast irrelevant. I could only hope he hadn't started anything else boiling because I was way too hot to let him leave.

Much later, he left the room to feed and water the hound. The food portion of our breakfast was yet to come. I couldn't believe that my phone would ring again while it was still so early. I read the clock, which said nine. Time flies when you spend the morning at play.

"Whiskey? Stevie McCoy. I hope I'm not interrupting your day."

I assured her that she wasn't, but from there I didn't know what to say or not say. I decided that the safest route was to pretend that I didn't know the identity of the criminal captured on my lawn last night.

"This is so awkward," Stevie said. "But here goes. That was my son who vandalized your property, Whiskey. I am very, very sorry about his actions, and he is, too. We will find a way to make it up to you. Please believe me."

I did believe her. Except for the part about Tate's being "very, very sorry." I hadn't seen a single sign of shame in the teenager, but I could let that go.

"Are we still on?" I asked her.

Silence. Then she groaned.

"Oh my god. I completely forgot that we were supposed to get together today. I was up all night with Tate, so I'm taking the day off. Frankly, I can't face other parents right now."

I made sympathetic noises, and I meant them. I had already seen the PTO unsheathe their claws. If they were willing to gang up on the headmaster, what might they do to the admissions/recruitment/marketing director once they decided her son was toxic to the school? Make her job a living hell.

I envisaged Kimmi Kellum-Ramirez, Robin Wardrip and Loralee Lowe texting the news of Tate's arrest to every Bentwood School parent. Surely that had already happened unless Ronald Kittler had worked his magic. Was the criminal defense attorney adroit enough at damage control to keep Tate's arrest on the down-low? Jenx hadn't been specific about Kittler's approach. If he had figured out how to hide or disguise the news from parents and the media, he just might save the kid's reputation and his mom's job, at least for now.

"Let me take you to lunch," I told Stevie. "I owe you a meal."

She laughed bitterly. "Not anymore. Tate and I owe you for the damage he did to your property, which we will cover completely. I promise."

"No worries. Tate and I will work it out."

If he resisted, I knew how to break him, by belittling his learning disability and surrounding him with local dogs. Nah. That was cruel and unusual punishment.

Stevie thanked me for understanding and promised to get back to me about viewing properties as soon as things settled down. I could read between the lines. What she meant was that she would call if she still had her job next year. Fortunately, Tate was due to graduate in the spring. I figured he would matriculate into an academy where The Bentwood School parents weren't poised to track his criminal tendencies. Maybe that would ease Stevie's burden. Maybe not. I kept expecting the citizens of Magnet Springs to forget my dog was a felon. It never happened.

Jeb's promised pancake breakfast was almost as tasty as his appetizer. He rinsed dishes while I finished my second short stack, an especially fluffy batch soaked in strawberry syrup. My phone, which I'd left on the counter rang loudly, distracting us just long enough for Abra to snare with one snap of her aquiline jaws all that remained on my plate. Jeb and I both reached for my phone, and Abra got away with the pancake. I checked Caller ID.

"Hello, Anouk. If you're phoning for Abra, she can't talk right now. Her mouth is full."

I regarded my long-haired hound, noisily licking her chops. Sticky red syrup had migrated to her ears and paws.

"Napoleon is unhappy today. He demands an audience with his queen."

"Don't you mean his consort? Or concubine?"

Anouk was not amused. "For our dogs to thrive, we must respect their relationships. Can you have her here in half-an-hour?"

"Sure."

This appointment would be easier to keep than most. I already knew Abra's location. No need to scour the countryside.

In the past, I might have sniggered at the notion of Napoleon "needing" Abra. Not anymore. I realized that Abra needed Napoleon, too, if only to restore her sexual self-confidence in the wake of the Sandra Bullock-Officer Roscoe fiasco.

As a champion standard poodle, Napoleon had to be one studly dude. Naturally, he would demand a beautiful babe. With Abra spayed, there was no threat of mixing the breeds, the very definition of safe sex for dogs.

27

If, as Jenx theorized, Mark Vreelander's killer had fired the fatal arrow from *Tir à l'Arc*, then I wanted to see the archery range firsthand. I thought it might help me process, and then repress, what I'd witnessed on the Rail Trail. As sweet as the last two nights with Jeb had been, I was sick of dreaming of him as Mark Vreelander, rolling off a bike with an arrow in his back.

This was also a chance to sleuth for Jenx, and, if I could get past the silliness, to ask Anouk about psychic counseling for Abra and Sandra.

I felt a surge of curiosity as I flicked on my closet light. If what Chester had said last night proved true, I might find another new ensemble from Jeb, via Curvy Mommy. Okay, the name made me cringe, but the clothes apparently made me look good. Before last night, I couldn't recall when I'd gotten a compliment on something I wore. Now, rifling through a rack of too-small beige suits, I was pleased to discover another cool new jumper, this one dark mushroom with smocking across the bust line. I resolved not to check the size. No point in raining on my own parade. Jeb was trying to be a helpful expectant father, so what if he'd needed a boost from Chester?

I closed my eyes and tried to picture Jeb assisting me with our baby. No part of the image would come. Probably because I didn't know enough about babies to envision what we would be doing with one. My eyes flew open. Shit. I didn't even know how to change a diaper. How the hell were we going to figure this out? I couldn't expect Chester to teach us everything.

Whiskey and Soda

Jeb walked into my bedroom—our bedroom—grinning broadly and speaking into the receiver of my landline phone.

"You are so right, Irene. Whitney, it's your mother."

For Jeb's smile to be any wider, he would have required plastic surgery. I handed him my new Curvy Mommy clothes in exchange for the phone. If I'd known what he was going to do next, I would have dumped the clothes on the floor and shoved him out of the room. Well, probably not, but it is nigh on impossible to converse while being dressed by Jeb. With his sensuous musician's fingers playing my flesh, I had to stifle moans of pleasure, in addition to a few giggles. Meanwhile, Mom droned on about something to do with a shower. Suddenly, I understood the point of her call.

"Mom," I gasped, twisting away from Jeb. "I don't want a baby shower."

Silence. A rare thing when my mother's on the phone.

"Did you hear me?" I said.

"Yes, Whitney, I heard you. Of course, you'll want a baby shower, but it's too soon for that. I'm talking about your bridal shower. When do you want that?"

"A bridal shower?"

I shot Jeb a withering look. He winked at me.

"Who said anything about a bride?" I demanded.

"Oh, we all know you two are getting married," Mom said. "The only question is when."

I told my mom I'd have to get back to her.

"Well, make it soon, Whitney. Showers require planning and it's Christmas time. People are busy. By the way, I got another new listing for Odette this morning. If you'd get to the office on time like she does, I could get a listing for you."

After I closed the call, I realized that Mom might prove useful in ways that had nothing to do with real estate. I was reasonably sure she knew how to change a diaper and perform other feats of childcare. While I didn't expect her to babysit, I did hope she would show me the tricks of the trade.

I forgave Jeb for so obviously enjoying my mother's phone call. How could I not? He made love to me. He fed me. He even dressed me. He had also agreed to send Sandra Bullock away for the night. Despite his insistence that I let her come back, I did love having Jeb around. Pulling a brush through my stubborn curls, I asked him to prepare Abra for departure using the leash. She was not getting away from me today.

Moments later I stood in front of my coat closet, mentally debating how much outerwear I required. According to the update on my phone, it was already 46 degrees on its way to the upper 50s. I selected a lightweight leather jacket, plenty warm enough for this morning and easily discarded by the time the afternoon sun had worked its magic. In the kitchen, I found Abra wearing an understated leather leash attached to her rhinestone collar.

"Her hair looks worse than mine," I said, noting the kinds of bumps and knots I usually found in my own mane. Hers also featured chunks of dirt and dead leaves, a look I had never attempted, plus strawberry syrup highlights.

"We could put a hat on her," Jeb suggested. "I bought a slew of 'em for Sandra."

Did he honestly think an Affie would wear a hat? Let alone a hat purchased for a Frenchie? With admirable dignity, I kept my lip from curling. Abra behaved, too.

"She doesn't wear hats. She eats them," I told Jeb. "I can ask Anouk to groom her in return for sexual services."

"Wait. Who's having sex today?"

Leave it to a man to hear only one word.

"Napoleon needs a little sexual healing," I explained. When Jeb frowned, I added, "Napoleon the standard poodle? The champion who ran off with the goat who was really Abra? She stoked his fire, and now he wants more."

"Got it," Jeb said, handing over her lead.

Even a bucking Abra was manageable when leashed, which made me consider keeping the leather tether permanently attached to her collar. Why not let her drag it everywhere she went? All I'd have to do to when I needed to control her was dive for the other end. Right.

Once in my vehicle, she immediately settled down and dozed off. It was as if she knew that a little more beauty sleep could only help her cause. I tried not to imagine what an over-sexed Affie and a horny standard poodle would do all day. If Anouk confined them to a kennel, I hoped it had adequate sound-proofing. Abra in lust was way noisier than regular Abra. I glanced again at her gnarly coat. Unless Napoleon was into messy sex, Anouk might choose to clean up my hound before the event rather than after. Then again, if her boy liked strawberry syrup, their doggie foreplay could be extra fun.

Tir à l'Arc was located just off Orion Road, south of the lot where I had parked my car two nights earlier. In fact, the Rail Trail bisected the archery range. It had been many months since I'd ridden that far, but now I recalled the signs posted there. Although they didn't warn cyclists and hikers of death by arrow, they did announce the presence of the range and urge passersby to stay on the trail. A lot of good that had done Mark Vreelander.

A private club, *Tir à l'Arc* had its own small gravel parking lot. I was stunned to find it nearly full on a Wednesday morning in December. Pulling into the only remaining spot, between two minivans, I snapped off the engine and instantly heard the unmistakable voices of children. Lots of children. Shouldn't they be in school? Christmas break surely didn't start this early. And even if it did, why would they all be shooting arrows? With the weather still Florida-mild, weren't they more likely to ride their bikes?

Abra yawned without bothering to lift her elegant head from the leather seat. Children, with or without lethal weapons, were of no interest to her. Suddenly, though, the sonorous bark of another big dog reached us both. Abra was on her feet, sailing back and forth from the front of my car to the rear, whining pathetically. Apparently, Napoleon was pining for her. I snagged her leash, steeled myself, and unlocked the doors. Out we flew. Miraculously—or maybe thanks to her psychic powers—Anouk Gagné was walking rapidly in our direction. A quiver of arrows slung over one shoulder, she appeared as she had on the Rail Trail. I realized that she must be giving lessons. The range behind her featured four targets, each with a queue of children and mothers.

Even at this distance, I recognized Kimmi Kellum-Ramirez chatting animatedly with Loralee Lowe. Kimmi's many gold bracelets and necklaces glimmered in the winter-slanted sunlight. As usual, she wore ridiculously high heels. They pitched her forward at an improbable angle, made perilous by her disproportionately large breasts. Loralee wore a soft, flowing pastel dress under a dark pea coat. I noticed that her calves were well-muscled.

"Hello!" Anouk called out to me. On second thought, she was probably greeting Abra. The Affie gagged, straining on her leash.

"Let her go, Whiskey," Anouk said.

"Oh, I don't think so," I protested.

"Release!" Anouk commanded.

I did, along with four children who were holding loaded bows. Fortunately, all arrows were aimed away from us. Freed from my grip, Abra surged toward Anouk, a bounding blonde beauty panting for attention.

Anouk held out her arms to the Affie, saying something I couldn't hear. In the next instant, a dog that looked just like Abra but behaved nothing like her was sitting patiently, watching the French woman for her next command.

"Amazing," I told Anouk. "How is that possible?"

"Through practice and discipline."

"I was afraid you'd say that. Whenever something looks easy, I want to believe it really is."

"It really isn't," Anouk assured me.

"This must be a field trip from The Bentwood School," I surmised, indicating the hectic archery range.

"It's a seminar that Mark hired me to teach. We're having our fourth session."

She waved toward the children, now ready to fire again.

"Release!" she shouted, and they did. I couldn't help but notice that at least half the arrows veered far from their marks. How fortunate that Abra's eyes were obediently locked on Anouk's face. No way she would have resisted chasing those flying sticks.

"Are these parents learning archery, too?" I asked.

"The seminar is for the children. The adults are chaperones. However, archery is a fine family sport."

"Isn't it dangerous?"

"No more so than other sports."

I could have named a dozen sports in which participants ran no risk of being shot.

"How about those mothers over there?" I pretended to randomly choose Kimmi and Loralee. "Do they know archery?"

"Ms. Lowe, on the left, is athletic and strong for her size. I cannot say the same for Ms. Kellum-Ramirez. She has balance issues."

Indeed. I pressed Anouk for more information about

Loralee's archery skills. She was noncommittal, insisting that the teacher was there to supervise third and fourth graders. That was when I noticed the absence of Chester. Anouk explained that some children chose a music seminar instead, which made sense for my neighbor since his parents were professional musicians. I couldn't picture Chester shooting anything except a video.

"So, do Robin Wardrip's sons take this seminar?"

I hoped my interest sounded casual. Before Anouk could reply, Camo-Mom herself stepped out of a small outbuilding near the lines of archers. Carrying a bow and quiver, she wore a leather glove. I watched her purposefully approach the nearest line of children.

"Robin is my co-teacher," Anouk explained. "Those are her sons."

I followed her gaze to two brown-haired boys, almost the same height.

"You told me Robin used to be your protégée, but her anger issues made her unfit for the archery range."

"Did I say that?" Anouk asked, her dark eyes twinkling mischievously.

"You know you did."

She shrugged. "Robin and I have had our differences. She's very good with the children, however, particularly the boys."

I thought of a particularly challenging boy at The Bentwood School.

"Do you accept any student who wants to take this course?"

"Yes, provided they have no history of discipline issues."

That would explain the absence of Tate McCoy, even if he hadn't been busted the night before. Just to be clear, I asked Anouk whether he had signed up.

"He did, but I could not accept him."

"Because of his behavior?" I asked.

"Because his mother wouldn't give him permission."

Stunned, I asked why not.

"She has her reasons. It is not my role to question a parent's choice."

I wanted to question that parent. Stevie seemed so cool, so progressive, and yet some of her choices baffled me. She apparently trusted her son to spend evenings unsupervised and yet she denied him a school-approved archery seminar with a former Olympic trainer. Why? Maybe saying no to the class was her way of punishing Tate for previous bad behavior. I was starting to surmise that parent-child dynamics could be dauntingly complex.

Abra whined softly, awaiting her next cue from Anouk.

"Not yet," the archer said firmly, and my dog shut up.

I cleared my throat. "Stevie McCoy told me you're a pet psychic. Can I hire you?"

"You already have."

28

Abra heeled perfectly as Anouk Gagné walked her away from me, toward a modest two-story white frame house located a couple hundred feet from the archery range. Napoleon must have got a good whiff of my dog. He howled piteously in anticipation, presumably from an outdoor kennel.

As I turned to leave, I noticed that all three PTO moms were now conversing. Kimmi Kellum-Ramirez and Loralee Lowe had joined Robin Wardrip. Though not a fan of conspiracy theories, I couldn't help thinking I was the subject of their chat. I was sure of it when Kimmi called out.

"Hey. You. Realtor lady!"

I took a deep breath and started toward them. "The name's Whiskey Mattimoe."

"Whatever," Kimmi said. "You're one of Chester's personal assistants."

"I'm his neighbor and also his friend."

"Whatever," she said again, flipping her long white-blonde bangs back from her forehead. Gold jangled against gold as her many bracelets banged together. "Any news about who killed the headmaster?"

"How would I know?"

The three moms exchanged glances.

"We think you're the prime suspect," Robin Wardrip said,

her tone aggressive.

"I'm the eye witness. I phoned it in, remember?"

"Right. But you ran and you left your bike at the scene of the crime. Those wanted posters don't help your case."

"Those posters are irrelevant," I said. "Ask Chief Jenkins."

As soon as I spoke Jenx's name, Camo-Mom's face flushed. What was up with that?

"If you didn't kill him, who did?" Kimmi demanded.

"Why would I kill him? I didn't even know him."

"Maybe you did it for Chester."

"Are you nuts?" I cried. "Do you even know Chester? He liked the headmaster. Chester likes everybody, which is way more than you can say for the PTO."

"You've been talking with Pauline Vreelander, haven't you?" Loralee piped up.

I stared, picturing her heart-shaped face in the upstairs window on Fresno Avenue.

"How would you know that?" I demanded, wondering if I should call her out, announcing to her and the other mothers what I'd seen from the curb.

During the fracas at the front door, either Loralee had sneaked in, or Pauline had let her in. Or—another possibility—Loralee had been in the house, hiding or known to Pauline, since before I got there. In any case, Loralee had to be aware that I'd seen her because we'd made eye contact as I stood by my car. What was the name of this game, and how many people were playing it?

"Everybody knows Pauline phoned you," Robin said. "She asked folks at school how to spell your name so she could contact you about selling their house."

"Mrs. Vreelander and I discussed real estate," I confirmed with deliberate vagueness.

"And how much her husband hated the PTO?" Loralee asked.

"Why would you say that?" I said. "Were you there?"

A long silence ensued, during which I never looked away from Loralee, and she never blinked. Finally, Camo-Mom coughed.

Whiskey and Soda

"Listen, Mattimoe. We don't know how you got involved with Mark Vreelander, and, frankly, we don't care. We do care about what happens at The Bentwood School, and you got no business there."

I peered beyond the mothers to the unsupervised archery seminar, which was rapidly taking on the appearance of a riot. With weapons.

"Uh, aren't you responsible for those kids?"

"Oh my god!" Kimmi screeched, teetering on her stiletto heels.

Loralee moved like a natural athlete to break up four third-graders wrestling over a single quiver and a circle of older girls braiding arrows into each other's hair. Most of the other kids had picked sides and started a competition to see who could shoot an arrow the highest into the sky. That might have been innocent enough, but gravity, working the way it does, ensured a shower of pointy objects plummeting to earth at high velocity. Little girls were already screaming and covering their heads. Kimmi bellowed for her son and daughter because there was no way she could chase them, then she settled for saving her own skull, covering her head with wrists so heavily weighted by gold that she nearly knocked herself out.

Withdrawing a whistle from a pocket in her vest, Camo-Mom blew it to earsplitting effect. In the sudden silence, I couldn't resist commenting.

"Good job, moms. Letting your kids run loose with the same weapon that killed their headmaster."

Camo-Mom glared at me. "For your information, Mattimoe, those are not the same arrows. The kids are using target points. Vreelander was shot with a mechanical broadhead!"

I knew that, and of course Jenx did, too. She had been the one to tell me what type of arrow killed Mark, but the information had not been released to the public. So how did Camo-Mom know? And who else was in on the secret?

Before I could follow that line of thought, I heard a ping, followed by an intensifying whistle. I felt a narrow stabbing pain, more sudden than sharp. Glancing down, I saw an arrow protruding from my lower left belly. My baby! Without thinking, I grabbed the shaft and plucked. The arrow withdrew easily, leaving a small hole in my leather jacket and probably one in me. I felt a lingering sting.

I screamed. Not from pain, not because I saw blood, but from pure terror. I had been shot. My baby had been shot.

I must have shouted exactly that because Robin Wardrip was at my side, speaking firmly.

"Your baby wasn't shot, Mattimoe. The arrow was in your clothes."

"I was hit! Somebody shot me!"

The next sound I heard was that of a child wailing. A child, I reassured myself, not a baby. Not my baby.

The kid bawled, "It was an accident. I didn't mean to do it."

I peered past Camo-Mom to see Anouk Gagné gripping a young boy by the arm. In his hand, he clutched a bow. Face contorted, he cried messily. Kimmi Kellum-Ramirez stomped toward the boy as fast as her short legs and stilt-shoes would permit.

"Let go of him!" she shrieked at Anouk.

"Not until he understands what he did. Your son could have killed somebody."

"I just wanted to see if I could shoot far enough to hit her," the boy whined.

"You could have killed her," Anouk said.

"Stop shaking him," Kimmi cried. "Robin said these arrows aren't even dangerous."

"I never said that," Camo-Mom exclaimed.

Kimmi shot her a withering gaze. "Well, you said they're not like the one that killed Vreelander."

"That was a broadhead. I said broadheads are used for hunting. These are target arrows, used for target practice. But they're still arrows, not toys, you dumb bitch!"

Through the haze of my shock, I understood. Robin not only knew what kind of arrow felled the headmaster, but she had told the other mothers. Suddenly the archery range was deathly silent. Like a battlefield between campaigns. Two middle-school boys giggled over Camo-Mom's word choice, and a little girl whimpered fearfully, but the rest of the kids were struck dumb. When two sparrows tweeted in a tree, I idly thought about birds, then birds and bees, and I wondered what Abra and Napoleon were up to.

"Are you all right, Whiskey? Do you need a doctor?"

Whiskey and Soda

Anouk Gagné stood before me, petite and pulsing with energy.

I realized I was hugging my stomach with both trembling arms. Although I wasn't in pain anymore, I did feel sick.

Anouk gently removed my hands and discreetly did what was necessary to survey the damage. She stood so close that she blocked the view from other enquiring eyes. I turned my own gaze away, holding my breath.

"You are fine," Anouk pronounced. "Thank God you wore leather."

She spun toward Kimmi, whose son clung pathetically to her hips.

"Lucky for you, this was not a tragedy," Anouk said.

"You can't blame Raphael," Kimmi snapped. "He's just a kid. Kids aren't responsible for what they do!"

"You might want to rethink your approach to child-rearing," a new voice declared.

Chief Jenkins strode toward us. Where had she found a parking space? I was sure I'd grabbed the last one.

"Who called the cops?" Kimmi shot Anouk an accusatory glare.

"Nobody," Jenx said. "I'm here to ask a few questions."

"It's her archery range." Kimmi nodded at Anouk. "She's responsible for everything that happens here!"

"Read the waiver you signed when you enrolled your son," Anouk said coolly.

"Well, she isn't even supposed to be here," Kimmi said, shifting her focus to me. "That one keeps popping up in all the wrong places. I don't know why you don't arrest her for killing the headmaster or for leaving the scene of the crime. We've all seen the posters of her bicycle."

"Shut up, Kimmi," Camo-Mom said.

"Why don't you shut up, Robin? I'm sick of you always acting like you're the boss of us. Just because you're old and ugly and couldn't get a husband if your life depended on it."

"I don't need a husband. I am a husband," Robin said through clenched teeth.

"Okay, ladies," Jenx said, her own face coloring. "Class

164

dismissed! Every one of you should expect a call from me later today. Leave your cell phones on and don't leave town."

Anouk systematically collected archery equipment while Jenx herded the horde of privileged kids and moms off the property. Before that happened, however, Anouk escorted me to a bench so that I could rest while watching the unhappy exodus. What was wrong with these families? They left a wake of misery wherever they went.

Jenx joined me on the bench. We sat in silence for a few minutes, looking on as Anouk cleaned up the range.

"Okay," Jenx said finally. "I cheated on Hen. I had a little fling with Robin."

That was not what I had expected to hear. Ergo, I had no ready response, and I couldn't summon a single intelligent thing to say. For once, I wisely said nothing.

After a moment Jenx went on.

"Back in October Hen and I hit a rough patch. I got sick of her expecting me to help run the inn when I had my own job to do. If I opened my mouth to complain, she'd tell me I should try the New Age crap that worked so well for her. Hen wanted me to spend my days off replacing the windows in the inn. All the windows. You got any idea how many that is? I did the math and figured I'd be working seven days a week for the next six months. Hen accused me of not loving her enough to be supportive. Bullshit. I got so mad I almost took a swing at her. That scared me.

"So I went for a jog on the Rail Trail, to blow off steam. Robin was out running, too. We hadn't talked since we broke up—what?—ten years ago? All of a sudden, we're running together, like old times. She tells me about her partner and her kids. I tell her about Hen. Hell, I complain about Hen. She complains about her partner. We go grab a few beers, and one thing leads to another. You know how it goes."

When I still didn't reply, Jenx shot me a sidelong glance.

"It's the same with gays, Whiskey. We just use different equipment."

"Mostly the same equipment," I said.

Jenx grinned. "Anyhow, we got together a few times. It was good, real good, but we started feeling guilty. No, Robin started feeling guilty. I was in love. I was ready to leave Hen, it felt so right, but Robin would never leave her family."

"So you broke it off?" I asked.

"Robin did. No drama. She just stopped taking my calls and replying to my texts. And my emails. And my registered letters."

"You passionate fool," I said with affection.

Jenx shrugged. "Robin was right. She should be with her family."

"How about you?"

"I love Hen. Hell, we all got issues."

"Tell me about it."

"Does it hurt where you got hit?" Jenx looked at my bump, which I cradled with both hands.

"Still stings a little," I admitted. "I don't even know if it bled. Maybe I don't want to know."

"You should disinfect a flesh wound," Jenx said. "Got a hand-mirror for a good view?"

"Do I look like someone who checks herself in a mirror? I don't even carry a comb."

"That makes two of us," Jenx said.

I chuckled. "Girls on the verge of being a mess."

Just then, in a kennel I was glad I couldn't see, a dog howled. Next came Abra's cry, a sustained and intense rhoo-rhoo of ecstasy.

The chief said, "That girl's a mess."

29

From the range where she was moving a large leather target, Anouk paused to flash me a thumb's up. Apparently, she was every bit as satisfied as Napoleon, and that was my cue to leave.

Jenx asked if I'd remembered to pack the two flash drives from the headmaster's house. I had.

"You could give 'em to me now, and I could give 'em to Brady when I get back to the station tonight," she said. "Or you could take 'em to Brady at the station. That would be the right choice."

"I have a business to run," I reminded her.

"We all know your mom and your best agent are running your business."

"Not since Jeb started dressing me. Now I look good enough to be seen in public."

"You do look good," Jenx conceded. "Curvy Mommy?"

"How would you know?"

She pulled a face. "You think lesbians can't get pregnant?"

I agreed to take the flash drives straight to the police station, which was just down the street from Mattimoe Realty. When I waved good-bye to Anouk, she called out, "Come back for your bitch any time after four."

Jenx told me to call Jeb and let him know everything was all right.

"Why?"

"By now somebody's told him you got shot in the bump. He's probably left three voicemails on your phone already."

In fact, he had left four voicemails and two text messages. I had left my phone in my car. When I finally got hold of Jeb, he was en route to the archery range to check my condition for himself, before whisking me off to the E.R.

I did my best to assure him that I was fine. So fine in fact that I was heading to the office as soon as I concluded a little totally trivial business at the police station.

"You took an arrow in the womb," Jeb insisted. "You need to see a doctor."

"No, I took an arrow mostly in the leather jacket and a little in the epidermis. I'm all right."

"Babe, I'm driving you to the hospital. We need to make sure the baby wasn't traumatized."

I took a deep breath. "The baby wasn't touched. You're the one acting traumatized, and frankly, you're freaking me out. You'd better be a whole lot calmer than this when I go into labor."

We compromised. I would drive to the police station and Jeb would meet me there. Brady Swancott, part-time peace officer and father of two, would arbitrate our next move. At least we could agree on that.

I was the first to arrive at the police station. When I walked in the door, the place appeared empty, which was not unusual. Most of the time there was no crime in Magnet Springs, so Brady spent his desk-duty shifts cooking or surfing the net. I sniffed. Nothing yummy coming from the kitchen today. I heard a soft woof, followed by the scrabble of dog paws on a linoleum floor. Officer Roscoe trotted toward me from the back office, tail wagging. As his brown eyes darted around the room, his tail action slowed like a pendulum winding down. Poor guy. He must have recognized my scent and assumed I came with the stocky four-legged tart.

"Sorry, dude. No Sandra," I said. "I don't even have the other one today. Abra's working for a living."

"Whiskey? Is that you?" Brady called out.

"It is."

"Jenx called. She said you got shot in the bump by a fourth-grader."

I followed his voice into the converted storage closet that was the station's second office.

"I'm fine. Jeb wants me to see a doctor, but he'll settle for your opinion."

Frowning, Brady glanced up from his computer screen.

"I'm not sure my coursework in art history has prepared me for this."

"How about your experience as a husband and father?"

"Brenda and I didn't have any archery incidents while we were pregnant."

I excused myself to use the restroom so I could clean the wound. My plan was to use the mirror above the sink to see whatever needed washing. That proved tricky since the wall mirror had been installed to reflect faces rather than bellies. It was hung much too high for my purpose unless I could climb up on the sink. I was in the process of doing that when the bathroom door flew open and Jeb rushed in.

"What the hell are you doing? You're going to fall!"

Just because I was kneeling on the narrow edge of a slightly shaky pedestal sink didn't mean I might fall, but I let Jeb help me down, anyhow. He positioned me to take best advantage of the overhead florescent light, and he knelt down to get a close look at my teeny-tiny wound. In less ridiculous circumstances, his posture might have heralded a good time. In this situation, it just made me laugh.

"There's nothing funny about this," Jeb scolded.

"Seriously? You're on your knees in a police station bathroom trying to find an arrow-hole in my tummy."

"Whiskey—" he began sternly, but when he glanced up at my face, he laughed, too. "Only you, babe. Only you could deliver your dog for a sex-date and get shot in your bump with an arrow."

Giggling, I said, "I can't take all the credit. I owe a big shout-out to Raphael Ramirez and his incredibly annoying mom. You can't expect a woman with tits that size and shoes that high to keep track of her kid."

I was laughing so hard my eyes watered.

"Hey, that's a public restroom!" Brady called from his desk.

Whiskey and Soda

"Don't make me come in there."

Jeb tenderly kissed my bare belly and cleaned the very small, shallow wound with soap and warm water. When we emerged from the restroom, Brady was still on the computer, the German shepherd at his feet.

"Roscoe's been depressed since last night," Brady explained. "He's got a crush on Sandra Bullock."

"More like an obscene obsession," I said. "He can't even walk on four legs when he sees her."

Brady shrugged. "The blood rushes away from his brain."

"What's new with Tate McCoy?" I said, eager to change the subject.

"We're waiting for a call from his attorney. If Kittler can convince Jenx that Tate will make full and immediate restitution, plus do community service, we're gonna drop the charges. He's fifteen, and he's got no record."

I shook my head. "I like Stevie a lot, but I've got a bad feeling about Tate."

"Like a psychic feeling?" Brady asked.

"You know I got no intuition. This is more like common sense. Tate practically started a mutiny during the school assembly, then we find out he's been destroying property. I think he's a bad kid."

"Maybe he's going through a phase," Jeb said.

"Or maybe he's bad to the bone," I said.

"A sociopath," Brady theorized. "A kid with no conscience. Speaking of which, I hear you stole something."

He held out a hand.

"Jenx told me to get something she could use when I toured the headmaster's house."

"She meant something like information," Brady said.

I dropped the two flash drives in his palm. "Here's your information."

"If we're lucky."

Brady popped one into a USB port and clicked a few keys. "Of course nothing we find here is admissible in court, but we're not officially working this case, anyway."

He cocked his head at the computer screen.

"It's encrypted. Somebody wanted to protect this."

"Can you un-encrypt it?" I said.

"Decrypt it, you mean. I can't, but I know someone who can."

"Another cop?"

"Sort of. Chester."

"Our Chester?"

"He took an online encryption seminar last summer. Jenx and I were hoping we'd come up with something he could try his skills on and here it is."

"This could be sophisticated stuff," Jeb said.

"Probably not. Whiskey stole it from the headmaster of a private elementary school. We're not talking corporate espionage."

"Vreelander was career Army," I reminded Brady. "What if this is military software? State of the art, top secret stuff?"

"We'll let Chester take a crack at it. Hand me the second flash drive."

He removed the first, replacing it with my other "theft." By now, all three of us were watching the screen, waiting for the flash drive to load.

"That's more like it," Brady said. "No encryption here. Large files, probably media."

As he spoke, he clicked open Folder A.

"That's it. Videos and photos."

I was imagining elementary school sports events, classroom presentations, holiday plays. What bloomed on the screen was something else altogether: Pauline Vreelander in the buff. Sprawled like a Rubeneque beauty on a leather divan, she dangled a bunch of red grapes over her head with one hand and caressed each piece of fruit with her tongue, moaning as she did so. I turned away before I could look for her other hand.

The boys in the room had their own responses, neither professional nor mature. Their eyes stayed on the screen.

"I don't think we're supposed to see this," I said.

"I don't think you were supposed to steal this," Jeb rejoined, laughing. "You found Vreelander's secret stash."

"Home grown," Brady added. "Man, there must be twenty

Whiskey and Soda

videos on here."

The guys guffawed like middle-schoolers. Suddenly, I did feel like a criminal. I had invaded the Vreelanders' private lives. On the bright side, I had inadvertently answered my own questions about the nature of their marriage. Mark had found his wife alluring, and he had found a way to sustain himself during their long separations.

"Turn it off," I barked at Brady.

"Just making sure there's nothing illegal in the rest of these files," Brady said.

"Now," I growled.

All the males in the room, including Roscoe, snarled at me and then settled down.

"I'll take that, thank you." My hand was out, ready to receive the X-rated flash drive. "I wonder why this one isn't encrypted."

"Are you kidding?" Brady and Jeb said in unison.

I wasn't kidding. I wanted to know. The guys exchanged glances.

Jeb said, "Whiskey, you only encrypt what you want to hide."

"Yeah? So?"

"Vreelander didn't want to hide this. He used it."

"Ewww. Got it. Now give it to me."

Brady did. I had an overwhelming urge to find hand sanitizer.

"What are you gonna do with it?" Brady said. "Ring Mrs. Vreelander's doorbell and tell her you took it by mistake?"

The guys laughed again. It wasn't like I was a prude. While married to Leo, I was the subject of similarly sexy videos and photos, made for our eyes only. Staged simply for our own spontaneous fun. Not for Leo's later stealth-use. Or were they? Whatever happened to those little films? A wave of anxiety rolled through me. What if Leo's nasty daughter Avery had found them during the months when she lazed around my house with her infant twins letting the nanny I'd hired do all her work? Avery might do anything with those movies. She might show them to my friends, show them to my enemies or even post them online. Chester had said she was an online buzz-maker. I shuddered.

"You okay, babe?" Jeb asked. "You don't look so good.

Better sit down."

I let him lead me to the sofa in Jenx's office, where I lay down. I didn't feel well at all. Screw the arrow wound. Guilt plus worry will fell the strongest among us.

I deeply wanted to get back, fast and hard, into the Real Estate game, but I also had karma to settle or restore or rebalance. Whatever it is you have to do to fix that stuff. All I knew was that I had overstepped a cosmic boundary in removing at least one of those flash drives, and I needed to make things right.

As I lay, eyes closed, on the too-short couch in Jenx's office, my shoeless feet balanced on the threadbare arms, my cell phone rang.

"Want me to get that for you, babe?" Jeb asked. He was keeping me company on an adjacent chair, doing good-daddy duty massaging my size tens.

Shifting my weight, I slid the phone out of my hip pocket. Caller ID announced Pauline Vreelander. My first response was to drop the phone on the floor in a panic of guilt. My second response was to scoop it up, answer it, and fix my world.

"Hello, Pauline. What can I do for you?"

I assumed she wanted the name of the real estate attorney who could handle the immediate cash sale of her house to George Bentwood on behalf of The Bentwood School. But if Pauline had been calling to demand the return of her flash drives, I wouldn't have batted an eye. I would have crawled over there on all fours and begged her forgiveness, then I would have hunted down Avery and demanded to know if she'd ever found her father's stash.

"Whiskey, I've decided not to sell the house to The Bentwood School. I would like you to list it and sell it."

I was on my feet moving toward the door so fast that Jeb had to follow me with my shoes. Of course, I would list the Fresno Avenue property, I told Pauline, and I would sell it for more than George Bentwood had offered.

I had a secret weapon—Irene Houston, office manager and receptionist. I might not understand how my mother's juju worked, but Odette wasn't the only salesperson getting great business vibes, and this deal came with a bonus, a legit excuse for me to re-enter the Vreelanders' home and replace the flash drive that rightfully belonged to the widow.

I just hoped I wouldn't picture her naked the next time we met.

30

The one snag in my business plan—and, hence, my karma—was that Pauline Vreelander couldn't meet with me until that evening. First, she had to handle the remaining details concerning her husband's remains. His wish was to be cremated and to have his ashes scattered on the family farm in his home state of Kentucky. Or was it Kansas? Truth be told, I was only half listening. The other half of my attention was on Brady as he conversed with somebody phoning in an anonymous tip about the president of The Bentwood School.

Sensing my interest, Brady switched to speaker phone. The woman caller, who refused to give her name, seemed to be altering her voice. I guessed that she was lowering it while speaking through a muffling piece of cloth. She might also have faked the thick accent although we do have Germans in this part of the state.

"George Bentwood is not who he says he is," she intoned. "You must do a thorough background check. The man is up to no good."

"Ma'am, a background check won't reveal what anybody's up to," Brady said. "It can only show what somebody has already done."

"Well, he has done plenty that he should be ashamed of, and he won't stop. He uses money and privilege to cover his tracks."

"Can you be more specific?" Brady said.

The woman had hung up.

"I think that's about his womanizing," I told Brady, forgetting that I still had Pauline Vreelander on the phone.

"Pardon?" Pauline said. "Who's a womanizer?"

"Sorry. I was just talking about . . . um . . ."

My eyes scanned the room for a bailout. They lighted on Jeb, still helpfully holding up my shoes.

"Jeb," I told Pauline, not wanting to leak the latest police station developments.

"Your husband is a womanizer?" she asked.

"My ex-husband. Well, he used to be. I don't know if that's true now—"

"You don't know?" Jeb demanded.

Before I could reply, he dropped both my shoes and exited the police station. Hastily, I concluded my phone business with Pauline and started to go after him. Roscoe blocked my way, growling.

This wasn't our first fight since Jeb's return; it was just our first fight since his return that had nothing to do with dogs. This one was entirely my fault, at least that was how Brady and Roscoe saw it, and they were eye witnesses.

What had possessed me to use that moment with Pauline to question Jeb's loyalty? Brady thought I was punishing Jeb rather than questioning him, and Roscoe gave me a look that telegraphed the same message. They were probably right, but why would I do that? Jeb was knocking himself out to please me in almost every way. I had no reason to believe that he'd had any female other than Sandra Bullock in his bed for months.

Back in the good-old, bad-old days of our marriage, Jeb used to frequent a couple cheap bars down by the docks. If he needed to go there to blow off steam today, maybe I should follow. I didn't, though, and not just because Roscoe blocked my way. Mom called and ordered me to come straight to work.

I left the station with all the dignity I could muster, carrying my shoes in my hands.

Ensconced at the receptionist's desk at Mattimoe Realty, Mom looked surprisingly youthful. Maybe it was her new hair and lipstick or the two vases of fresh pink roses that framed her face.

"I'm busy, Mom," I said, attempting to walk on by.

"Indeed you are, Whitney. I've prepared the paperwork for the Vreelander listing. It's in this file."

She extended a manila folder to me, like a flotation device to a drowning man.

I stopped. "Who told you about this?"

"Pauline Vreelander. She came by looking for you. I told her you were out servicing a client. She doesn't need to know how you waste your time."

"I wasn't wasting my time, Mom. I got shot—"

"In the belly with an arrow. Yes, I know about that, too. It wouldn't have happened if you'd been at your desk, dear, where you're supposed to be."

I snatched the file a little more forcefully than necessary. My mother made a distinct tsk-ing sound.

"What's that about?" I demanded.

"That is the sound of me recognizing you making the same mistakes all over again," Mom said. "By the way, Jeb phoned. He's too upset to talk with you right now. I told him I know the feeling. He forgives you, though, and he's got a special dinner planned for you tonight. Better change your appointment with Mrs. Vreelander."

A whirlwind of emotions spun my heart around. Mostly, I felt relief. I hadn't behaved my best, or even like a grownup. Surely, though, Mom was wrong about my making the same mistakes again.

"Thank you," I forced myself to say.

"Just doing my job," she replied. "By the way, Odette is out servicing clients."

"See? That's what we real estate professionals do."

"That's what Odette does, dear. You just get in trouble. Sorry to hear you got shot. I hope you learned something."

As I turned away, willing my jaws to stay locked, Mom added, "We need to talk about your bridal shower. Tick-tock."

I walked rapidly to my office, where I locked the door. Like that would help.

For the next two hours, I immersed myself in business.

It felt wonderful to work hard again. The only snag was that I couldn't leave my desk for fear of being scolded my mother.

Note to self: Fix that.

Happily for me, Pauline Vreelander was flexible about my coming over with the paperwork for her to sign. I told her to expect me just before dinner.

Shortly after one o'clock, Mom buzzed my phone.

"I'm taking my lunch hour now. Would you like me to bring you back something from Peg's?"

She was referring to the Goh Cup, the quaint coffee shop run by her friend and our town mayor. I recalled Mom's telling me that she planned to rent a room in Peg's house, so I decided to play nice and ask how that was working out. Big mistake.

"It's not working out. Peg is so depressed. Frankly, she's bringing me down."

"Depressed about her business?"

"Of course, she's depressed about that. But Peg's got bigger issues. She needs a man."

"She does?"

I knew that Peg's coffee shop and tattoo parlor were foundering, and that she missed her weird little Devon rex cat. I was mainly to blame for her having lost that cat although Odette had made sure she was compensated in the transaction. However, I had never once thought that Peg needed a man. A long-time widow like my mom, she seemed too busy to have time in her life for a guy.

"It's a problem," Mom insisted. "Peg is jealous of me and Howard."

"How can she be jealous? Howard isn't even here."

"He isn't here yet," Mom said. "But he sends flowers every day. Even you must have noticed the roses on my desk. Peg won't let me keep them in my room. She says she's allergic, but I know that's not true. She's sick with envy."

A dull ache crept from the top of my skull toward my forehead.

"Go enjoy your lunch, Mom, and take your time. I'll get myself something to eat when I'm ready."

"That's not how it works when you're expecting. You've got to feed that baby first, often, and well. I thought you knew that much."

I managed to get off the phone by promising to leave within five minutes for a nutritious hot lunch at Mother Tucker's. The fact that Mom wasn't hell-bent on joining me signaled that even she needed a break.

In fact, I was hungry. As I walked the half-dozen blocks to my favorite restaurant, I entertained myself by mentally sampling each item on the menu and imagining which one would taste best today. My mouth was watering for the pulled pork sandwich with curly fries and German coleslaw when my phone rang. Wishing it were Jeb but knowing it wouldn't be, I read the caller's name.

"Chester, shouldn't you be in school?"

"We get out early on Wednesdays because of the seminars," he said. "Are you okay? I can't believe Raphael Ramirez shot your baby with an arrow."

I assured him that my leather jacket was the actual target, and that every part of me was fine. Chester was a chronic over-reactor. Given his mom's penchant for drama on stage and off, he had a right to be theatrical. I knew he meant well.

"The Bentwood School is complicating your life," he exclaimed. "And I'm responsible. Things started going wrong when I brought you to the school assembly."

"Actually, things started going wrong as soon as I hit the Rail Trail. You couldn't have known what would happen."

"I should have known," Chester said. "Everybody but you has some intuition. The Bentwood School has bad karma, and now you and your baby do, too."

"No, Chester," I said firmly. "My baby and I do not have bad karma. We have good karma. We have survived two flying arrows."

Chester was troubled by the notion that he had placed us in the path of those arrows.

I reminded him that I had free will. Clearly, Chester needed comfort. I invited him to meet me for lunch at Mother Tucker's. We would both feel better after pulled pork.

At age nine, Chester couldn't yet drive himself, so he conferred with one of Cassina's employees.

"I can join you for lunch, Whiskey, but there's a string attached."

"No leashes, Chester. You cannot bring dogs to the restaurant."

"I'm talking about Avery. She'll drive me to Mother Tucker's, but she wants a word with you."

Many words, I was sure. Most of which would be nasty. My ex-step and I hadn't laid eyes on each other in almost two months. An inspiring record, but one that I would break in order to spend time with Chester.

I remembered my earlier concern about the disposition of Leo's X-rated home movies. Was Avery's need to speak with me a coincidence? Or more karma?

31

Even before I was pregnant, I rarely imbibed while the sun was in the sky. Now, waiting at my table at Mother Tucker's for my late lunch with Chester, I needed all my willpower to resist ordering a fortifying shot of something with my name on it. Facing Avery Mattimoe had never been easy. Going back to when she was a teen and I was her new stepmom, she had blamed me for breaking up her parents' marriage. I hadn't. In fact, her mom had left Leo for another man, but Avery still saw me as the villain who stole her dad.

I did feel sad on her behalf that Leo had died without knowing he had twin grandkids on the way, so I did my level best to help by providing a home and a nanny until she could get on her feet. The catch was that Avery didn't want to get on her feet. She wanted to sit on her ass while others took care of her and her babies.

Her recent employment at The Castle marked the first time in her life that Avery was self-supporting. I could only hope that status wouldn't change.

Now, here she was, crossing toward my table in her usual graceless and aggressive way, perpetual scowl in place. Avery was a large young woman in her early twenties, almost as tall as I but a good fifty pounds heavier even than my current weight.

Usually her thin blonde hair hung limp. Not today. A stylish geometric cut de-emphasized the fleshiness of her face, which looked smooth, probably thanks to a coat of foundation. Avery's soft black sweater and pants had a slimming effect. Silver drop earrings and a long chain necklace caught my eye. She had artfully tossed a red and gray paisley scarf over one shoulder, and on her feet were black leather boots with silver buckles and thin heels.

Quite a change from the usual stained sweatshirt, baggy jeans and Crocs. Cassina must be dressing her, but who was I to talk?

As my ex-step drew close, I spotted kohl eyeliner and dark terracotta-colored eye shadow skillfully applied. For once, her piggy little orbs claimed dramatic focus in her round face. Earth-tone lipstick defined her narrow mouth. If Avery could have managed a smile, she might have verged on attractive, but that wouldn't happen.

She flicked her tongue at me. Not in disrespect, although that was surely what she felt. Avery stuck her tongue out at everyone. It was her singularly repulsive personal tic.

"Where's Chester?" I said by way of greeting.

With Avery it's wise to get in the first line. Otherwise, she'll launch her attack and block every divergence.

"There's a stray cat in the parking lot. Naturally, he stopped to pet it."

Thrown off her rhythm, she took a breath and evaluated my appearance.

"You're fat."

"I'm six months pregnant."

"At least you finally got tits."

Willing myself to stay civil, I asked how her babies were.

"Still cutting teeth. Wait 'til you go through that stage. It lasts forever. You'll wish you were dead, or dead drunk."

I skipped ahead. "What do you want, Avery?"

"Sandra Bullock."

For a moment I thought she meant the movie star. Then I got it.

"The dog? You want the dog?"

"Duh."

My heart soared. Maybe Avery would take the little beastie off my back. Oh wait. Not so fast. Sandra Bullock wasn't mine to give away.

"That's Jeb's department," I said.

"Really? Cuz Chester thinks you and Jeb are getting married." A wicked grin twisted Avery's face. "I knew that wouldn't happen. No way you can keep a man, even if you're having his baby."

Before I could say what I wanted to say—"Like you know how to keep a man?"—the phrase I'd penned on my palm the day before returned to haunt me.

So I did the right thing, or at least I didn't do the easy wrong thing, even though it would have felt wonderful.

"What about Sandra Bullock?" I asked through gritted teeth.

"Cassina's crazy about how cute she looks in costume. She wants to use Sandra on the cover of her next CD. Dressed like an angel, with halo, wings, the works. The photo shoot's this afternoon. Somebody's gotta sign this waiver."

Avery produced what appeared to be a legal contract.

"You'll need to ask Jeb," I said. "He's her manager even though she's our family dog."

Man, that was hard to say, but I could almost accept it. After all, I had taken the first giant step by hiring a pet psychic to get us over the bumps. Jeb would be ecstatic about Sandra's new gig. Abra would just have to deal with it.

Avery fixed me with a hard gaze. "So you and Jeb are sharing things now?"

I nodded emphatically.

"Really?" she said.

"Really," I said, crossing my arms over my chest. My C cup-size chest.

"Really?" Avery repeated as if sure she could catch me in a lie.

"Hey, Whiskey. Did Avery tell you the good news?"

Chester appeared, panting, at my elbow. He was covered from shoulders to waist in thick white cat fur.

"Yeah, she told me about the photo shoot."

"Sandra Bullock's going to be famous," Chester said. "I mean, the canine version of Sandra Bullock."

"Got it," I said. "Jeb and I are so proud."

"Did she tell you the other good news?"

"There's more?"

"Tell her, Avery."

A devious smile lighted my ex-step's face.

"Well, I was going to surprise you later, but you might as well hear it now. I'm getting married!"

For a second I thought I had entered one of those mind warps where nothing in the known universe makes sense. Who the hell would marry Avery? I might have even said that out loud.

"Who do you think?" she asked coyly.

"Really, I have no idea."

She and Chester exchanged knowing glances, which I found annoying.

"MacArthur, of course." Avery flicked her pink tongue at me. The tic did double duty. It made her look hideous, and it pissed me off. "You knew MacArthur tattooed me on one arm and the twins on the other."

I did know that, and I had often wondered about his choice of disfigurement. The hunky yet mysterious Scot had worked for Cassina as bodyguard, driver, and fixer of messy moral errors. Then, suddenly, he was gone. Now I wondered if Chester, like Avery, had always known he would return. To marry her?

A blinding flash filled my field of vision. Avery was wiggling her fat left hand in my face. On the third finger a diamond sparkled. It was the size of a pea.

"Congratulations," I said, because I had been raised that way. Irene Houston taught her daughter to wish people well, at least in public.

"Bigger than any stone you've ever had," Avery said, sticking her tongue out again.

I imagined myself hurling a much larger stone straight at her head, until I remembered to "do the right thing" and decided to kill her with kindness.

"How nice for you," I said.

"Speaking of diamonds," Avery said. "What happened to the one my dad gave you? You didn't pawn it, did you? Cuz I think I might be entitled to half."

"You're not. But no, I didn't pawn it. I saved it. In memory of Leo."

"Good. You can give it to Leah."

There was an upside to Avery's outrageous rudeness. If she had found Leo's secret stash of marriage porn, she would have used it by now to blackmail me. I could cross that off my worry list.

"You're not joining us for lunch, are you, Avery?" That was Chester's question. He looked a little nervous for my sake that she might say yes.

"Hell, no. I got better things to do than hang out with Whiskey. MacArthur wants me to surf the web for honeymoon locations. We both love a good nude beach."

I loved watching her walk away. Such a simple thing, and yet guaranteed to improve my mood. After Chester and I placed our lunch orders, I asked if he had known MacArthur was coming back.

"Sometimes you don't know how or when something will happen," Chester said. "But you just know it will. I always knew MacArthur would return."

Our lunches arrived. We didn't speak again until we had cleaned our plates. For the record, I did make Chester wash his hands before he ate even though there wasn't much I could do about the cat fur all over his clothes. While he sipped a second glass of milk, I enjoyed a leisurely cup of herbal tea. Only then did we talk shop. Brady had called Chester about decrypting the flash drive, and my neighbor couldn't wait to get started.

"It's probably open-source encryption," Chester said. "The easiest kind to crack. Something more complicated might take me a couple hours."

"A couple hours? I expected you to say days."

"Please, Whiskey. I aced the course, and got advance-placement credit at M.I.T."

"Did your instructor know you were nine?"

"It never came up."

Chester accompanied me back to the office, where he enjoyed chatting up my mom. Ever the little gentleman, he complimented her hair, her roses, and her smile.

"Aren't you adorable?" Mom cooed. "Just wait until you're old enough to date. Oh my, the ladies are going to love you."

"The ladies already love me. I'm looking forward to attracting bad girls. It's how a guy learns."

After he left for the police station, Mom said, "I never told you this, Whitney, but I always wanted a son. Of course, there's nothing feminine about you, so I almost got my wish."

Odette the Good Agent was still out servicing clients. She had left Mom a message that she'd come in later to complete paperwork. She hadn't left me a message, but, hey, I was just the boss.

I told myself this was as it should be. Now that Mattimoe Realty had an efficient office staff, there was no need for the top gun to track everything. Truth be told, I had never tracked everything, or even much of anything. I wasn't a natural like Odette when it came to sales, but I knew how to leverage the local market, and I was a darned good closer. Adjourning to my office, I prepared to dazzle Pauline Vreelander. I would come up with a strategy for getting her a fine price fast.

When I heard the knock on my door, I was startled to see that almost two hours had passed. I hadn't made a whole lot of headway. Mom stood in the hall, ready to leave for the day.

"Have a good time tonight, Whitney. More important, make sure Jeb has a good time."

"He's treating me," I reminded her.

She gave me a look that made me want to check over my shoulder, just in case she had hired the Relationship Police to keep me in line.

After Mom left, I reviewed my Fresno Avenue notes one more time. Earlier in the day, I had called a few local residents whom I thought might like the house, and also a couple ambitious Realtors employed at other agencies. I wanted to start a buzz. The problem, of course, was that Christmas was a week away. Realistically, we couldn't expect much action until after the first of the year. In that sense, Pauline Vreelander might have been smarter to take Bentwood's cash. I suspected, however, that she just plain disliked the man and his school so much that she couldn't accept his check.

After I delivered the paperwork to Pauline and told her about my sales strategy, I would retrieve my hound from the doggie sex farm. Hopefully, Abra would be exhausted after making whoopee with Napoleon all day. If Anouk were as pleased as I hoped, she might have even groomed Abra. Sleepy bitch.

Sexually satisfied bitch. Clean bitch. What could be better? I would schedule a pet psychic session for Abra and Sandra just as soon as Anouk could put it on her calendar. Jeb and I were going to make everything work out for our dogs as well as ourselves.

An incoming text message from Jeb startled and confused me:

Meet me @ Anouk's ASAP

Uh-oh. Had Abra managed to take off with Napoleon again? Surely they were too tired to run. Besides, Anouk would have called my cell if that had happened. Wouldn't she? Unless Anouk couldn't call because something was terribly wrong.

32

Enough with the crazy-making speculation. I started my car and phoned Jeb. Maddeningly, the call went straight to his voicemail.

"I'm on my way to meet you," I said and clicked off.

I just hoped that all the humans I cared about were safe. Jeb's text message jarred my nerves. Add the fact that his phone was off, and things didn't feel right.

What I found in the unlighted archery range parking lot caught me by surprise. The sun had set and faded, so the only illumination came from a pair of high-beam headlights aimed straight at me. They didn't look like Jeb's headlights or any headlights I knew, and it was impossible to discern the shape of the car or anything that lay beyond it.

I fumbled with my phone and managed to dial Jeb's number again.

Voicemail.

"I'm here," I said tersely. "In the parking lot at Anouk's. Where are you?"

A door slammed. A dark form that could have been a man or a woman emerged from the driver's side of the shadowy vehicle. If I'd been thinking, I would have simply moved my car so that my headlights exposed the other person. Instead, I did the most aggressive thing. I hit my high beams and leaned into the horn.

The shadow jumped. A dog jumped, too. Straight into the

beam of my headlights.

It was Sandra Bullock, gargoyle angel. Dressed in a gauzy silver gown with sparkling wings and a glimmering halo, she froze like the proverbial deer. Her bug eyes shone blankly, reminding me of alien orbs. My ex-step joined the Frenchie in the blinding whiteness.

Shielding her own eyes, Avery bellowed, "Cut the lights. You're spooking your dog!"

Leaning out the window, I suggested a compromise, that we both notch it down to parking-light level. Avery stooped to scoop up Sandra Bullock. The dog did a forward somersault right out of her grasp.

"Freakin' Frenchie," Avery muttered, collecting the beast on her second try. "I keep forgetting they're front-loaded."

After we'd both cut our engines and reduced our lights, we faced off in the lot, Avery holding Sandra.

"Where's Jeb?" I said.

"You don't know?"

"He texted me to meet him here. I thought it was an emergency."

"Yeah, well, you might say that. Think about who else was here."

"Anouk and Napoleon . . . and Abra. Abra! Oh no, don't tell me—"

"I won't," Avery said. "It's too much fun watching you guess."

She stuck out her tongue and told me anyhow.

"Chester phoned me from the police station. I forget what he was doing there, but he said he wouldn't need a ride home. Jeb was going to pick him up, and they were coming here to fetch Abra. So I came here to get Jeb's signature on the waiver for Sandra's photo shoot."

"You didn't have that yet?" I arched an eyebrow at her.

"I still don't. Hey, it's better to ask forgiveness than permission. Not my fault all hell broke loose when Abra saw Sandra."

I cringed at the mental image of my Satanic sex fiend attacking Jeb's little angel, who was dressed for the part. No doubt Abra ate her halo.

"So Abra tried to kill her?"

"After she tried to kill Napoleon for going gaga over Sandra. Abra rammed him so hard she rolled him right over. She attacked Sandra, but Jeb rescued her and asked me to hold her."

In Avery's arms, Sandra snort-snuffled. I thought she sounded smugly victorious. For Avery's sake, I hoped she'd fart.

My ex-step said, "Abra charged Napoleon, and he took off running. They're both gone."

"Affies can outrun and outlast standard poodles," I said.

"Yeah. Anouk's worried Abra's going to hurt him."

"She should be worried. She should be very worried."

By now I had sagged against Avery's car, my strength ebbing. "Anouk, Jeb and Chester are out trying to find them?"

"Yeah, and good luck to 'em. Anouk took her bike. Chester went with Jeb in his car."

At the mention of her master's name, Sandra whined piteously, and it hit me, my latest epiphany. Avery Mattimoe was like Sandra Bullock, the French bulldog. Both were lumpy, ugly and yet inexplicably attractive to certain members of the opposite sex. Also, they both looked better when accessorized.

"Whose car is this?" I wondered aloud. I was leaning against an extremely expensive vehicle. A Bentley.

"Cassina's. She keeps it for my use," Avery said, her tongue flicking. "When MacArthur comes back, we'll share it, and we'll live in our own wing of The Castle. Working for Cassina is like a fairy tale."

More like a circle of hell. Celebrities as spoiled and addled as Cassina invite chaos, and MacArthur would likely remain a man of many secrets. I couldn't imagine Avery ever being content for long.

When I heard what sounded like a tiny bell, I assumed it was part of Sandra's costume until I spotted the pinpoint of light coming toward us on the Rail Trail. A cyclist approached.

"I know where they are, and we will need my van!"

The French accent revealed her identity before she drew close. Anouk wasn't upset, just slightly winded from her fast ride. I jogged alongside her up the path toward her house, which was barely visible in the night.

"Whiskey, wait!" Avery shouted from the parking lot.

Whiskey and Soda

"What about the waiver for Sandra Bullock? What should I do?"

"Your job!" I yelled back.

Dismounting, Anouk assured me that both big dogs were fine.

"How about Jeb and Chester?" I said.

"Also fine, and with the dogs, not far from here. Jeb called my cell. He cannot transport them in his Z4."

When I pictured the two humans wrestling the two canines into that tiny sports car, the Keystone Cops came to mind.

"The dogs will require crating," Anouk said.

I had expected her to say "sedation." Although I would have offered to transport Abra in my own vehicle, it lacked anything resembling a crate. I loathed the prospect of trying to drive while she bounced off every interior surface, so I rode shotgun in Anouk's well-equipped van.

"Now that I have seen the interaction between Abra and Sandra, I understand your concerns," Anouk said.

"They only have one kind of interaction," I said. "Abra attacks Sandra."

"Clearly, Abra feels a deep psychic conflict."

"Really? I think she's just jealous. All the boys love Sandra, including Napoleon."

"It's a French thing," Anouk said.

"What is?"

"French bulldog, French poodle. Like French people, French canines are natural lovers. Free with their bodies and their hearts."

"That also describes my Afghan hound, except she's a thief and she wants to kill Sandra."

"She was also furious with Napoleon tonight," Anouk said.

She fell silent. I couldn't tell whether she was pondering my dog's many issues or concentrating on the dark highway. As near as I could tell, we were on County Road H heading into wine country. Anouk had said that the dogs weren't far away.

"Where exactly are Abra and Napoleon?" I said. "I know Abra's fast, but I don't think she could have run all the way over here."

Anouk drove on without speaking. I was about to pipe up

again when she turned her van onto a gravel road and cut the engine.

"The dogs are here?" I asked.

I knew they weren't. I knew I was in trouble.

"I brought you here because I need your full attention," Anouk said. "I couldn't get that with your obnoxious stepdaughter in the way."

"Obnoxious ex-stepdaughter," I said.

Anouk flipped on the overhead light, and I blinked. She held something out to me, something shiny and gold. A bangle bracelet almost a half-inch wide.

"Read the inscription," she said.

I held the bracelet near the dome light, tilting it back and forth to find the optimal angle. Although my vision was keen, the engraved letters were tiny and difficult to decipher.

"Love . . . Gale. No, wait—Yale."

Anouk said, "Does that mean anything to you?"

"Should it? What's this about?"

"Whiskey, I believe that bracelet belongs to the person who killed Mark."

33

I stared at the engraved gold bracelet.

"Where did this come from?"

"Abra found it when she took off with Napoleon. I saw her snatch something shiny from the grass where the archery range meets the Rail Trail, so I commanded her to drop it."

"And she did?"

Amazing. Abra never surrendered sparkly objects on request.

"What makes you think it belongs to Mark Vreelander's killer?" I said.

"I know who Yale is, and that narrows the field of suspects."

Did it? I had never heard of anyone named Yale in Lanagan County, and I told Anouk as much. In response, she insisted on showing me what I needed to know. First, though, I insisted on seeing Jeb and Chester.

"They are fine," she assured me. "The dogs ran to a barn on Uphill Road."

"Jeb can't put them in his Z4," I reminded her.

"Which is why I called Robin to retrieve them."

"You called Camo-Mom?"

Even after hearing Jenx's story, I wasn't sure I trusted Robin Wardrip any more than I trusted this woman, or any woman I'd met lately except Stevie McCoy.

"Camo-Mom?" Anouk was amused by the nickname. "Robin has two poodles sired by Napoleon and a big SUV with dog crates in the back. Plus, she owes me."

I detested Anouk's games and wondered if she were setting me up. But for what? If she wanted my dog, all she had to do was ask.

Restarting her van, Anouk continued along the unpaved, unnamed and extremely dark rural road. I had a vague idea where we were—east of the lake (Lake Michigan, that is) and north of County Road H—but there was nary a yard light in sight. This was wine country; that much I knew. What could Anouk plan to show me at night among acres and acres of dormant grapevines?

The road turned right and switched back on itself before curving left and dipping sharply into a grove of tall trees that appeared from nowhere I could imagine. We slowed at an intersection enclosed by pines. Anouk turned the wheel left and braked, clicking off her headlights. Before us a Tudor-style home glowed gracefully, outlined in thousands of tiny blue and white lights. The same Christmas illumination shone on leafless trees and evergreens that edged the expansive lawn. If there had been snow on the ground, the scene would have been perfect.

"Yale lives here," Anouk said.

I thought about the countryside that lay beyond this cozy enclave.

"Is he a vintner?"

"No. Although his family once owned much of the land we passed by, they were never in that business. Little by little, Yale sold off all but this parcel. It makes for a lovely, secluded home, don't you think?"

"'Secluded' is one word for it. Who is this guy?"

"You have no idea?"

"Absolutely none."

Although we sat in darkness, I felt Anouk's eyes boring into me. Was I in the company of a crazy person? A criminal? Or just someone French?

"I don't know who Yale is," I said keeping my voice even, "or why you made me come here, or why you think a bracelet found by my dog has something to do with a murder, but I have a very bad feeling about this. Please don't take me hostage."

At that point, I pulled out the only weapon I carried, my

Whiskey and Soda

smart phone. I noticed in consternation that it had no signal.

"You think I would kidnap you?" Anouk asked, dismayed.

"I have no idea what you would do."

Without explaining anything—or even turning her headlights back on—Anouk shifted the van into reverse. She made a ninety-degree left turn, flipped her high beams on, and roared forward. We were leaving much faster than we had come, too fast for road conditions. I covered my bump with one hand and gripped the door handle with the other.

"Please slow down."

"*Pardon*," she murmured in French, easing her foot off the accelerator. "Sometimes I get so angry—"

I wasn't sure I wanted to hear the end of that sentence, so I started one of my own.

"What road are we on?"

"Yale."

"Yale Road? Never heard of it."

"The road is named for a proud family tradition."

"Tradition? You mean like going to Yale University?"

She nodded. I couldn't think of a single local family with that tradition, and then, suddenly, I did.

"The Bentwoods?" I asked.

"Yes. Three generations of Bentwoods attended Yale."

"So, that was George Bentwood's house?"

"One of them. His wife prefers a milder climate. She is rarely at home on Yale Road although she is due back for Christmas, so Georgie bought the lights."

I wanted to laugh at Anouk's use of the nickname until I recalled how she and Bentwood had kissed when they met in the school hallway. Far too enthusiastically for casual acquaintances, even if one them were French.

"Are you Bentwood's lover?"

The question flew from my mouth before I could edit it. Her response was a small laugh.

"Am I one of his lovers, you mean? No, I am not."

"Then what does any of—"

"I used to be one of his lovers, long ago. I know where the

bodies are buried, as Americans like to say."

That intriguing comment, combined with an invitation, was how I ended up drinking at Anouk's house. Pouring Bordeaux wine for herself and soda for me, she shared her own local history. Napoleon, sans Abra, arrived at the archery range only moments after we did, courtesy of Camo-Mom, who had already delivered Abra to Vestige. I let Anouk handle that transaction while I did the right thing by making a couple quick calls.

First, I phoned Jeb to make sure that he, Chester, and the dogs were all right. They were fine though weary from Abra's wild chase. Next, I did exactly what my mother didn't want me to do. I took a deep breath and asked Jeb to postpone our dinner. Specifically, I requested a two-hour delay to pursue my work as a volunteer deputy. He asked me no questions, just gave me his blessing. What a guy.

Next, I called Pauline Vreelander and arranged to come by her house at ten A. M. She wasn't thrilled with the delay, but she accepted it. Although I couldn't tell her so, my hope was that by morning I would have more to offer than a real estate contract. I hoped to be able to point her toward the person who had killed her husband.

I considered phoning Jenx to say I might be on to something huge, but she would have asked a whole lot of questions, and I didn't have any answers. Yet. Besides, if that bracelet turned out to belong to the killer, I had accidentally put my fingerprints all over it.

Anouk had a dim galley-style kitchen and no breakfast nook. I noticed that the dented off-white appliances were old, circa 1980. The brown cabinets were made of faux walnut veneer, and the green laminate countertop was chipped. While she poured our beverages, she parked me in the living room in front of a gas fireplace that appeared long disused. A scarred oak coffee table was made level courtesy of three poker chips under one leg. The sofa and two stuffed chairs matched, but their striped upholstery was faded and badly worn. The carpet, mottled with dark stains, needed replacing, too. A gnawed nylar bone lay on the tattered hearth rug, the only sign of Napoleon, who had retired for the night to his "poodle man-cave" in the basement.

The living room boasted no photos of humans or hounds. I knew that Anouk had a son and daughter, both graduates of The Bentwood School. A professional recycler and a manicurist, she had said, lending credence to Chester's claim that recent alumni were not going into more pricey professions. Certainly, this house was modest compared to the homes of Chester's peers. I wondered how Anouk had afforded her children's education. Was the solution linked to her affair with "Yale"?

"Sorry I have no lemon for this," Anouk said, presenting a plastic glass filled with ice and soda. She settled into the chair on my right.

"Not a problem," I said. "Do your children still live with you?"

"They are grown. My son lives in Paw-Paw with his girlfriend. My daughter has an apartment in Sugar Grove, but sometimes she spends the night here. She gets nervous."

I recalled that Anouk's daughter had phoned the police the evening when Abra seduced Napoleon.

"My daughter is suggestible," Anouk said. "She heard there was a long-haired goat on the loose, so she thought that was what she saw when she spotted Abra."

"Abra is hard to explain," I conceded. "Please. Tell me about George Bentwood and the bracelet."

Anouk sipped her Bordeaux, a label I recognized from my many hours at Mother Tucker's bar.

"It's a long story. I married a man who loved archery the way I did. The way Mark Vreelander also did. We three met during the '84 Olympics. My husband was a trainer, like me. After we married, we bought this rundown little archery club and changed its name to *Tir à l'Arc.*"

"Did you keep in touch with Vreelander?" I said.

Anouk nodded. "Always. We three remained friends. When Mark was in the Army, we exchanged letters. A few times over the years, we managed to get together face-to-face. Once he came here and saw our range. He liked it very much. Of course, he was hopeful last summer when he applied for the position at The Bentwood School."

"Did you and your ex-husband also know Pauline?"

"My ex never met her. I met her only once, when Mark interviewed for the job. She was pleasant, but . . . "

"But what?" I prompted.

"I thought she seemed a little jealous of Mark and me, because we shared a passion. For archery."

I waited while Anouk drank more wine.

"What can you tell me about George Bentwood? And the bracelet?" I said.

"I will get to the bracelet. As for Georgie, he is who he seems to be."

When I didn't comment, Anouk added, "A spoiled, rich boy."

"George Bentwood's a little old to be called a boy."

"Exactly. Georgie never grew up because he didn't have to. When he was young, Georgie married a woman who required little of him. She wanted a husband from her own social class who would mostly leave her alone. She did, however, insist that he never embarrass her."

"Has he embarrassed her?" I said.

Anouk smiled. "To be embarrassed, one must be aware. Georgie's wife has mostly not been aware. She is seldom with him, and they have few friends in common."

"Which is why she doesn't know about Loralee Lowe's daughter, Gigi," I surmised.

"Oh, but she does know about Gigi. Now."

"Because of Loralee?"

"Because of someone named MacArthur."

I nearly choked on my soda.

"Mrs. Bentwood hired him as an investigator," Anouk said. "Georgie had become careless."

I hadn't known that MacArthur's services were available for hire. This might explain his temporary absence and his imminent return.

"How do you know about MacArthur?" I said.

"He investigated me. A pleasant Scotsman and so handsome, he inquired about Georgie as a father."

"Why would MacArthur ask you?"

She smiled and raised her glass. "Two of Georgie's children are mine."

34

"Bentwood is the father of your children?" I asked Anouk Gagné.

Although I tried to keep my tone judgment-free, it didn't come out that way.

"Yes. But my ex-husband raised them as his own."

"Does he know?"

Anouk crossed to what looked like an antique hope chest in one corner of her living room. She raised the lid and reached inside. Straightening, she turned back to me, a thick black scrapbook in her hands. She opened it, flipped through a few pages, and smiled at what she saw. She brought the book to me.

"You asked if my ex knew the children were not his. Here they are, when they were much younger. Do you still wonder?"

I peered at a close-up color photo of two beautiful smiling children, their arms around each other's shoulders. The dark-haired boy looked about eight; the sandy-haired girl, about six. Despite the differences in their hair color, they bore a strong resemblance not only to each other but also to George Bentwood. They had his winning smile and his distinctly handsome face.

"Good-looking children," I said although that was obvious. "Do they know who their father is?"

"My ex-husband is their father, legally and emotionally."

I nodded although I wasn't sure what I was agreeing with. "Did your husband know George Bentwood?"

"He met him at the archery range. Georgie was taking lessons from me. That was how we fell in love. Later Pierre and I sent the children to The Bentwood School. A strong private education was important to us."

Her story was so confusing, and so French.

"Did your husband ever confront you or Bentwood?"

"Never. The children could have been Pierre's in that we had a passionate marriage, especially in the early years."

She peered into her wine glass. "Pierre did leave me, eventually, but not because he resented Georgie or the children. He left when he met a woman he truly loved."

"Were you attracted to Bentwood's money?" I ventured.

"Not at all. You must understand that money means little to me. What I loved about Georgie was his playful spirit, the little bad boy in him."

Anouk smiled at memories playing in her head.

"While we were lovers, he gave me jewelry, but I don't wear jewelry, so I pawned it to pay my bills."

After an awkward pause—awkward for me, that is—I said, "I'm sorry. I just . . . I guess I don't know the right thing to say."

"You are uncomfortable, of course, and so Midwestern." I couldn't miss the pity in her voice. "We French are both passionate and casual about affairs of the heart. May I get you more soda?"

I declined her offer, trying not to think about how much I missed my daily dose of Pinot Noir.

"Will you tell me about the bracelet?"

"I'm coming to that part," Anouk said. "First, you need to know that Georgie was a wonderful lover. Still is, I am sure, although I foreswore that pleasure years ago."

"Why stop seeing him now, when you're no longer married?"

"Married, not married. It's irrelevant." She waved her left hand distractedly. "What matters is what the heart desires. Georgie wanted younger, fresher lovers. I wanted not to care what he wanted."

"He wanted Loralee Lowe?" I asked.

"Oh, there were many before Loralee. As for the bracelet,

Whiskey and Soda

Georgie likes to give gifts of gold to the women he loves. Engraved with his nickname, Yale."

"His alma mater," I said.

"His family tradition, yes." She sniffed. "However, one cannot wear a bangle bracelet when firing an arrow. I am certain that someone involved with Georgie dropped that bracelet, while preparing to fire at Mark."

"Kimmi Kellum-Ramirez wears bangle bracelets," I said. "Is she Georgie's—George's—lover? Or an archer?"

Anouk was sipping her wine, so I bumbled on. "We know that Loralee Lowe is the mother of his daughter. Is Loralee an archer?"

"No, no, and, I don't know," Anouk said finally. "Kimmi cannot shoot an arrow, and she's not involved with Georgie. Trust me, she's not his type. Loralee is his type. I watched her with the children on the range today. She seems to know something about archery. How much, I cannot say."

"So whose bracelet is it? It can't be Robin Wardrip's. She's an accomplished archer, but she doesn't like men and she wears camouflage gear, not gold."

Anouk raised both palms to signal either that she didn't know or that it didn't matter.

"You are on the hunt, Whiskey. You will need to follow the trail all the way to the killer."

I rolled my eyes in exasperation. "Just give me one good clue."

"I have given you every clue that is mine to give, but here's a thought. You are looking for someone whom Georgie helps in return for the help she gives him. It is a circular relationship, I think."

"So this woman is not Bentwood's lover? Or not his lover anymore?"

Anouk gazed solemnly at her smiling children in the open scrapbook on the coffee table.

"Find out what Georgie needs, and you will be able to figure out who she is, and also why she killed Mark."

I left Anouk's house, my brain buzzing with new information. A woman had killed Mark. A woman who loved George Bentwood, or used to.

Because I was less than two hours late for my originally scheduled date with Jeb, I was now early for the postponement. That made me feel virtuous. Approaching Vestige, I noted happily that my exterior lighting had been restored. I honked as I pulled in the driveway. Before I could exit the vehicle, Jeb stepped out on the porch accompanied by Abra.

Throwing open my door, I shouted, "Where's her leash?"

I hadn't completed the question before she leapt off the porch and flew toward the darkest recesses of my front yard. She was aiming for the forest beyond, where I knew she would vanish.

"Jeb!" I cried. He hadn't even moved.

"You let her get away again!" I stomped toward him.

Without answering, he held up a finger and slowly, dramatically pointed it toward the distant grove of trees. As if by magical command, Abra reappeared and loped toward the porch.

"How about that, babe?"

Jeb turned his thousand-watt grin on me. In the restored porch light, I could fully appreciate his good looks. He looked like James Taylor back in the Carly Simon days.

"How the hell—?" I began.

What I hoped was about to happen didn't. Instead of returning to us on the porch like a much anticipated miracle, Abra swerved away again. Her golden hair lifting like a curtain, her long legs stroked the night air. Without slowing her pace, she traced a wide, graceful circle around the yard. No question. The Affie was poetry in motion. The problem was that I never knew where the poem was going, or where it would end.

"No worries, babe," Jeb said, pulling me toward him. "She won't leave the yard. We now have a dog containment system."

"We do?"

"It's called a hidden fence. Did you see the new collar she's wearing?"

"Sorry, no, she went by in a blur."

As we watched Abra loop the yard, Jeb explained that Camo-Mom had suggested he try installing a flexible and temporary hidden fence system. The delay I had requested in starting our date gave Jeb time to buy the best kind available and set it up.

I couldn't help being skeptical. After all, I had been living with the bounding beast. In my experience, Abra could find her way out of any "containment system."

Listening to my concerns, Jeb remained optimistic.

"So far, so good," he said.

Abra was now on her fifth lap. I studied her as she rounded the bend near the porch. For a split second, we made eye contact, and I got a chilling vibe.

"Jeb, she's playing us, just humoring us humans 'til we're lulled into submission. Then she's going to take off again."

"I don't think so," he said.

With that, he stuck three fingers in his mouth and blew a show-stopping whistle. I had completely forgotten he had that talent. It achieved the immediate desired result. Abra turned herself back toward the house, sailed onto the porch and flew through the front door that Jeb held open.

"Great job," I told him.

But I still believed she was conspiring against us.

35

Once we were inside the house, Jeb removed my leather jacket, led me to my favorite recliner, and brought me another glass of soda, this one served with a sprig of fresh mint. I didn't have the heart to tell him I'd been drinking bubbly water until I thought my bladder would burst. While I relaxed with yet another bland carbonated beverage, he took care of securing Abra for the night.

He settled on the floor to massage my feet.

"I didn't get to finish this job when we were at the police station."

"I am so sorry," I said.

"'Least said, soonest mended.'"

He wouldn't let me apologize, but he did let me plant a big warm wet one on his handsome musician's mouth.

When we finally paused the kiss, Jeb said, "Speaking of mending, Tate McCoy's mom sent over a guy to fix your lights this afternoon. He measured the door on Leo's workshop, too, and said he'll be back tomorrow to install a replacement."

"Good restitution," I murmured, my eyes still closed, but I was way more interested in the kind of restitution Jeb and I had begun.

"Don't get too comfy, babe. I'm about to whisk you away for a wonderful dinner."

"Aw, Jeb," I purred. "I love you, and God knows I love good restaurants because I sure do hate to cook, but tonight I'm just too tired to go out again."

"Who said anything about going out? I'm whisking you away to a gourmet dinner served in your own king-size bed."

I opened my eyes. He was holding up a menu. Not just any menu, but one that I recognized as belonging to my favorite restaurant. The one I had visited for lunch.

"I know you had pulled pork this afternoon," Jeb said, "so we're doing something different tonight. I hope it's all right that I took the liberty of ordering for you. Any minute now, the doorbell should ring, and—"

Right on cue, the doorbell did ring.

"Now that's what I call timing," he announced, jumping up to answer the door. "Start dreaming about crab cakes and smashed Yukon golds because that's what we are about to devour. Why don't you go on up to bed and get comfortable? I'll serve you in a minute."

When I'm invited for dinner, nobody has to ask me twice. The same applies when Mr. Right makes a date in the boudoir. I was halfway up the stairs before Jeb had even reached the foyer. This was shaping up to be a perfect ending to a rather unsettling day, which meant I could now flush the emotional bad stuff and focus on paradise.

I flew past Abra's room into my own boudoir, dove into my featherbed, and pulled the down comforter all the way up to my chin. I proceeded to slither out of my clothing and toss each item toward a different corner of the room. I was thrilled when my larger-than-ever bra snagged on a corner of the dresser mirror. After that, I deliberately aimed my panties at the floor lamp next to the door. Two more points! I was now officially naked, famished, and ready to score in a way that counted.

A female voice drifted up the stairs and into my room. A familiar female voice, as in that of the woman who had raised me. Since when did Irene Houston deliver meals for Mother Tucker's? I sat up straight, clutching the quilt to my bare chest. Surely Jeb would tip Mom and send her on her way. I was puzzling over the delay when Jeb appeared in our bedroom doorway. He offered no crab cakes, just a perplexed expression.

"Whiskey, you're not going to believe this," he began.

"I heard her voice," I said, rolling my eyes. "I can't believe she's got a second job already. Do you need more money for the tip?"

"Your mom isn't here delivering food. She's here because she needs a place to stay."

"Peg threw her out?"

"Peg threw them out," Jeb said. "Howard is with her. They're in their pajamas."

"What?"

Jeb was trying hard not to laugh.

"According to your mom, they were in her room at Peg's house 'making whoopee.' And that popped Peg's cork. She had some kind of meltdown and made 'em leave before they could even get their clothes on."

"So there's no dinner?" I asked.

"Oh, your dinner's on its way, but where do you want me to put your mom and her boyfriend?"

"Fiancé. Howard is my fiancé, and Peg should have respected that."

I shrieked. Mom was standing inside my bedroom wearing a sheer peach-tinted bathrobe and negligee. Victoria Secret sheer. Next to her stood a tall, stocky bald man with an unnaturally deep tan. I could see a lot of his tan because he wore only fleece pants, and they came only as high as a couple inches below his navel. The fleece pants sported palm trees with red and white Christmas lights.

"How ya doin'?" he said, his voice deep and husky. "The name's Howard Nusbaum. I love your mother."

He crossed to the bed to shake my hand. A dicey proposition since I was using my hand to hold the quilt over my breasts. I bunched the fabric into my left hand, slid farther down into the bed, and lamely offered my right palm. As a Realtor, I have developed a power-handshake, but that wasn't what Howard got.

"I love her, too," I stammered. "But, honestly, Mom, couldn't you have grabbed some clothes?"

"No, we couldn't. You should have seen Peg. She went completely ballistic. She was swinging her broom at us, wasn't she Howard?"

He nodded gravely.

"Did you forget to close the bedroom door?" I said.

"Of course not. We weren't born in a barn." Mom looked insulted.

"We did forget to lock the door, though," Howard said. "That's how come Peg was able to barge right in, waving the broom."

"I told you she was jealous, Whitney," Mom said. "But I never expected a fit like that."

"If she was ten years younger, I'd uh blamed it on The Change," Howard said. "She screamed like a banshee. You'd uh thought we were swappin'."

"Swappin'?" I repeated.

"Yeah, you know, swappin' sex partners. Like back in the '70s."

I longed to stick my fingers in my ears and sing "la-la-la."

Jeb cut in. "How about I show Irene and Howard to the guest room, Whiskey? The guest room at the far end of the hall?"

"The far end is a good idea," Howard said. "That way we won't bother you guys. Irene likes to make a little noise, don't ya, doll?"

"Only for you, Hunbun," my mother said. She surveyed my undergarments hanging about the room. "I never could teach her to put things away."

I pulled the quilt over my head. It was so dark, warm and soft under there—a welcome retreat from flying arrows, running dogs, and sexually-active senior citizens. I must have dozed off. The next thing I knew, Jeb was gently peeling back the bedspread, filling my head with the tantalizing scent of our dinner.

"I'm going to feed you," he said.

Which was exactly what he proceeded to do. Slowly. Sensually. I highly recommend smashed potatoes as foreplay-food. Sure, the meal was a little messy, but Jeb and I aren't the types to mind rolling around on a few crumbs and spills. Who needs dessert when you are dessert? Eventually I fell asleep in Jeb's loving arms, Mom and Howard long forgotten. If they did make noise, I never heard it.

If only I could have slept without dreaming. Sometime before dawn, the nightmare played again in my head, and the newest version was the worst.

Jeb was riding toward me on the headmaster's bike, wearing the same yellow and white Spandex. When he raised both hands,

I knew he was going to fall to the trail, dead. Before I could shout a warning, an arrow struck my belly. I felt no pain, but gazing down, I realized the arrow had penetrated so deeply that only a few inches of the shaft were visible. I grasped it firmly with my right hand and pulled. The shaft wouldn't budge. So I pulled again, using both hands this time, straining with all my might. Still no movement. Deep within me, a baby wailed—a loud and terrible cry—the desperate breathless bawling of a wounded infant. My child.

"Whiskey! Whiskey, wake up."

Jeb was rattling my shoulder and speaking straight into my face.

"You're dreaming, babe. It's okay. Everything's okay."

"That was awful," I whimpered. "The baby—this time, it was the baby who—"

Jeb folded me into him, caressing my hair.

"Shh," he whispered. "The baby's fine. You're fine. I'm fine. We're all fine."

"When will I stop dreaming about death and arrows?"

"Soon, I promise, very soon."

But even as Jeb held me, I wondered when my night terrors would end. Most likely, not until I could be certain that the person who had killed Mark Vreelander would never hurt anyone again.

36

There's nothing quite like post-coital breakfast with your lover, your mother, and your mother's lover. That's right. All four of us managed to arrive in the kitchen at the same time very early in the morning. Jeb and I were in our robes. Mom and Howard were in the scant nightwear they had arrived in. I tried not to look at my mother's negligee for any number of reasons.

Mom peered into my fridge.

"I can tell Jeb's living here now," she said. "You have food."

She proceeded to make us all scrambled eggs, bacon and toast, and I let her. Hell, I hadn't even known we still had food in the house. While she cooked, Howard lasciviously watched, and I tried to ignore that.

We didn't say much, not only because the situation was awkward, but also—and more importantly—because my mother didn't talk while cooking. A real chatterbox at almost any other time, Mom put herself in the zone when she cooked, and she detested interruptions.

Apparently, Howard had been trained. He seemed content with his designated role as silent and lusty observer. No doubt he also knew that Mom was a good cook, so whether they went back to bed or not, he was about to be made deliriously happy.

Chewing and swallowing further removed the necessity for conversation. By the time we'd all had two helpings of everything and multiple cups of coffee, I felt sufficiently fortified to deal with my mother.

"When are you going to get your clothes?"

"Just as soon as we finish our coffee, dear."

"Dealing with Peg might be awkward," Jeb said, "Do you want me to fetch your stuff?"

"No need," Mom said cheerfully. "She texted me. Our clothes are in the front yard."

Howard said, "I got a text, too. Our clothes are all over the front yard. Peg threw 'em out the window."

"Where are you going to stay?" I said.

Jeb cleared his throat meaningfully. So meaningfully that I looked at him, and I didn't like what I saw. During the long pause that followed, I had the unsettling sensation that I was supposed to answer my own question. When I didn't, Jeb did.

"You know, Irene, there's plenty of room here."

"Howard and I need privacy," my mother said. "I'm sure Odette can find us a nice cabin or condo to rent 'til we're ready to head back south."

"Mom, I can find you a place. I'm a real estate broker."

She ignored that remark, turning instead to Howard. "We'll get our clothes, and I'll go to the office. Odette will be there. She's always on time."

"Mom," I tried again. "You're more than welcome to stay here."

My mother gave me the look she'd always given me when I lied to her.

"I'm not lying," I cried.

"Whitney, I love you, but parents shouldn't live with their adult children. It's unnatural. Besides, Howard is allergic to dogs, and you don't even know how many dogs you have."

Howard said, "No problem last night. I took an antihistamine. Good thing it didn't interfere with that little blue pill."

"It sure didn't," Irene cooed.

Jeb asked Howard how he planned to spend the day while Irene was at work.

"Sightseeing, I guess, unless you got a better idea."

"I just might," Jeb said.

Whiskey and Soda

When I excused myself to get ready for work, Mom reminded me that I needed to set a date for my bridal shower. In response, I kept walking.

My day promised to be more hectic than usual. I had a real estate deal to seal and a murder to solve, or at least help solve. As I showered, I made a mental list of the nagging questions that, when answered, might point us toward Vreelander's killer. In no particular order, these sprang to mind:

- Who made the Blitzen poster, and why did he or she put Mark Vreelander's cell phone number on it? Who has that phone, anyway? Pauline Vreelander said she would produce it, but so far she hasn't. Was it the same person who left the note on my windshield?

- What was Loralee Lowe doing at the Fresno Avenue property? And how did she get in? Did Pauline Vreelander know that she was there?

- What is on the encrypted flash drive recovered from the headmaster's home office?

- If Anouk is correct that the inscribed gold bangle bracelet belongs to one of Bentwood's lovers, who is that person, and did she in fact drop the bracelet while shooting Vreelander?

Fresh from my shower, I stepped into fuzzy slippers and wrapped myself in an oversized towel. To my surprise, the bed was made. For an instant, I suspected my mother of making it, either out of nostalgia or as a silent rebuke of my housekeeping skills, but I spotted a note on the bed. Inside a folded piece of notepaper, Jeb had printed: Check the closet. Curvy Mommy delivers again.

On the inside of the closet door hung my third brand-new beige maternity ensemble this week, a bulky turtleneck sweater with darker skinny-leg pants. A brown and ivory checked silk scarf was draped gracefully across the sweater. It gave me pause. I loved Jeb and his shopping muse, Chester, but how could either of them expect me, in my second trimester, to undertake accessorizing? It was a concept as foreign to me as, well, weekly grocery shopping, and yet reflecting on how good Avery had looked in her scarf, I knew I probably ought to give it a try.

Howard and Mom were on their way to Peg's to retrieve their clothes by the time I kissed Jeb good-bye. He had already fed and watered Abra. She was out running laps around the frontyard, courtesy of Camo-Mom's flexible "containment system."

Once again our weather was better suited to April than December, a bane to anyone who stood to profit from Christmas spirit. The continuing mild temperatures would work in Howard and Mom's favor, however, since Magnet Springs had a surplus of cabins and condos for wintertime tourists who couldn't find winter here.

Grabbing my leather jacket, shoulder bag and briefcase, I headed toward my car, parked overnight in the driveway. Abra zoomed past me in an apparently happy lap around the yard. As if she just loved to be contained. Sure she did.

Jeb waved from the porch, and I backed out. I had barely shifted into drive when my cell rang.

"A good morning to you, Volunteer Deputy," Jenx began.

The cheery greeting was so out of character that I applied the brake.

"What happened?" I said.

"Aside from your mom and her boyfriend starting an altercation at the mayor's house, you mean?"

"That's not the way I heard it," I said.

"Well, if you'd actually heard it, you would know how loud it got. Peg's neighbors thought they were listening to domestic violence. A three-way tryst gone terribly wrong."

"Yeesh."

"When I got there, Irene and her beau were drivin' away, but Peg was still swingin' her broom. I never knew she had a temper like that. She said they disrespected her and her house. But, as consenting adults, they didn't break any laws."

"You didn't see my mom's negligee."

"And you didn't see how whacked-out Peg was. Our mayor is seriously overstressed. The bad economy is tanking both her businesses. Says she can't sell enough coffee or tattoos to pay the rent. On top of that, she has to listen to all the other Main Street merchants whine."

"Should I have a talk with her?" I said.

"She'll think you're there to take your mom's side. Better wait a few days, then buy everybody you know gift certificates for coffee and tattoos. They sell some tats that wash off, ya know."

Changing the subject, I asked Jenx if she'd heard any news

about the encrypted flash drive from her favorite volunteer deputy.

"Chester called this morning. He's got study hall third period, and he thinks he can knock it out before math class."

I proceeded to inform Jenx about Anouk's discovery of the engraved gold bangle bracelet and her theory about the shooter.

"Did you know that 'Yale' is Bentwood's nickname, and he lives on Yale Road?" I added.

"Everybody knows that," Jenx said.

I declined to mention that I didn't or that I hadn't even known there was a Yale Road.

"This morning the State Boys sent me their forensics update. Just a courtesy," she growled, "since they took my case away. No fingerprints on the arrow that killed Vreelander. That's not a surprise. Serious archers wear gloves. But the trajectory report is interesting."

"Why?"

"It would seem to confirm Anouk's theory about where the killer fired the arrow."

"Near the spot where she found the bracelet?" I said.

"Bingo. The arrow was fired with maximum force and precision."

I urged Jenx to talk with Anouk if she wanted more details. No way was I going to pass along her tale of Bentwood, his spawn, his disgruntled wife, and MacArthur.

Jenx said, "After I interview Anouk, I'm gonna talk to the PTO moms again."

I thought about the chief's history with Camo-Mom but decided not to mention any part of that, either. Instead I said, "What are you hoping to hear that they haven't already told you?"

"Second interviews are always a good idea. People remember things they forgot to tell you the first time around. Plus, if they change their story, you know they were lying."

"Somebody must be lying," I said.

"Everybody lies about something," she said. "Especially about how they feel, like whether they hated somebody enough to kill 'em. I'm still trying to figure out what happened to the headmaster's phone. By the way, using a disposable cell that we confiscated in another case, I called the number that was on your note and the Blitzen poster. It went straight to default voicemail. Either somebody's just watching the calls come in, or that phone is lost."

"If it's lost," I said, "the note and poster must be some kind of joke."

"Maybe," Jenx said. "Or maybe somebody's trying to rattle you."

"Me? Why?"

"Maybe they don't like you, Whiskey, or maybe they're trying to deflect attention away from themselves. Anyhow, I gotta see Vreelander's home office for myself."

"You won't tell Pauline that I borrowed anything, will you?"

"Hell, no. That's your crime."

I winced at her word choice. Fortunately, I had a plan to replant the first flash drive, the X-rated one, in Mark's home office. My strategy was to convince Pauline to walk me through the whole house one more time. While we were in the office, I would distract her just long to drop it somewhere. Anywhere. She or the movers would find it when the house was packed up, and it would be back in her possession where it belonged. Karma restored.

By the time Jenx and I concluded our call, I was turning left onto Fresno Avenue. A silver PT Cruiser pulled away from the curb in front of the Vreelanders' home. Although only the back of the driver's head was visible, I could have sworn I saw Loralee Lowe's golden waves. I didn't know her license plate, but this looked like the car she'd been driving the day the PTO reconnoitered on Broken Arrow Highway before heading off the headmaster. Shouldn't she be at work? I supposed that even teachers got a break during the day, one that lasted long enough for her to drive the short distance from The Bentwood School to speak with Pauline. Was she delivering a message on behalf of "Yale"?

I made up my mind to ask Pauline why Loralee Lowe was here in the middle of a school day. Depending on her reaction, I might reveal that I'd seen Loralee in the window of Mark's office when I left the last time. Had Pauline known she was in the house? What the heck was going on that day? This time I wouldn't let her lie to me.

Note to self: Get Pauline's signature on all listing documents first, just in case I ticked her off.

As it turned out, I didn't have an opportunity to do any of those things. I rang and rang the doorbell, but nobody answered. I switched to pounding my fist on the door, and I rang the bell a few more times. No reply. The knob wouldn't turn when I tried it.

Given that Pauline's husband had been murdered three days ago, and I had just seen one of the suspects leaving the scene, my senses shot into overdrive. Everything here looked normal, but quiet. Too quiet.

I picked my way around the house, hoping to find a window that I could peer into. Unfortunately, every first-floor shade was down, as had been the case on my previous visit.

At the back door I pounded repeatedly. It was also locked. The detached garage had no windows, making it impossible to know whether a vehicle was parked inside.

After I completed the circle, I rang the bell and knocked again, just in case Pauline had been indisposed. No result.

Time to try the telephone. First, I dialed their landline. Mark Vreelander's energetic voice lived on, inviting me to leave a message after the beep. I declined. Next, I tried Pauline's cell. It rang a few times and went to voicemail.

"Pauline? Whiskey Mattimoe. We had an appointment at ten this morning. It's a few minutes after that now. I'm at your door, but you're not answering. I'm a little concerned. Is everything all right? Please give me a call back. Thanks."

I forced myself to breathe deeply. Pauline was expecting me. She hadn't phoned or texted about any delay, but before I jumped to full alarm mode and called the cops, I would try my Classic Card Trick. Credit card, that is. Using plastic from my wallet, I did my best to slip the front and back locks. No go.

Holding my phone, I stood in the front yard and studied my options. Ordinarily I would chock this scenario up to either a client scheduling conflict or a client "blow-off." However, Pauline wasn't the type to miss appointments, and a cold-blooded killer had recently whacked her man. If Mark Vreelander never changed the locks, Loralee might still have a key. For all I knew, the PTO mom had just met with Pauline, and now Pauline wasn't answering the door.

I was ready to dial Jenx when the phone jangled in my hand. The caller ID said Pauline Vreelander.

I clicked to answer and heard a low sustained moan, the kind of sound I imagined a dying lion might make.

"Pauline? Pauline! Is that you?"

The moan turned into a series of whimpers.

"Pauline, this is Whiskey Mattimoe. Can you hear me?"

"Help . . . me. Help me."

"Where are you?" I said, my heart rattling my whole body.

"Help me." The moaning began anew.

"Pauline? Can you hear me? Are you in your house? Pauline?"

"Uhhhhhh," the moan was almost a word.

I was sure she meant yes.

Keeping that line open while I dialed the police, I thanked the demigods of technology for giving us smart phones. Jenx took so long to answer her desk phone that I was almost ready to try her cell.

"Yo, Whiskey. Kinda busy here. Can you call back?"

"No! Listen, this is an emergency!"

I proceeded to explain, as succinctly as possible, that I believed Pauline Vreelander was seriously injured inside her own home.

"Gotcha. I'll dispatch EMTs, the State Boys, and Brady. You stay there. Keep her talking."

More like moaning and whimpering, but I vowed to do my best. Returning to Pauline's line I heard only silence.

"Pauline? Pauline, are you there?"

Nothing. I repeated her name but got no response. Fighting panic and realizing that I had turned clammy all over, I scanned the windows again. It had been too long since my last first aid class, and I had an unfortunate tendency to puke or faint at the sight of gore. However, if I could get inside, I might be able to help or comfort Pauline. At the very least, I could open the front door for the arriving emergency crew. That would free up a few life-saving moments.

I rushed around the house, checking every first-floor window. All were locked. I would have to break one. That may sound like a simple task, but it requires an appropriate window-smashing tool, which I didn't have. The Vreelanders' yard boasted no rocks or small statuary suitable to the task, but in the backyard garden I spotted a lone plaster urn less than a foot tall. Fortunately, it was empty and easy to wield.

Next, I did what any self-respecting former high school volleyball star would do. With all my might, I spiked it through a side window and used my briefcase to whack away remaining shards of glass for a clear passage.

I had chosen a low side window that looked small enough to shatter yet large enough to climb through. When I imagined the climbing-through part, I pictured myself at my normal weight and shape. Now I glanced down at my baby bump. Of course, the hips and thighs were wider, too, and I was generally less limber. For a split second, I wasn't sure whether this strange new version of me could slip through the allotted space. No time to waste wondering. I did have one thought, though, as I hoisted myself up and through. Jeb, your gift timing is impeccable. Loved the jumpers, but so glad I got pants today.

Coming through the broken-out window, I shouted, "Pauline, it's me—Whiskey Mattimoe! I'm in your house. Pauline! I'm going to find you and help you!"

Well, I hoped I could help her. Stepping over the shattered glass, I scanned the living room, where I had landed. Everything seemed normal, minus my messy handiwork. Still calling for Pauline, I unlocked and opened the front door. She wasn't in the front of the house, so I dashed to the kitchen at the back. No sign of trouble there, and no sign of Pauline.

I thought of Mark's upstairs office, where I had seen Loralee. The room drew me like a hypnotist, and yet, as long as I was this close to the basement, I knew I should check it first. I crossed the kitchen and flipped the light switch at the top of the basement stairs.

Pauline lay at the bottom, her head turned sideways, mouth open, eyes closed. Her right arm was folded under her; the left arm was visible, a cell phone clutched in her hand. Blood encircled her head, staining her silvery-brown hair maroon. If I'd had to guess, I would have said she was dead.

37

I think I screamed. I couldn't be sure because sirens wailed in my ears. What I did know was that Pauline Vreelander was beyond any help I could give. My best response would be to stay out of everyone's way and answer whatever questions I could.

I had three huge questions myself. Had Loralee Lowe found and left Pauline like this? Or had she caused this? Or, if Loralee hadn't entered the house, how the hell had this happened?

I stood clear as the EMTs entered carrying their equipment. One paramedic asked me for basic information—my name, Pauline's name, her age, her health, what I knew about the situation. I shared what I could, withholding only my comments about Loralee. Those I wanted to share with the cops, still en route. Standing in the kitchen answering the EMT's questions, I suddenly smelled Pauline's blood, or thought I did, and my good ol' gag reflex kicked in. Either my reputation as a wuss had preceded me, or the paramedic just knew my type. He ordered me to sit down in the living room and breathe deeply.

"When you feel stronger, go sit outside. The fresh air will fix you right up."

I was sitting in a wingback chair, my head down as far as it would go, when Jenx walked in.

"Head between your knees, Mattimoe," she said by way of greeting.

I peered up at her. "Baby in the way."

"Oh, yeah. Puke yet?"

"Nope. And I'm not going to. Pauline's at the bottom of the basement stairs."

"Is she conscious?"

I shook my head. "There's a lot of blood. She looks bad. Hey, I thought you were sending Brady."

"I traded him my desk duties for this call. I wanna deal with the State Boys."

Two of them were striding toward us. Quickly she told them what I had told her. They nodded and moved on to Pauline. I grabbed Jenx's wrist before she could follow.

"Loralee Lowe was here. Her silver PT Cruiser was pulling away when I arrived."

"You sure?"

"Pretty sure. Who else do we know that drives a silver PT cruiser? But I don't know if she was in the house."

"We'll figure it out. Nice job smashing the window."

I just hoped I hadn't been too late. Checking my watch, I did the math. Pauline had managed to phone me back twelve minutes ago. Maybe she could still be saved.

When Jenx joined the State Boys, I took a few more steadying breaths and stepped outdoors, where I leaned against a porch post. The mild December weather was as confusing as this case. If Anouk were right, one of "Yale's" lovers or ex-lovers had murdered the headmaster. Had the same person pushed his widow down a flight of stairs?

I recalled Pauline theorizing that the killer needed to please or protect George. Anouk had observed that Loralee was athletic, but she couldn't vouch for her archery skills. Bottom line: Loralee had been here, alone, with Pauline. She could have been in position on the Rail Trail the night Vreelander died. The question was whether she had the motive, mindset, and ability to kill two people.

My cell phone announced a call from Chester. I swallowed hard, willing myself to sound more calm and cheerful than I felt. My sensitive little neighbor wouldn't find out about our town's latest violence from me.

"Hey, Volunteer Deputy," I said brightly. "Whassup?"

"Nobody's answering at the station, and I promised Jenx and Brady I'd phone in my decryption results ASAP."

"Well, I happen to know that this is Brady's morning off," I said, still forcing a smile into my voice. "And Jenx is probably busy."

At that moment the EMTs approached from inside the house, rolling Pauline Vreelander on a gurney across the hardwood floor. One paramedic jogged alongside, holding tubes and bottles in place. I couldn't help but notice that Pauline looked more dead than alive.

"What's that noise?" Chester said.

"Noise?"

I scurried out of the paramedics' way.

"Yeah. It sounded like thunder, but it's not going to rain."

Realizing that sirens were about to scream, I decided that my best strategy was to get Chester off the line.

"Hey, buddy, gotta run. I'm kind of in the middle of something. Can I have Jenx call you?"

"Is she there?" His tone registered surprise rather than suspicion. Such a trusting child.

"Of course not, but I'll call her and have her call you. Bye now."

I clicked off just as the ambulance unleashed its siren. Covering my ears, I asked my higher power to forgive my sins, especially lying to Chester.

I jumped when Jenx tapped me on the shoulder.

"She's probably going to make it," the chief shouted.

"Thank god. What happened?"

"Hard to say. We think her phone was in her pocket. When you called, she managed to fish it out and hit redial."

"How bad is she hurt?"

Jenx wiped her brow. "Won't know 'til they do X-rays and a C-scan. Looks like a skull fracture. EMTs think she might have a broken hip, broken arm, broken collarbone, and some broken ribs. There could be internal bleeding."

"Where did all the blood come from?"

"Head wounds bleed a lot," Jenx said. "She banged up her face. Her nose is probably busted."

I shuddered.

Jenx went on, "Your timing was perfect. You probably saved her life."

"If my timing was perfect, I would have gotten here before it happened."

The chief sighed. "I know the feeling, but we do what we can."

I told her about Chester's call and the fact that I hadn't told him anything. She glanced at the State Boys conferring on the front porch.

"I'll call Chester. You need to tell those guys what you suspect about Lowe. If they think there's a link, they'll bring in their crime scene investigators."

When I hesitated, she said. "I know. We want to be the ones to solve this, but the State Boys got the big guns. It's the right thing to do."

The men in blue and gray did look impeccable in their pale neckties and crisp caps. Maybe they deserved to solve this case. Somebody needed to solve it soon so that Magnet Springs could celebrate Christmas with open hearts and no fear.

Troopers Carter and Pawlicki were pleasant and professional when I approached. Jenx had briefed them on my experiences over the past few days. They seemed genuinely interested in what I had seen as well as any insights I could share. Although they listened much more than they talked, I was left with the impression that they planned to interview both Loralee and Anouk—Loralee, regarding her whereabouts today and at the time of the headmaster's death; Anouk, regarding the gold bangle bracelet she had found and anything else she observed the evening Mark Vreelander died.

When the troopers dismissed me, I was ready to leave. Until I remembered I still had the marriage-porn flash drive in my pocket. In light of the day's tragic events, it seemed silly to worry about replacing it, but I was mightily aware of my karma. I owed Pauline two flash drives. This was my opportunity to drop the first one back where it belonged. I would return the encrypted one later.

The EMTs had left, Jenx was on the phone with Chester, and the two troopers were deep in discussion. I slipped back inside and hurried up the staircase to the second floor. The door to Mark Vreelander's office was closed. What if it were locked? I was fully prepared to shunt the flash drive under the door, if necessary. As I reached for the knob, a small voice in my head—probably Chester's—reminded me that my fingers leave prints, so for once they didn't. I slipped my right hand under my sweater before trying the knob. It turned, and I entered.

What lay before me bore little resemblance to the messy home office I had seen two days earlier. The space had been ransacked. Drawers were removed, and their contents dumped on the floor. Furniture was pulled away from the walls; many pieces were inverted, as if an intruder had demanded a view of the underside. The couch had lost its cushions, and the lamps were now missing their shades. A person or persons had turned Mark's office inside-out in search of something specific. A flash drive? Surely not the one I held. Using my sweater-covered hand, I wiped it as free of prints as I could and dropped it into a desk drawer that now lay on its side. I could only hope that Pauline Vreelander would recover sufficiently to take comfort in discovering the location of that pictorial romp.

"What the hell are you doing?"

I whirled to face Jenx. "The right thing."

Jenx surveyed the room. "Whoa. You said this room was a mess. You didn't say it was a disaster."

"It didn't look like this," I said. "Someone came after I left."

"Is that the window where you saw Lowe?" Jenx said.

I nodded. She peered out and turned back to me.

"The bad news is Carter and Pawlicki are securing the house, so we gotta go. The good news is I talked to Chester. Study hall was a success."

"He decrypted the flash drive?"

"Shhhh. Let's take it outside."

We passed the troopers on their way upstairs.

"Looks like somebody ransacked that office," Jenx remarked. "Have fun, boys."

Outside, Jenx paused to sniff the air.

"Spring is comin' to an end," she declared. "Get ready for a change in the weather."

"Not until next week," I said. "I checked the Weather Channel."

I glanced at Jenx's face. She was wearing an expression that said I shouldn't doubt her grasp of certain forces.

"What do you know that I don't?" I whispered.

"Don't get me started."

"I mean, about the weather."

"Daffodils don't bloom at Christmas, Whiskey. Something's gotta change soon."

She motioned for me to join her in the patrol car.

"Let's talk about Chester. I'm not sharing this with the MSP."

Once we had settled inside, Jenx rolled up the windows and locked the doors. She took out her pocket notebook and squinted at her own cramped writing.

"Chester gave me a shitload of info. He said the decryption process was easy. The flash drive has what he called 'on-the-fly-encryption.' All you need is the right software. Chester figured out the encryption keys in half an hour."

"Amazing," I said.

Jenx shrugged. "Not according to Chester. He said we should expect nothing less from an MIT course graduate."

She glanced back at her notes.

"Looks like Mark Vreelander stumbled into a mess of nasty truths about The Bentwood School. Chester thinks he had info that could have closed down the academy."

"Why would Vreelander want to close the school?" I said. "It was his job to run it."

"Nobody's saying he wanted to close it," Jenx said. "More likely, he wanted to save it, and that was his mistake."

"What's on the flash drive?" I said.

Jenx held up a hand like she was stopping traffic.

"I'll get to that. We know Vreelander had already launched a campaign to improve the school, right?"

"Right," I said impatiently. "Including getting the kids physically fit and assigning them homework."

"Tip of the iceberg. According to Chester, there were much bigger problems."

"Like what?" I was on the verge of grabbing the chief's notebook to read it for myself.

"Well, to start with, somebody was fixing student transcripts and standardized test scores."

"What do you mean, 'fixing'?"

"Tampering with. Making them look a lot better than they were."

"How can you mess with standardized test scores? Aren't they recorded by the test provider?"

"Yup. But you can falsely report the results."

"You mean the school was faking reports for the parents?"

"And lying about test results in their publicity. Student transcripts weren't accurate, either. Chester says there are notes on the flash drive about teachers being pressured to inflate grades."

"Which teachers?" I wondered aloud.

"Pretty much all of 'em," Jenx said. "And that's not the end of it. Chester says there's stuff on the flash drive about faking faculty credentials."

"What do you mean?"

"That alphabet soup after people's names? Mostly bogus. They didn't all earn those degrees. Chester thinks Vreelander figured it out fast."

"He was the boss," I said. "The buck stopped there."

"Did it, Whiskey? Who did Vreelander answer to?"

I thought about it. "The PTO! Stevie McCoy says the parents practically run that school. It's all about their money and their egos."

Jenx checked her notes. "For fifteen thou a year, they're buying a 'tradition of excellence.' They don't wanna believe that's not what they're getting. They also hate change, even when they need it."

"Right," I said, putting puzzle pieces together. "Chester told me the Board brought in a new headmaster because they knew the curriculum was getting soft and parents weren't happy with high school placement. But you're saying the problems were way worse than that. The PTO pressured teachers to raise grades and test scores, and exaggerate their credentials."

"Not just the PTO," Jenx said. "The school president, our pal 'Yale.' Only he's not a Yalie, after all. George Bentwood is the first generation of Magnet Springs Bentwoods not to graduate from Yale, or any university

38

I blinked at Jenx. "You're saying 'Yale' isn't even a college graduate? He's perpetrating fraud at The Bentwood School?"

"Yup. But think about it, Whiskey. He couldn't pull it off without help."

"So there's a cover-up. A conspiracy."

Jenx nodded.

"How come the Board never figured it out?" I said.

"Bentwood took over for his grandmother, the school founder. She ran the place 'til she croaked. Bentwood handpicked his Board, with input from 'selected' parents and alums. The roster reads like a 'Who's Who' of Old Money in Magnet Springs."

"You're saying the Board is in Bentwood's pocket?"

"Yup. And some of 'em just don't care. Chester says Vreelander made suggestions at every meeting. Nobody listened to him."

"How's that possible? The headmaster's the captain of the ship."

"More like the figurehead in this case," Jenx said. "Bentwood's name is on the school. Hell, he is the school."

I thought about it. "Vreelander was an outsider. From the working class."

Jenx nodded. "Nobody that anybody on the Board or PTO

was gonna respect, but they hired him because their parents wanted a strong-looking leader."

"Yes. Vreelander fit the bill. He was career Army and a professional educator. He looked like somebody who would bring The Bentwood School into the twenty-first century. Emphasis on looked like. Vreelander's credentials were all that mattered to George, the Board, and the PTO."

"Right," Jenx said. "Nobody wanted him to change a thing."

"Except admission test scores to private secondary schools," I said.

"Only because Bentwood hadn't found a way to fudge those," Jenx said.

"The school looked respectable for hiring Vreelander," I summarized. "And the PTO bought into it so long as he didn't cause them or their kids any pain. But then he did cause them pain, or at least inconvenience. He tried an end run around the Board and the PTO in order to reform the school."

"'Til somebody stopped him," Jenx said.

"We're back where we started! One of the PTO moms must have offed him. If Anouk's right, it's a mom who had an affair with Bentwood."

"It's an archer, Whiskey, and maybe also a mom who's involved with Bentwood."

"Loralee Lowe," I insisted.

"If's she's an archer," Jenx said.

I ran through the incriminating stuff we had on Lowe. She was Bentwood's lover, the mother of his child, a vocal member of the PTO and a teacher whom Vreelander was threatening to terminate. Not to mention she had made two visits to the Fresno Avenue house that sure didn't look like coincidences.

"Two days ago, I see her in Vreelander's home office, where she doesn't belong. This morning I see her leaving his house, and I find Pauline seriously hurt and the office ransacked."

Jenx called my attention to a sticky little issue called cause and effect, which apparently depends upon another little issue called proof.

Fair enough, but I was no fan of coincidence. Loralee looked better for two crimes than anybody else we could think of, even though seeing the State Boys bust Kimmi would have been so satisfying.

Whiskey and Soda

"If Loralee didn't do it, who did?" I demanded.

Jenx was quiet for so long I wondered where her mind had gone. I was about to repeat the question when she said, "Tell me again what Anouk told you. About the kind of clue you should be looking for."

"She said to look for somebody in a 'circular relationship' with Yale—I mean, Bentwood. He needs something from her, and she needs something from him."

As soon as I said the words out loud, my brain clicked.

"Jenx—Pauline said almost the same thing. How did she put it? She said the killer was probably someone who needed to please or protect George. Who would need to protect him?"

Jenx frowned. "Not his wife, if what you heard about her hiring MacArthur to investigate him is true. She's not an archer, anyhow. But Anouk is. She might need to protect Bentwood if he's throwing money at her or her kids."

"I don't think he is," I said quickly. "But Loralee needs Bentwood to support her daughter. She needs to protect him and the school."

"But we don't know if she could land an arrow in Vreelander's back. We're looking for somebody with the skill to do that."

That was the catch, all right.

Somebody's knuckles rapped the passenger side window. I yelped. Trooper Pawlicki was bending down to peer in. Jenx lowered my window.

"We've secured the house," Pawlicki told her. "Except for the broken window. Our crime scene team will take care of that when they finish. They're en route now."

Jenx and Pawlicki exchanged a few remarks across invisible, irrelevant me before the chief raised the window again.

"Let's get outta here, Whiskey. We got leads to follow. I wanna beat the State Boys at this game."

"Do we have to tell them what's on Chester's flash drive?"

She gave me the kind of look I would expect from an officer about to make an arrest.

"Don't ya mean the victim's flash drive? The one you illegally removed from the premises?"

"Like you said, you got leads to follow," I told her, reaching for the door handle. "And I got real estate to sell."

"Did ya call Jeb yet? Ya know he's gonna hear about this from somebody. It oughta be you."

Obediently I whipped out my cell and dialed. When Jeb answered, I took a deep breath and dove into the shortest, least alarming version of events.

"Better call your mom," Jeb said. "She just texted me that something bad went down at your appointment. One of her friends picked it off the police scanner."

Many residents got their news that way. The usual "10-whatever" code didn't apply in Magnet Springs, where we went beyond the standard numerical system. I didn't have a scanner, but Chester did. He swore that most regular listeners knew the codes for Abra's assorted escapades, as well as my own dances with danger.

I assured Jeb that I was fine and told him I would see Mom in person at the office. He was in his car, en route to The Castle to retrieve Sandra Bullock. Avery had phoned him when the second photo shoot wrapped. She said she was sorry—right!—if Jeb didn't like the idea of Sandra in costume on the cover of Cassina's next CD, but the pop diva would make it worth his while.

"Anouk called," Jeb added. "She told me to bring Sandra straight over for her first pet psychic session. Later I'll get Abra, and she'll have a session, too. Anouk's also going to try a joint appointment."

"Will that solve the problem?" I asked.

"Anouk isn't making any promises. She says the process can take time."

Ka-ching, ka-ching, I thought and then felt petty. Anouk had been honest with me so far. At least it seemed that way. In Magnet Springs more than a few folks had paranormal talents. Maybe Anouk's name belonged on that roster. We needed help with our dogs—yes, our dogs, I thought, wincing—and Stevie McCoy had recommended Anouk. For starters, maybe she could teach Sandra to wear fewer hats and Abra not to eat them.

I told Jeb I loved him and would see him soon. When I tucked my phone back into my pocket, Jenx was grinning at me.

"What?" I said.

"Feels good to have a partner again, doesn't it, Whiskey?"

I started to say that Jeb was my boyfriend, not my partner; that Leo was the only man who had earned that title, and Jenx should mind her own freakin' business. Except, of course, she was right.

Pushing open the passenger door was a lot harder than it should have been, thanks to a sudden frigid wind. The trees were bending over, and the temperature was dropping fast.

Before I could close the door, Jenx shouted, "Change in the weather. I was right about that, too."

Drawing my leather jacket tight around me, I wished I had left home with earmuffs and mittens. It was beginning to feel a lot like Michigan, if not Christmas.

39

Doing the right thing. An inconvenient notion, yet ever since I'd scrawled that note on my palm, I'd felt compelled to follow it. Never mind that the words had washed off days ago.

Next stop, Mattimoe Realty. I only hoped I wouldn't find my mother doing receptionist duty in her negligee. Even Odette might fire her for that.

Mom was wearing what she called "Florida business casual"—Capri pants with a bright cotton shirt. Thankfully, she and Howard had managed to pick up their clothes before the rising wind could scatter them across town. She was even more chipper than usual.

"Whitney, isn't the weather wonderful?"

I waited a beat, in case there was a punch line coming. Nothing happened.

"Mom, the weather's getting worse. Those are fifty-mile-an-hour gusts."

"Exactly. We might have sleet soon." She positively beamed at me.

"And that's wonderful because . . . ?"

"You of all people should know. The weather is turning out exactly like it's supposed to at this time of year."

"Not quite, Mom. For the past three weeks, it was supposed to be cold and snowy so that Magnet Springs merchants could sell Christmas to tourists. Now that Christmas is almost here, and there are no tourists in Magnet Springs, what's the point of having crappy weather?"

Irene Houston smiled and sighed. The phone on her desk rang. She answered it with more cheer than I could bear, so I walked rapidly toward my office.

"One moment, please," I heard her tell the caller. "Whitney, there's a Stevie McCoy on the line for you. Such a happy-sounding woman. I do hope you won't bring her down."

Through gritted teeth, I said I'd take the call in my office. I closed and locked the door.

"Hey, Stevie. Thanks for taking care of the repairs to my property so fast."

"Whiskey, that is the absolute least we can do for you. Tate still owes you a formal apology."

Indeed, he did, although I wasn't sure I wanted to be around the kid long enough for him to offer one.

"The reason I'm calling," Stevie continued, "is that I'd like to buy you lunch."

"You bought me dinner the other night," I reminded her.

"Well, that hardly counts, given everything that's happened." She lowered her voice. "Listen, Tate is doing community service in addition to making restitution, but I want to personally thank you for your goodwill. You have been so gracious about this."

"No problem," I said.

"I wish I could sign you as my Realtor, but I don't know if I'll still have a job here next year."

My ears pricked up in the hope of hearing new gossip that might translate into new clues to the Vreelander case.

"Why? Is the school down-sizing?"

"No. Well, let's just say that it doesn't help the career of The Bentwood School's P.R., Marketing and Recruitment Director when her son, who attends the school, gets arrested."

"Are you afraid George Bentwood will fire you?"

"He might have to if the PTO pressures him."

"I thought the police agreed not to press charges, provided you and Tate settle everything with the affected homeowners."

"That's true," Stevie said. "But you know our PTO. If they get a whiff of this, I'm afraid they'll make such a stink about

Tate smearing the school's reputation that we'll both be history."

I didn't know how to respond. Kimmi, Loralee, and Camo-Mom were only three members of the PTO, but they were the three members I knew and they scared me shitless. All of them were mean, not to mention that I was pretty sure Loralee was a cold-blooded killer.

When I didn't reply, she said, "Please don't think I'm trying to make you feel sorry for me. Everybody's fighting some kind of battle, right? The police have been very reasonable, especially Chief Jenkins. She's your friend, isn't she?"

"Jenx and I go way back," I said.

"I thought so. How's her investigation into Mark's death? Does she have a suspect?"

Before I could comment, Stevie said, "Sorry. You're probably not allowed to say anything, are you?"

"The Michigan State Police took over the case," I said.

"I see. Well, I hope they catch the guy soon. Just knowing there's a killer out there makes people nervous. Our whole school is tense."

"I think the whole town is tense," I said.

Stevie surprised me with a short laugh. "Yeah, it isn't just a problem for The Bentwood School, is it? Although, I've got to tell you, it's not helping recruitment."

"Really? It didn't happen on your campus, and none of your students got hurt."

"I know. Once everything settles down, I'm sure we'll look good again. George is going to be Acting Headmaster for the rest of the school year, and that will give us stability. We'll launch an official search for Mark's replacement in the spring."

She paused.

"Whiskey, I enjoyed our dinner the other night. If this thing with Tate hadn't happened, I was hoping we could become friends."

"We still can," I told her.

"Great. Then I won't take no for an answer. Even if I can't buy real estate right now, I can buy you lunch. Today. Would you mind picking me up? We could eat at that new Italian café, if you're up for it."

"Sure, I've been meaning to try that place. You're at work?"

I said.

"I took another personal day to make sure the handyman I hired finishes all the repairs, but I live on campus, remember?"

I did remember. She told me how to find her cottage and added, "Tate's back in class today. He's such a strong kid. Nothing scares him for long."

Because he's a sociopath, I thought.

"You know, Tate might be home by the time we finish our lunch," Stevie continued. "If he is, I'll have him apologize to you in person."

I looked forward to that about as much as I looked forward to an episiotomy. When Stevie said she would be ready to go to lunch in an hour, I told her that would work. In the meantime, I would tackle the stack of papers on my desk.

I had barely made a dent in the pile when I heard a knock on my door. Not Odette's distinct three-rap rhythm but the same knock I used to hear on my locked bedroom door way back in my teen years.

"Yes, Mom?"

"Whitney, there's something here that requires your attention."

"Slip it under the door."

"That's funny, dear. No, this is something you'll need to step outside to see."

"I'm in the middle of a contract. Can it wait?"

"Probably not."

I heaved the kind of loud, aggrieved sigh that usually belongs to a teenager, before I walked to the door, unlocked it, and cracked it open. My mother stood there smiling.

"What?" I said.

"You're going to have to come to my desk," she said. She spun on her neatly pedicured heel and headed for the lobby.

Muttering, I followed her. Even before I reached the front office, I saw what she wanted me to see. Beyond our storefront window, the first blizzard of the season was in progress as a howling wind powered a slanting curtain of white.

But that wasn't Mom's point. Standing on the sidewalk in the driving snow with a wide grin on his face and both arms raised, Jeb held up a hand-lettered sign.

I LOVE YOU, WHISKEY HOUSTON HALLORAN MATTIMOE!

PLEASE BE MY WIFE. THIS TIME IT'S FOREVER & EVER!

So help me, I started crying. I—who can scream, barf or faint without warning—almost never cry. Yet now I was bawling. Mom had her arms around me. By god, she was crying, too. Jeb was laughing, but through my tears and the snow, I saw his tears. They coursed down his red cheeks.

"Yes! Yes!" I shouted, nodding my head hard in case he couldn't hear me.

"That boy has always loved you," Mom said.

"Only since sixth grade," I reminded her.

"Whatever. I'm going to be a grandmother! And I win the bet!"

I stepped back. "What bet?"

"Oh, I might as well tell you now. Years and years ago, a bunch of us mothers who had daughters about your age were at a party. We had a few drinks and made some wagers. We bet on whether or not our kids would ever have kids."

"Wait. The mothers bet on their daughters?"

"Well, sure. Who knows ya better than your mom? Anyhow, I bet that you'd give me a grandchild and a son-in-law even though everybody else bet against you."

I gaped at my mother for what seemed like a full minute. I could feel the saliva drying in my open mouth.

"Nobody thought I'd even get married?"

"Well, you were always extremely tall," Mom said. "And flat-chested. Screw 'em. I believed in you. Enough to place a sizable wager."

"How much?"

She whispered an amount equal to a respectable monthly house payment.

"And it's been earning interest through the years," she added, her eyes twinkling.

"Mom, you are something else. I'm just not sure what."

I doubled over in laughter.

"Oh, look at that," Mom cried.

Turning my head, I peered sideways through the front window. In the blowing snow, Jeb had adjusted the sign for my ninety-degree viewing angle, and he had turned it over. The flip side read:

Now let your mom give you a bridal shower

"Oh no!" I shot straight up and confronted Mom. "No bridal shower! I hate showers. You know that."

"That's because you've never been to a fun one."

"There's no such thing as a 'fun' bridal shower."

"Not true, Whitney, and I can prove it."

Jeb pulled open the front door. The wind roared, and he entered in a cloud of cold air and snow. Before I could speak, he had dropped the sign and was holding me. Pressed against mine, his mouth tasted like fresh ice and hot love.

"So you'll give me the chance to get it right this time?" he whispered.

"Oh yes."

"Sorry my hands are cold."

With that he took my left hand in his left hand and, with his right hand, slipped a sparkling diamond solitaire onto the appropriate finger.

"This time you get an engagement ring," he said.

"A nice one," I cooed.

It was beyond nice. Although I'm not a girl who knows much about jewels, all girls know something about diamonds. This was a two-carat princess-cut on a platinum band.

"Whitney said yes to the shower, too," Mom announced.

I hadn't said yes to that, but Jeb and I were kissing again, so I couldn't argue.

Behind me, I heard the door open and felt another blast of

arctic air.

"This is supposed to be a place of business," Odette intoned. "Please get a room."

Still kissing Jeb, I waved my ring finger at her.

"When's the bridal shower?" she inquired.

"Mom made you say that."

"Whitney, you know I can't make anyone do anything," my mother lied.

Odette, who knows the value of everything, scrutinized my ring. To Jeb she said, "Even if you can't dress her every day, she will look good in that. We who must work with her thank you."

When the phone rang, Mom answered it in her perfect office manager mode. She passed it to me.

"I hear congrats are in order," Jenx said. "About damn time."

"Did Jeb tell you this was coming down?"

"He didn't have to. Everybody in town knew he was gonna pop the question. I'm calling about Pauline Vreelander. The docs think she'll be able to talk soon, so I'm gonna hang around the hospital. I wanna hear how she landed at the bottom of the stairs."

After I disconnected, Mom reminded me of my lunch date with Stevie. She also checked the Weather Channel. Conditions were supposed to improve soon. While visibility was still a problem, there would be little snow accumulation because the ground was warm. Jeb walked me to my car. Huddling against each other and still holding hands, we forced our way into the wind.

"I love your sign!" I shouted over the roar. "I'll want to keep that!"

"Howard showed me how to use the table saw in Leo's workshop. Nice guy. He'll be good to your mom."

If the weather had been better, we would have stood outside kissing, and I might have been late for lunch, but that wasn't a temptation in the howling winter wind. Besides, Jeb had to go fetch Abra from home and take her to her pet psychic session. Sandra was with Anouk already. I tried not to imagine what the Frenchie might psychically impart to her "shrink." No doubt she'd describe me as the mean stepmother—a role I seemed doomed to repeat. At least my doggie stepdaughter had agreed to get help.

    I climbed into my car, waved good-bye to my fiancé, and rolled away toward The Bentwood School, eager to show off my brand-new rock to my brand-new friend.

40

High winds and low visibility meant that I had to concentrate during the drive from downtown Magnet Springs. All I wanted to do was stare at my ring. The vehicle rocked ominously, and I strained to see even two car-lengths ahead through the dense snowfall.

I was about halfway to The Bentwood School, driving less than twenty miles an hour on a rural road, when I passed something low and yellow-gold moving along the berm in the same direction I was heading. Both shape and speed were familiar, but the location was wrong. What I had just seen belonged in a containment system. In my front yard.

Swerving sharply off the road, I squinted into my rear-view mirror. Abra appeared again, bursting through the wall of snow, long legs churning. Her ears floated like a shoulder-length mane, and her paws barely struck earth. I admired her timeless grace.

Then I flung open the door and tackled her.

She didn't give up without a fight, but the fight was mainly for show, and for our mutual self-respect. If she had simply surrendered, neither of us would have been satisfied. Sandra Bullock notwithstanding, Abra and I needed to keep our relationship spiky. Otherwise, hating the Frenchie would be no fun at all.

A woman wrestling an Afghan hound into her vehicle during a snow squall isn't a frequent sight, even in Magnet Springs. Hell, I hardly ever caught up with Abra, but to the driver coming toward me on the country road, it must have been a show-stopper. The man in the beat-up black pick-up braked, opened his door and shouted at me through the wind, "Hey, lady! That dog don't wanna go with you. Try buying a pet!"

I thought about explaining the situation, but really what was the point? He watched for a while, shaking his head at my stubbornness. As if she were a contestant on reality TV, Abra amplified her performance with impressive snarls and lip curls.

"Crazy!" the driver yelled. I knew he meant me.

Finally, the man drove on, and the dog relaxed.

"Happy now?" I said.

Although I was being sarcastic, Abra did seem content stretched out on the back seat. I noticed that the "containment collar" was gone, proving that Jeb had a few things to learn about this beast. She wore Leo's rhinestone-studded collar, a gift from the one human she would always adore, the good man who never came back. I hoped she would come to love Jeb, too.

That thought, plus estrogen in overdrive, made me suddenly weepy. I got past it by looking again at the new ornament on my hand. It wasn't the diamond that mattered; it was Jeb. Somehow he had kept on loving me through rages and across miles, all the way home again, and now we were building a family together. Just like Irene Houston had wagered we would. Besides having a baby, we were adopting two dogs who happened to hate each other, which reminded me that Abra was supposed to be on her way to pet psychic therapy.

"No wonder you bolted," I said over my shoulder just as my cell phone rang.

"You're not going to believe this," Jeb began.

"Yes, I will, but you're not going to believe this."

I told him my story first in order to relieve his pain. Jeb had returned to Vestige to find the front yard Abra-free. At first he thought he just couldn't see her through the veil of snow, then he decided she must have returned, via the doggie flap, to our warm dry kitchen. Sure enough, her "containment collar" was in the kitchen, but not her royal highness.

"I can't figure out how she got it off," Jeb said.

"Here's everything you need to know about that: she's an Afghan hound, the Houdini of dog breeds."

Jeb pointed out that she was due at Anouk's within an hour.

For a musician, my fiancé often exhibited an amazing awareness of time. Because I didn't want to be late for Stevie, and he didn't want to keep Anouk waiting, we crafted a plan. Jeb would drive to The Bentwood School and transfer Abra from my vehicle to his. According to Stevie's directions, I would have to park in the school lot and walk about a hundred yards to her cottage on campus. Jeb would probably arrive minutes after I got there; I would leave my car unlocked so that he could unload the furry cargo. Man and dog would be gone by the time Stevie and I left for lunch.

Abra had spent herself on the run from Vestige and the faux fight with me. When I pulled into The Bentwood School lot, she was sleeping so hard that she didn't respond to the vehicle's stopping. Typically she was ready to tear out the door the instant I applied the brakes.

Thick snow was still flying in a gusty wind, making it hard to see even as far as the main building on campus. The grand Victorian mansion loomed ahead of me like a pale shadow. I shook off a flash of creepiness by reminding myself that the building was filled with children.

Stevie had told me to follow the sidewalk around the right side of the mansion to the quadrangle in the back. Her cottage would be the second structure on my right, just past Alumni Hall. I gave thanks that the wind and snow were at my back, pushing me along and making it slightly less difficult to see. Passing the mansion, I noticed that the windows were too high for me to peer inside. Idly I wondered which classroom Chester was in right now, and which room Tate was in.

A long low frame building—yellow with pale blue trim, like the school—hove into view. This had to be Alumni Hall, plain and functional. Was it used as a gathering place for self-congratulatory graduates? More likely, alumni had donated the funds to construct it, and the building housed auxiliary classrooms or maybe a meeting space.

Beyond it, as Stevie had promised, lay her house. Drawing close, I could appreciate how quaint it was. Designed to resemble a small English cottage, it, too, featured the school's colors in the yellow wood siding, pale blue shutters and blue peaked roof.

Curtains were drawn in the windows. A sign only slightly smaller than the one Jeb had used to propose hung next to the front door.

YALE COTTAGE

Aha, I thought, as I rang the bell. Here was another misrepresentation, or perhaps not. If the data on the flash drive were accurate, only the latest Bentwood had failed at that fine institution. For all I knew, back in the glory days of George's family and their school, many alumni may have graduated from Ivy League colleges.

Stevie's face registered surprise when she opened the door.

"Am I early?" I said.

"No. Your hair is full of snow." She laughed. "I didn't know the weather had changed. I've been on the computer. Come in and sit down. You need to get warm."

The door opened directly into a comfy living room, appointed in floral patterns and overstuffed upholstery. All that it lacked was a roaring fire in the country-style hearth. Stevie indicated the wood already in place.

"If you have time after lunch, I'd like to light that," she said. "We can have coffee or hot chocolate."

She asked if I were still willing to drive to the Italian café. I was; I didn't expect the storm to worsen.

"I hear their ravioli alla ricotta is to die for," Stevie said.

"Sounds good, but I'm in the mood for meat or at least meat sauce."

"Oh my god, Whiskey," Stevie said suddenly. "Are you engaged?"

Before I could reply, she reached for her purse on the coffee table. From it she withdrew a pair of darkly tinted sunglasses, which she slipped on.

"Much better. The glare of your rock was blinding me. Let me see that."

Studying the ring, Stevie made all those sounds that signal appreciation.

"I always wanted one like that," she sighed, releasing my hand and removing her shades.

"You were married, right?" I said.

"Yes, but I never got an engagement ring."

"Jeb and I tried this before. No engagement ring that time, so maybe this is our lucky charm."

"Your child will be your lucky charm," Stevie said. "Your marriage is going to work because you both want to be parents. Together."

For just a second, her voice veered toward melancholy, then she put her usual smile back in place and stood.

"Shall we go? Ready to brave the elements?"

Nodding, I stood, also. Stevie picked up a tan trench coat that she had folded over a wingback chair and laughed.

"I don't think this will be warm enough now, do you? Let me grab my parka."

I took a few steps toward the front door and stopped. Contemplating the living room décor, I said, "Such a pleasant room. Did you put it together?"

Before I could say all the words, Stevie opened the coat closet. Hanging on the inside of the door was a crossbow. Built like a combination rifle and bow, it was nearly identical to the one my father had hunted with when I was a kid. It even had a similar scope for precision shooting, but this crossbow was loaded. My father had unloaded his after every use.

"Wow, you shoot a crossbow—" I began.

Pulling her parka from the hanger, Stevie froze, and my heart lurched. I knew enough about crossbows to appreciate both their accuracy and their force. Unlike conventional bows, they could be used to lethal effect by a person with no archery skill. A person who decided to kill another person by firing at him on his bicycle from the woodsy edge of an archery club.

"My dad had one of those," I babbled. "Man, it is not easy to bag a buck. I admire you for hunting. Hey, let's go eat!"

Stevie didn't move.

"You weren't supposed to see that," she said slowly. "And I really, really wish you hadn't."

Like my dad's crossbow, this one no doubt required a little time to load, and that was why she kept an arrow in it with the safety on. Just in case she needed to defend herself or her kid or both of them. Who knew how Stevie's mind worked? All I knew was she might want to kill me, so I had to go.

In a single motion, Stevie dropped her parka and spun toward the crossbow, snagging it from the door. Continuing the arc of movement, she turned the weapon in her hands, assumed shooting stance, released the safety, sited at me, and cocked.

I wasn't standing still, but given her proximity to me and the distance to the front door, I knew I'd never make it out. So I did what any self-respecting expectant mother would do if

Whiskey and Soda

cornered with a crossbow in a living room. I dove behind the big sofa. The crossbow pinged, and the upholstery exploded. I felt rather than heard the arrow erupt through the back side of the couch and bury itself in the plaster wall just inches above my bowed head. Foam and dust filled the air.

I could have been shot clean through. Only I wasn't. I was alive and intact, and trapped in Stevie's cottage. But, unless she had an arrow in hand and was deft at loading it, I might have time to get the hell out. I pulled myself to my feet and lunged toward the door, screaming so hard and long that my throat burned.

Stevie recoiled, her face twisted. She had already withdrawn another arrow. Notching it in would take maybe twenty seconds if her hands weren't shaking. Twenty seconds would just about see me out the door and off the front porch. After that, I was running prey.

"Fuck!" Stevie yelled, fumbling the arrow. I flung open the door and threw myself into the howling wind. Pushing with all my might, I ran against the stinging wall of snow toward the mansion that housed The Bentwood School. Visibility had decreased since I'd been inside, and now the force of the weather was full in my face. I opened my mouth to call for help, but the wind sucked my voice away.

Alumni Hall was coming up on my left. My best chance would be to vanish inside and find someone, anyone, to help me. Hugging the building as I ran made me feel smaller and less like a target. My left palm grazed the wall, my heart thudding. She hadn't shot me yet. Panting, I located the concrete steps to the main door and stumbled up them. I missed the top step and crashed onto my right knee. From somewhere not far enough behind me came the muffled zoop of a powerful bow being released. Flattening myself against the cement stoop, I vibrated with the arrow as it penetrated the wood siding near my neck.

"Help!" I shouted, pushing myself upright. The double door had no window. I tried the brass knobs. Locked. Pounding with both fists, I screamed again. My only option now was to run and to hope, once more, that my assailant would be slow to reload.

Glancing over my shoulder, I spotted Stevie standing on the green, notching another arrow. In the wind, her auburn hair stood out from her head like dancing snakes. Medusa with a lethal weapon, she had absolutely no reason to quit.

I pounded the sidewalk toward the main building, which seemed unfairly far away considering a crazy woman was firing a crossbow at me, and my right knee hurt like hell. Snow still blasted my face, forcing me to turn my head sideways as I ran.

My eyes watered, my nose leaked, my lungs ached. No question that I was slower than I'd ever been in my life, and yet I was running for my life. Running for two lives.

A man's voice reached my ears, his words muted and blurred by the wind. The sound came again, like a chant. I could see no one ahead of me, and, oh, how I longed to see anyone.

Suddenly a blonde blob emerged like a shot from around the far side of the mansion, bolting down the middle of the green. The man called again, and this time I understood him.

"Abra!"

My shaken brain put it together. Jeb had lost control of our bitch in the parking lot. She was running free, and he was running after her straight into the path of an arrow about to be fired with deadly force. The good news was that my family had arrived when I needed them. The bad news was that we were all in mortal danger, and two of us didn't even know it.

My fiancé appeared, running hard after our Afghan hound.

"Jeb!" I waved frantically. "Jeb! Be careful!"

He spotted me, waved and slowed. I wasn't sure he saw Stevie or grasped her intent. Jeb was used to my chasing Abra, so seeing me run might not strike him as strange. Today I was supposed to be with a friend. Instead I was being hunted by one.

"Be careful!" I shouted again into the gale. I was still running alongside Alumni Hall, aiming toward the nearest part of mansion. "Stevie's trying to kiiiiiiiilll meeeeeeee!"

Whether or not he understood my words, he accelerated, charging in a diagonal path straight for me. Making himself a clear target for Stevie. Would she kill him? Was she desperate enough now to take out anyone who got in her way? Or would Jeb's arrival jolt her back to her senses?

Abra chose that instant to rhoo-rhoo, her eerie bark rising on the wind.

"Fucking dog!" I heard Stevie cry.

When I turned my head, I saw Abra like a yellow missile launching herself toward the wild woman with the crossbow cocked in her hands.

"No!" I shrieked.

But the wind swallowed my prayer.

41

Everything that ever made sense suddenly didn't. A nice person, the only new friend I'd made in months, was a cold-blooded killer, and the moment I figured that out, she tried to murder me.

Thank god she didn't kill my dog. When Abra vaulted straight into Stevie's face, she knocked the crossbow to the ground before Stevie could pull the trigger. Jeb reached me seconds later and held me tight as I gasped for breath between hysterical sobs. Meanwhile, Abra contained the killer, intimidating her with snarls and snapping jaws rarely seen in an Afghan hound. Don't let the breed fool you. They manage their energy, and they know how to get what they want.

Abra's barks attracted attention. My screams helped. The rear door of The Bentwood School opened, and adults spilled out, led by George Bentwood and Loralee Lowe. Jeb called Jenx on his cell phone; she would alert all authorities. I heard Bentwood shout to his teachers that the school was now in lockdown, but a student burst past him through the door. Coatless, Tate McCoy dashed into the blowing snow and down the green toward his prone mother, calling for her. Two young men I hadn't met bolted after him. Before he could reach Stevie, they caught and restrained Tate, who kicked hard. I later learned that they were education majors observing classes for a college course. No doubt their time at The Bentwood School taught them volumes.

Jenx was first officer at the scene. Brady and Roscoe arrived right behind her, followed shortly by paramedics and the

Michigan State Police. Jeb kept reminding the EMTs attending me that I was pregnant, as if they couldn't tell. My right knee was bruised and swollen, and I did show signs of shock. Otherwise, I emerged unscathed. Or, as I liked to put it, un-penetrated by any arrow.

Once Abra was pulled off criminal containment duty, Stevie tried to kick, hit, and bite her human captors. She required a sedative before they could cuff and transport her. By comparison, her son's arrest at Vestige had been downright uneventful.

In the days that followed, we learned a lot about Tate McCoy and his troubled mother. As Anouk had theorized, the engraved gold bangle found near the Rail Trail did indeed belong to the killer, who was one of Bentwood's sexual conquests. We had all been misled by the coincidence of an arrow fired from Tir à l'Arc. Stevie was no archer, just a reasonably experienced crossbow hunter on a mission.

A free spirit when she was young, Stevie never planned to have children. The marriage she mentioned to me was a mere blip right out of college. In her thirties, she met George Bentwood, and that relationship became the love of her life, or at least her single obsession.

For Bentwood, though, Stevie and Anouk filled exactly the same purpose. They were on-again, off-again mistresses whom he enjoyed year after year. Along the way, Tate "happened," as did Anouk's two kids. In essence, Anouk and Stevie shared Bentwood until Loralee replaced them both. While Anouk could afford to give him up, Stevie relied on George—emotionally and professionally. Tate, who had learning issues, needed the small class size and individual attention afforded by The Bentwood School. As long as Stevie worked there, she could send Tate for free, and, courtesy of George, she had access to heavily subsidized on-campus housing.

"Sure, Stevie knew about George's scams at the school," Jenx said. "She directed publicity and managed their web site and social media, remember?"

The chief and I were sharing a booth and updates on the Vreelander case over a couple mugs of peppermint mocha at the Goh Cup. Four days had passed since the showdown at The Bentwood School. Another winter storm had rolled through, and that one had blanketed the ground with a few downy inches. Now, two days before Christmas, the sky was as blue as George Bentwood's eyes, and the mood in downtown Magnet Springs matched the holiday music piped into the streets.

"Stevie saw herself as Bentwood's ally, if not his savior," I theorized. "And she contrived a plan to rid the school of Vreelander, who was hellbent on exposing lies and fixing weaknesses."

"She needed to keep the school going to keep her job," Jenx said. "But there was a lot more to her plan than killing the headmaster. She stole the contents of his school office so nobody could read his notes."

"That's why his office was bare when you checked it," I said.

The chief nodded. "Stevie also stole his cell phone, which he left in his desk drawer. She made the Blitzen poster and put his number on it."

"But how did she get Anouk's photo from the Rail Trail for the poster?"

"Anouk texted her fellow archers, remember? That included Robin. Robin texted the PTO, and Stevie—duh—is a member."

I gasped. "Of course she is. Her son goes to the school. But why make the poster? What was the point?"

"Stevie wanted to confuse the issue, to deflect attention away from the school."

"She got the PTO moms excited, all right," I recalled. "They were almost ready to lynch me at that assembly."

Jenx slurped her mocha. "Stevie also wrote the note you found on your car the night you had dinner with her."

"Huh? She arrived at the restaurant before I did, and left after."

Then I remembered her taking a long mid-meal break, presumably to go to the bathroom. Given how mild the weather was that night, I wouldn't have noticed reddened cheeks or hands when she sneaked back inside.

"What was the point of the note on my car?"

"She wanted to create drama and mess with your head."

"Back up. You say Stevie stripped Mark's school office looking for what she needed. Who ransacked his home office?"

"Stevie. After she pushed Pauline down the basement stairs. We got that much from Pauline, who, by the way, likes the roses you sent. She'll be in the hospital a few more days, but she said to tell you she's ready to sign the listing papers."

Jenx explained that Stevie had rung Pauline's doorbell an hour before the widow's appointment with me. It was also Stevie at the door the day I waited upstairs in Mark's office near the end of Pauline's house tour. On both occasions, Pauline refused Stevie entry. She didn't want a visit from anybody at The Bentwood School, but Stevie was desperate to know what Mark kept in his home office. After Pauline denied her access the second time, Stevie sneaked around the back of the house and admitted herself, using a copy she'd made of Loralee's old house key, 'borrowed' without Loralee's knowledge.

Pauline heard Stevie coming in. The two argued, and Stevie struck Pauline in the head with a skillet as Pauline moved toward the wall phone to call 9-1-1. Stevie shoved the unconscious woman down the basement stairs. After that, she tossed Mark's office and grabbed anything that looked potentially dangerous to George or the school.

"Stevie took the skillet, too, and she remembered to wear gloves," Jenx said. "Like you never do. The State Boys couldn't find her prints on anything. She screwed up, though. She was sure she'd killed Pauline, but Pauline lived to identify her."

I sipped my peppermint mocha, which smelled and tasted even better this year than last. Either Peg had a new recipe, or I owed the pleasure to being pregnant.

"What about Loralee?" I said. "What was she doing in Vreelander's home office right after I finished my tour?"

"Loralee admitted to me that she let herself in with her old key, the one she used when she lived in the house, back when it belonged to George."

"The key Stevie copied," I guessed. "That's breaking and entering."

"Pauline won't press charges. Loralee only did it because George Bentwood sent her. He didn't know Stevie was on the same mission."

"Was Loralee in the house the whole time I was there?"

"Yup. She hid in a closet while Pauline gave you the tour. When you left, Pauline went to the bathroom, and Loralee scoped out Mark's office. She didn't have much time to look and she didn't find much before she got the hell out. But she came back the morning you saw her PT Cruiser. That was supposed to be a 'courtesy call' on George's behalf, requesting that Pauline reconsider his cash offer. Of course, Pauline couldn't come to the door."

"Because she was lying at the bottom of the basement stairs," I said. "Why was George so determined to buy back the house?"

"If the school owns it and Loralee works at the school, George can figure out a way to keep her and the kid in it. Like the way Stevie and Tate lived in that cottage on campus. Everybody knows Tate is George's son. They got the same eyes."

The twinkle, I thought. Over dinner, Stevie had mentioned that her son's eyes were his best feature. To her, they were the feature that marked him as George's own.

"Who's taking care of Tate now?" I said.

"That's where things get interesting. George is gonna be single soon, thanks to a little legal action called divorce. Stevie aided that effort, by the way. Your friend MacArthur interviewed her about George, and she spilled his secrets."

"Anouk helped, too," I said.

"Yup," Jenx said. "By the way, that was George's wife who made the anonymous call to the station telling us to check George's background. She was mad as hell at him and wanted to make extra trouble. She forgot we have Caller ID."

According to Jenx, the court would no doubt decide that George was Tate's father and award him custody. In the meantime, Tate's attorney—paid for by George—had worked a deal so that the kid could stay with Loralee and Gigi.

"Maybe Anouk's grown children can move in with them, too," I said. "And make one big dysfunctional family."

The Goh Cup's front door opened, and in came Chester with two dogs on leads.

"Hey, buddy," Jenx said. "I don't think you can bring dogs in here."

"Yes, he can," Peg piped up from behind the counter, where she was brewing more coffee. "I've changed my policy. The Goh Cup is now a pet-friendly establishment."

Even so, I couldn't take my eyes off the dogs. Chester had managed to leash and civilize a most unlikely pair, Abra and Sandra Bullock.

The dogs appeared to have had their bodies taken over by tranquil aliens. Abra looked normal, albeit much better groomed, and Sandra was smartly dressed in a Santa suit, complete with shiny black boots and a tasseled cap. Both hounds wagged their tails and checked the air for delicious scents. Abra sniffed delicately, whereas the French bulldog snort-snuffled.

"How—?" I began.

My young neighbor wrinkled his nose to skooch his fogged wire-rimmed glasses back into place. Both mittened hands were occupied with leashes.

"Jeb dropped us off. We just came from pet therapy," Chester announced. "Anouk says the girls had a breakthrough."

Either that or double lobotomies, I thought.

"What happened?"

He frowned. "You know Anouk can't say. Patient confidentiality."

"They're my pets, and she's a pet psychic," I pointed out.

"Okay," he sighed. "She did past-life regressions, and it turns out Abra and Sandra Bullock were sisters, once upon a time."

"Sisters," I repeated. "Were they Affies or Frenchies?"

Trying to imagine either of their personalities switching breeds made my head hurt.

"Neither. They weren't even dogs. They were movie stars. Abra was Olivia de Havilland, and Sandra was Joan Fontaine."

"Ooooh, that's bad," Peg murmured, approaching our table with a fresh carafe of coffee. "Those two were jealous of each other their whole careers. Check IMDB."

"Or Wikipedia," Chester said. "The rivalry goes back to their childhoods. Olivia used to tear up Joan's clothes, so Joan had to sew them back together. Apparently, Olivia was their mother's favorite, and that created a whole lifetime of trouble. Several lifetimes of trouble."

Everyone stared at me, including the dogs.

"Hey, it's not my fault they hate each other."

"But you're perpetuating the cycle," Chester explained, "unless you stop favoring Abra."

I studied the Affie. Her long blonde tresses gleamed in the morning light streaming through the Goh Cup's big windows. In her rhinestone collar with her patrician profile and stately bearing, she did indeed look like a leading lady.

My gaze shifted to the stocky Frenchie. She peered up at me from under the faux fur trim of her red Santa hat. Born to play comedy, she was more a Sandra Bullock than a Joan Fontaine, for sure. Even so, the boys she met in this life instantly sniffed out her sex appeal.

"De Havilland and Fontaine might still be alive," I said.

"I think they are," Chester confirmed. "But that doesn't matter. Anouk says animal spirits can visit many lives."

I sighed. "What's the next step?"

"Anouk recommends family psychic therapy, you and Jeb included," Chester said. "In the meantime, just try to be fair. Let Sandra know you accept and welcome her. Abra should follow your lead."

"Abra has never followed my lead," I said. "Even when I leash her."

"We speak metaphorically, Whiskey."

Peg perked up the whole affair by serving doggie biscuits to the bitches and a huge mug of hot chocolate to Chester. I cheerfully imbibed another round of peppermint mocha, and Jenx did the same. Thank goodness Peg's business was better, and so was her mental outlook. Surrounding herself with thirsty people and their pets seemed to be exactly what she needed. Now, if she would just agree to speak with Mom again.

42

Our little group at the Goh Cup had just finished our hot beverages and doggie treats when Jeb walked in. Apparently coached by Anouk, my fiancé made a huge show of hugging both hounds at the same time. So far, so good. He invited me to take a drive with him.

"What about Joan and Olivia?" I whispered.

"I'll get Chester and the girls home," Jenx offered. "Two days before Christmas, it's a little slow at the station."

Jeb had a plan. Once we settled in his Z4, he proposed we take a nice long drive up the coast.

"I have work waiting for me on my desk," I objected. "Any minute now, Mom will call to nag me."

"Turn off your phone. We need to relax and talk about where we want to go on our honeymoon."

"Honeymoon? We haven't even picked a date for the wedding."

"Start planning," Jeb said. "You don't want that license to expire."

He was referring to our marriage license. The day after my brush with death at The Bentwood School, Jeb had convinced me to follow up on his proposal by getting our marriage license.

"It's good for thirty-three days," I said.

"And we have thirty left." Jeb patted my belly. "I'm guessing

Whiskey and Soda

you might want to do the deed before this little guy or gal ends up in the wedding party."

I had already made clear that I wanted a private ceremony officiated by a Justice of the Peace and witnessed by two close friends to be named later. Jeb had no problem with any of that, so I supposed I should humor him and start checking my calendar. Like a good fiancée, I opened the scheduling app on my phone and thumbed through the touch-sensitive pages. He turned the car onto Broken Arrow Highway, and we headed north.

He must have driven us in a big circle, however. The next time I glanced up, we were pulling into the parking lot at Mother Tucker's, which was empty.

"Why are we here?" I said. "Where's all their business? It's almost lunch time."

"I almost forgot. Walter and Jonnie asked me to stop by and talk with them about playing a New Year's Eve gig. It'll just take a minute, Whiskey. You might as well come in."

Considering how much I liked the couple who owned my favorite restaurant and how little I'd seen of them lately, I was fine with this side trip. However, I was puzzled by their lack of customers. Trade at every other local establishment had improved since the weather turned Christmassy.

I paused at the front door, where a handwritten sign read

CLOSED UNTIL 5 PM

"Weird," I mumbled.

Jeb opened the door, and I stepped inside, momentarily blinded by the shift from sunlight and white snow to restaurant dimness. The place was silent.

"Hello!" Jeb called out.

"Surprise!" a chorus of voices replied.

I made out a large shadowy crowd moving toward us. It felt like a friendly crowd.

"Surprise?" I repeated the word as a question. "Surprise what?"

"Welcome to your surprise bridal shower, Whitney," Mom said, throwing her arms around me. "Jeb helped me plan this, didn't you, son?"

I glared at my fiancé, whose face was becoming clear as my eyes adjusted. He wore an ear-to-ear grin.

Howard stood next to Mom. Beyond them, the room was filled with almost everybody I knew and loved in Magnet Springs—and even a few folks I wouldn't have invited.

Noonan was there, of course, giving me the peace sign, or maybe it was a V for victory. Her permanent spouse Fenton Flagg had returned to town for this event, which meant that his companion dog, Norman the Golden, was around here somewhere. That was good news for Abra since Norman was her true canine love.

Fenton, with whom I had once spent an excruciatingly awkward night, offered me a bear hug and reminded me that he had been the first to identify Jeb as my "permanent spouse."

"This is your fate, Whiskey. Now go with the matrimonial flow."

Odette, wearing Dolce & Gabbana, had brought her handsome husband Reginald, a psychiatrist who rarely attended public events. With them were several of Mattimoe Realty's high-rolling clients. Our property manager Luís Regalo was there, too, along with part-time handyman Roy Vickers, who was also Chester's formerly estranged grandfather.

Brady and Roscoe were present, of course. I noticed that Brady kept the K9 officer on a short leash. Also in attendance was Martha Glenn, senile octogenarian owner/operator of Town 'n' Gown, our local upscale clothier. She wore a party hat and a T-shirt that said "Kiss me. Life begins at 40."

My heart jumped for joy when I spotted Dr. David Newquist, our town veterinarian, and his girlfriend Deely Smarr, the Coast Guard nanny I hired for Avery's newborn twins. I knew they had been abroad promoting radical animal rights. Deely congratulated me and showed off her own shiny shackle.

"We just got back from the Rain Forest, ma'am. It was so inspiring, we got married."

"That's white," Dr. David said. "Good wuhks and a honeymoon, aww wode into one."

Translation: "That's right. Good works and a honeymoon all rolled into one." I no longer had trouble understanding his speech impediment.

Avery was there, too, with the twins. Fourteen-month-old Leah and Leo were as tickled to see me as I was to see them.

Their mom perched on a barstool, texting, while mostly ignoring me, which I considered a major favor. I assumed she was communicating with her own fiancé, MacArthur.

Wells Verbelow, the first man I dated after Leo's death, and the judge who presided over Abra's purse-snatching trials, had brought an attractive professional-looking woman as his date. He whispered to me that she was an attorney in the next county, and he was smitten. He planned to pop the question on Christmas Eve. I squeezed his hand and wished him luck.

Of course, I laughed and cried with my good ol' buds, Walter and Jonnie St. Mary. The sweetest gay couple—make that, the sweetest couple—I knew, they had kept me well-fed and sane through the numb months of my new widowhood. Although their restaurant was open for lunch and dinner only, they had made sure I got breakfast every day, too, for almost six months. Now they were only too pleased to host a celebration of brighter, happier times.

"But where did everybody park?" I asked Walter.

"Give your mother credit for that deception," he said, his thick white hair shining. "She ordered a shuttle bus to pick everyone up."

"There will be a few stragglers," Jonnie predicted. He was usually nervous and under-confident about everything except his cooking skills, which were world-class.

Walter winked at me. "You'll be happy to see 'em. Most of 'em."

With that, the front door opened, and in rushed Chester with Abra and Sandra still on leashes, looking exactly as I had left them at the Goh Cup. Peg and Jenx followed. My mom rushed to hug Peg, and the two stood embracing for a long, wonderful moment.

Anouk arrived, too, with Napoleon. A red leather collar complemented his black pompadour. I held my breath, but the girl dogs from Vestige behaved like ladies, even though one of them was dressed as Santa. Today Abra only had eyes for Norman, much as I only had eyes for Jeb.

Our final guests arrived, Cassina, the pop harpist diva, and her black-clad entourage. I noticed that Rupert, Chester's nominal father—read: sperm donor—did not appear. Cassina was Chester's mother of record, if not his actual on-duty mom. Day servants and dogs generally filled that role. Today, for a casual public appearance, she wore a modified mummy suit, a body-length wrap of pigment-free fabric that exposed only her dainty hands, feet and most of her alabaster face, plus a few loose strands of scarlet hair. Cassina's wide eyes were astonishingly deep green, and she tinted her fingernails and toenails to match. Slender gold and emerald rings adorned all twenty digits. Even in late December with snow on the ground, Cassina wore leather sandals.

As if on a cloud, she drifted over to me and delicately placed a wrapped package in my hands.

"It's not a puppy, is it?" I asked, recalling her one and only previous "present."

"Hell, no," she replied in that trademark breathy voice. "This is something with your name on it. For when you can drink again, like a normal woman. Raising a kid requires sedation."

"Amen, sister!" Avery shouted from the bar.

When my ex-step flicked her pink tongue, I did the same back at her. Cassina's eyes wandered to the many shiny bottles behind the bar, and she was gone.

Velcro and Prince Harry were present, no doubt escorted by one of Cassina's aides. The dogs ran in circles, mostly, but they didn't bother anybody. I also glimpsed Wells Verbelow's trained tracking dog, Mooney the Rotthound, slobbering all over the polished wood floor. I only hoped that Martha Glenn wouldn't slip and crack a hip. In all, we had eight canines present, and every one of them behaved beautifully.

Maybe Peg was onto something. We could rebrand Magnet Springs as a pet-friendly mecca. I imagined humans and their four-leggers converging from around the world for recreation and renewal. It could happen.

"I told you, Whitney," Mom called out, "bridal showers can be fun."

She and Howard danced cheek to cheek to a little impromptu music provided by my fiancé. He must have stashed his acoustic guitar here earlier. Other couples danced, too; Jeb played every request he could honor. After about an hour, he held up his guitar and called out a request of his own.

"Hey, can somebody else play so I get a dance with my bride-to-be?"

To my surprise, Chester took the instrument.

Whiskey and Soda

"I can play 'Call and Answer,'" he said, referring to the Barenaked Ladies tune that Jeb and I considered "our" song.

It wasn't the best number for dancing, but it was the right song for us. On the dance floor we held each other close. Jeb placed his hand on my belly, and we both felt the kicks, a joyful little shuffle. Our baby was celebrating with us.

"Whaddaya say, Mattimoe? How about getting married right now?"

I studied Jeb's face. His handsome, clear-eyed, earnest face.

"Think about it," he said. "We got the license, the hall, a judge, and all your best friends. Plus, it's almost Christmas. What could be better?"

So it was that my bridal shower—a party I had never, ever wanted—turned into my wedding, an event I suddenly wanted with my whole heart. A surprise wedding with friends, family and canines. Jeb excused himself to confer with Wells before we began the proceedings. I had a little business to attend to myself.

Using her leash for a change, I walked Abra sedately to the ladies' room, which was conveniently vacant. We needed the facility for a human-canine tête à tête. With neither grace nor ease, I lowered myself to the slate floor and peered into Abra's alert eyes.

"Hey, this is a big day for me, girl. One of the biggest ever."

She cocked her sleek head suspiciously.

"How can I explain this?" I began, wondering why I even felt I had to. Yet it was something I still owed Leo, and this stubborn, stunning Affie was forever a part of him. "We all need somebody to love. You and I both loved Leo, and—oh my—how Leo loved us."

Nearly two years after her beloved master's death, the mere mention of his name still arrested Abra. She turned her head away, as if listening for his voice or hoping to catch a fleeting glimpse of him.

"Leo's gone forever, girl. He's the good man who had to leave us way too soon." I swiped at the tears suddenly tumbling down my cheeks. "But you and I are still here, and we need somebody to love. Wherever Leo is, believe me, he understands."

She gazed at me, and I stroked her graceful neck.

"I was lucky to find Jeb again. He's a good man, too, you know."

Abra responded with a sound I'd never heard before, something between a sigh of agreement and a groan of regret.

"His taste in canines may be questionable," I admitted. "But Jeb is to me what Norman the Golden is to you—my one true love."

Abra's whimper indicated that I had no right to speak on her behalf. Much as she loved Norman, maybe she wasn't ready for monogamy.

"You need to feel appreciated when Norman's not around? Is that it?"

She wagged her tail.

"I understand. Now here's the thing." It wasn't easy to lean forward, but I managed, hoping fervently that my dog would accept my proposal. "From now on, Abra, Jeb is going to live with us, and we're going to make a family."

By way of illustration, I patted my bump, which she sniffed indifferently.

"You'll learn to love that little one, I hope." I swallowed a shard of anxiety. "And then there's the Frenchie. I understand you've been sisters before, but this time will be better because I promise to be a good, fair, loving mother to you and Sandra, as well as the new two-legger. So how about it, Abra? Leo wants this for us, I know he does. He valued family above all."

Now I was crying for real, tears flowing in abundance. To my astonishment, Abra kissed my wet cheeks with her smooth, insistent tongue. A cynic might say she was thirsty for saltwater, but I knew otherwise. The Affie was giving me her blessing, or at least a tentative seal of approval. I kissed her back, planting a loving *mwah* on the top of that maddeningly beautiful blonde head.

After washing my face and finger-combing my hair, I met Jeb in the dining room, ready to join my life with his in front of God and everybody. I asked Mom to be my matron of honor. That seemed only fair since she had been right about the bridal shower and a few other things.

Abra and Sandra were my bridesmaids, of course. Coached by Anouk, and cheered by the whole crowd, they strutted down the makeshift aisle with perfect doggie dignity. Jeb whispered to me that he wished he'd had time to buy Sandra a frilly dress and veil. We could argue about her wardrobe later. Or maybe Abra and I would both learn to let that go.

Author Bio

Nina Wright is a former professional actor turned playwright and novelist. Her published works include six books in the humorous Whiskey Mattimoe mystery series starring Abra the Afghan hound as well as two urban fantasies, Homefree and Sensitive. Nina leads writing workshops at conferences, schools, libraries and corporations. Follow her on Facebook and Twitter

CPSIA information can be obtained at www.ICGtesting.com
Printed in the USA
LVOW131714210612

287117LV00011B/2/P

9 781937 070199